P9-CQP-921

"I know how you like a man's hands on your body, Silver," Nicholas said. "And how you love it when he possesses you."

But not with any man, she thought. Only with Nicholas. Her knees felt suddenly weak as she remembered the wildness, the rhythm. . . . "I think I'll go back to the ballroom."

"Not yet." He took a step closer. "This garden reminds me of that night on the bank of the Mississippi. Do you remember that night, Silver?"

She didn't want to remember, but pictures came flooding back to her. Soft moss beneath her naked back, Nicholas's face in the firelight.

Nicholas gazed at her, his lips curved in a smile that was infinitely sensual. "It's been a long time since I saw you like that. I want to see you like that now."

She felt an ache deep inside her begin to throb as he spread her sable cloak beneath a cherry tree. "I don't want . . ." She stopped as she met his knowing eyes. "I won't do this."

"I think you will. You want me, Silver. You're as hungry for me as I am for you. It will be good for you, I promise."

"But you're angry."

"Yes, I am." Something wild and hot flickered in his eyes. "Angry, and frustrated, and raw, but I would never hurt you. It might even make it better. You can't deny you like it wild."

No, she couldn't deny it, Silver realized helplessly. She wanted to be touched by him in any way he chose to touch her. Wild or gentle. Soft or hard. . . .

THE DELANEYS, THE UNTAMED YEARS II

Satin Ice

Iris Johansen

BANTAM BOOKS
TORONTO • NEW YORK • LONDON • SYDNEY • AUCKLAND

SATIN ICE

A Bantam Book / November 1988

ISBN 0-553-21978-2

Published simultaneously in the United States and Canada

Bantam Books are published by Bantam Books, a division of
Bantam Doubleday Dell Publishing Group, Inc. Its trademark,
consisting of the words "Bantam Books" and the portrayal
of a rooster, is Registered in U.S. Patent and Trademark Office
and in other countries. Marca Registrada. Bantam Books,
666 Fifth Avenue, New York, New York 10103.

PRINTED IN THE UNITED STATES OF AMERICA

O   0 9 8 7 6 5 4 3 2 1

Satin Ice

THE DELANEY DYNASTY

Shamus Delaney m. 1828 Malvina Kelly

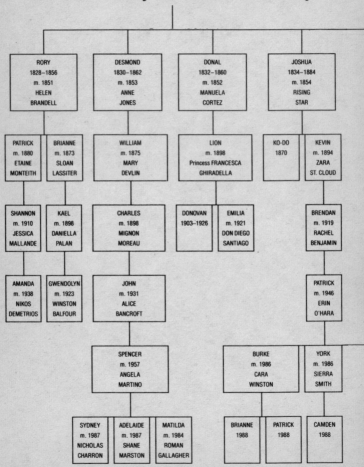

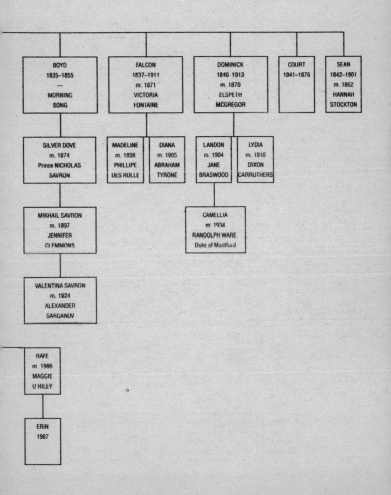

1

St. Petersburg, Russia
July 10, 1874

"Why isn't it dark?" Silver peered curiously out of the window of the carriage. "Surely it must be close to midnight. It was well after ten when the ship docked."

"It's the time of the white nights." Valentin Marinov smiled indulgently as he looked at the eager expression on Silver's face. His gaze followed hers to the deserted streets of his native city, now bathed in pearly light that imbued even the cobblestones with iridescent beauty. "For a few weeks each year there is no darkness here in St. Petersburg," Valentin added by way of explanation.

"How peculiar." Silver shot him a mischievous glance. "But just what I would have expected from a land that breeds men as contrary as you and Nicholas. America is far more reliable. When it's supposed to get dark, it gets dark."

"Reliable, perhaps, but not nearly as interesting. Admit it, Silver. You've never seen a city as beautiful as St. Petersburg, have you?"

1

"How can I tell? I've scarcely had a chance to see more than a few miles of your precious city." Yet the little she had seen had been both fascinating and intimidating, she thought. Everything was so . . . different. Buildings sported towers of strange exotic shapes, stunning the eyes with their brilliance in shades of yellow, green, red, and turquoise. There seemed to be an abundance of wide avenues, broad squares, and verdant parks; misty-wreathed canals crisscrossed the city, adding to the mysterious charm of St. Petersburg.

Yet its charm was exotic, quite outside anything she had experienced, and it suddenly made Silver feel very isolated, utterly alone. What was she doing here in this strange place so far from anything she knew or cared about? "It seems very . . . large. Even larger than New Orleans or St. Louis."

"They call it the Babylon of the snows," Valentin said softly. "No city on earth can compare with—" He stopped in amazement when he noticed how ramrod straight Silver was holding herself. He could almost feel the tension of her slim body across the carriage. He hadn't expected Silver to be subject to an attack of nerves. Another woman, perhaps, but not Silver, who was like no other woman he had ever met in the boldness of her ways and the independence of her spirit. He supposed he shouldn't have been surprised at her being apprehensive, he thought with sudden compassion. After all, Silver was only nineteen and pregnant with Nicholas's child. She was usually so full of vitality and confidence that he sometimes forgot how young she was and how little she had seen of the world. But—blast it!—Nicholas should have been more sensitive to Silver and come with them instead of going off somewhere with Mikhail the minute the ship had docked.

He frowned as he thought angrily about how his

friend Nicholas was treating Silver. She was his wife, dammit. He should have recognized his duty and . . . Duty? He must be mad to even think of Nicholas in terms of feeling bound by duty, when he had never submitted to wearing that yoke in all the years Valentin had known him. Well, if Nicholas were negligent in fulfilling his husbandly responsibilities, then Valentin would simply have to try to give Silver what comfort he could. "St. Petersburg is just like any other city," he said with deliberate lightness. "Your New Orleans also has a certain charm."

She laughed, her anxiety ebbing slightly. "You hated it. You told me so."

He made a face. "Not the city, the weather. So hot, so muggy I couldn't draw a decent breath. It's much dryer and cooler here in the summer. It's even cooler on Crystal Island."

"Crystal Island?"

"Like quite a few noblemen who have residences on private islands close to the city, Nicholas has a palace on an island in the River Neva. It's called Crystal Island because Nicholas's father had the palace completely rebuilt when he brought home his bride. He had so many large windows put in that the glass seems to shimmer like crystal, especially when the house is viewed from a boat on the river. Didn't Nicholas tell you about it?" Then, as Valentin saw her shuttered expression, he silently cursed himself. Why should he assume that Nicholas would have confided that or any other information to Silver, when their relationship appeared to have become both guarded and complex. Silver had occupied a lone cabin on the long trip from New Orleans to Liverpool and also on the ship from England to St. Petersburg. It made no sense to him. If Nicholas had wanted Silver enough to wed her, then why didn't he occupy her bed? He was certain Nicholas's lust for her had not dwindled. If anything, his friend's desire had increased, as was evidenced by Nicholas's short temper of the past months. The child? But Silver was a scant two months along.

"No, he didn't tell me anything about his home." Silver steadfastly gazed out the window at the grandiose buildings they were passing. "Perhaps he thought it might intimidate the poor little half-breed. We Apaches aren't accustomed to palaces, you know."

"I doubt if he was worried about that," Valentin said dryly. "He knows you are bold enough to take over the entire city and tweak the nose of the tsar himself if it happens to please you. What's a niggling little palace to an Apache like you?"

"Nothing." She lifted her chin proudly. "I care nothing for his palace or his fine title."

"It's your title too," he reminded her mildly. "You're now Her Highness, Princess Silver Savron. And your child will also carry the title."

Her face was suddenly illuminated with a light as softly radiant as the white night beyond the windows of the carriage. Her hand moved down to rest on her flat abdomen that as yet bore no sign of the child. "Yes," she whispered. "I forgot. It will help guard my child, won't it, Valentin? A title will make him safer."

"A title has its advantages," he said. "As long as it's accompanied by the Savron fortune. I find being a count opens certain social doors, but my lack of funds closes many others."

"I don't care about society." Silver's gray eyes were blazing fiercely. "All I want is for my child to be safe and free from shame."

"Nicholas will see that the child is protected, Silver," Valentin said quietly.

"No, *I* will see to it." Her voice was shimmering with force. "I will not rely on any man to fight my battles."

"Not even your husband?" Valentin asked softly.

The fierceness in Silver's face faded and was replaced by uncertainty, then a fleeting expression of pain. "Not even my husband." She added haltingly, "You should know that our marriage isn't ... ordinary."

"Quite extraordinary," he said. "But that doesn't change Nicholas's nature nor does it alter your own." He smiled. "I think I envy the child you're carrying, Silver. With you and Nicholas as parents, it will be the most carefully guarded and nurtured child in all of Russia."

"In the entire world." A sudden smile lit up her lovely golden face. "Don't underestimate us." Her smile faded. "Does Nicholas really want the child, Valentin? Has he said anything to you?"

He shook his head. "But of course he wants the child. Why shouldn't he? Every man wants an heir."

"Every man may want an offspring, but some men are particular about the mothers of their children," she said bitterly. "Princes usually don't choose illegitimate half-breeds like me to produce their heirs."

"Then they should. It would make for much more interesting progeny." She failed to respond as he'd hoped she would, so he added softly, "My dear Silver, if Nicholas hadn't wanted to acknowledge your child, he only would have had to turn his back on you and walk away. Unfortunately, it's done all the time in our world. Instead, he chose to marry you."

"But he didn't choose—" She broke off and tried to smile carelessly. "It doesn't really matter whether he wants the child or not. I merely wondered if he had spoken to you about it." Her gaze shifted quickly to the window again. "Is that the River Neva?"

It was clear she wished to abandon the subject, but for an instant he was tempted to pursue it. In the past months he had become very fond of this child-woman who had come so explosively into their lives, and he had a most uncharacteristic wish to comfort and reassure. Then he decided to ignore the impulse and gave a half shrug. Comfort and reassurance was Nicholas's duty, though he seemed to be making a damn poor job of it. "Yes, that's the Neva. We'll hire a boat to take us across to the island. I think you'll enjoy the trip. The city is quite beautiful from the water." He glanced at her taut face and deliberately resumed his casual patter. "Though in the winter the journey is more exciting. In November the river freezes over and we have to cross by sleigh. I think you'll find that very interesting."

"I may not be here in November."

"You and Nicholas aren't thinking of traveling this winter? I'd wait until spring if I were you. The winter season is very gay here in St. Petersburg."

"I didn't come here to enjoy myself." She leaned wearily back against the cushions of the carriage. "I came only to find Etaine and take her back to America."

"Did you?" His smile was cryptic. "I'm sure your concern for your circus waif is genuine and your purpose admirable. However, you're now Nicholas's wife and will bear his child. I've found Nicholas seldom gives up what is his. I think you'll still be here when the snow falls."

"You don't understand."

"No, I don't." Valentin smiled coaxingly. "Would you care to enlighten me?"

She gazed at him for a moment before slowly shaking her head.

He sighed. "I didn't think so. Oh, well, I've understood very little of what's transpired between you two from the beginning. Perhaps in time one of you will indulge my curiosity."

"Perhaps." Silver closed her eyes, shutting out the

alien panorama, shutting out Valentin's good-humored curiosity, shutting out the night that was like no night she had ever known. She wished desperately she could shut away her thoughts as well. She considered Valentin her friend, and she would have given him an answer if she had known what to say to him. How was she to make him understand what she didn't understand herself? Nicholas was as much of an enigma now as he had been the day she had forced him to marry her. On their three-month journey from St. Louis to St. Petersburg, he had been courteous, protective, even charming, but she had never been able to see beyond the mask he kept firmly in place.

Was he harboring a terrible anger behind that mask?

She had not thought so on the night of their marriage when Nicholas had put her to bed with such tenderness. He had been exquisitely gentle, but there had been an undercurrent of intense desire in his every action. He had wanted her at other times on the journey down the Mississippi on the *Rose* and on the journey across the sea. She *knew* he had wanted her, dammit. But if he had wanted her, why hadn't he taken her?

Not that she wanted him to make love to her, she assured herself quickly. It was nothing to her if his lust had faded as she had known it would. A man quickly could grow tired of a woman's body, she knew. Hadn't her father taken her mother and forgotten her as soon as he had spilled his seed into her? Besides, it hadn't been Nicholas who had taken her, it was she who had chosen to give herself. She would someday walk away from him with no more regret than her father had felt when he'd left her mother.

But not yet. She was not ready to walk away yet. It would do no harm to linger awhile with Nicholas. He

gave her kindness even if he withheld passion. It was
pleasant to be in his company and listen to his deep
voice and see the expressions flitting across his face
that was more beautiful than Lucifer's before the fall.

She was lying to herself, she realized with self-
disgust. His company was *not* pleasant. When she
was in his presence she alternated between feeling a
strange bittersweet pain and a fever of lust. If he had
grown tired of her, she could not say the same about
her desire for him. It was unfair for one partner to
grow weary and the other to still burn, she thought
fiercely. But then, when had life ever been anything
but unfair? She would get over this passion soon.
She would become tired of Nicholas and leave him
to his rich world of palaces and tsars. She would find
Etaine and take her away from the cruel bastard
who had fathered her and they would go back to
America, where there were no titles or beautiful
princes or days that had no end.

"Silver, wake up."

Valentin's voice brought her to the awareness that
the carriage had stopped. Her eyes flew open. "I
wasn't asleep. Is this where we hire the boat?"

He nodded. "We're at the quay." He opened the
door of the carriage and stepped down onto the cob-
blestone street. "Stay here. I want to find boatmen
with the voices of nightingales. Your first boatride
on the Neva should be an experience you'll always
remember."

The carriage door slammed behind Valentin and
she gazed after him in bewilderment as he walked
briskly toward a group of men dressed in brightly
colored tunics and tough homespun trousers who
were lounging lazily on the quay. Singing boatmen?
Well, why not? It would be no more strange than
anything else in this bizarre world of Nicholas's.

She leaned back against the cushions again, trying

to stifle her impatience while Valentin searched for his nightingales.

"Do you wish me to wake the cooks?" Mikhail shut the tall brass-studded door. "You have had nothing to eat tonight."

Nicholas shook his head as he gave his hat and gloves to the waiting servant before waving him away. "Go to bed. I'm not hungry."

Mikhail frowned. "You should eat."

"Go to bed," Nicholas repeated. "I have no need of you to mother me."

"No, but you have a great need for a little sense," the big Cossack said bluntly. "It is almost morning and you have not eaten since noon yesterday. This is foolishness."

"Mikhail, blast you, will you—" Nicholas broke off as he saw Mikhail's jaw set in determination. "I promise that I'll eat a breakfast fit for a *Hitman*. Will that satisfy you, my friend?"

"No."

Nicholas turned away. "It will have to be enough. I want to be sure Silver is well settled and then go to my own rest. Food will wait until later." He started up the sweeping grand staircase. "I'll see you in the morning, Mikhail."

"You should not have left her tonight."

Nicholas paused on the steps and turned to look at him. "It was necessary."

The light of the candles in the crystal chandelier above them glinted in Mikhail's flaming red hair as he shook his head. "She felt very much alone. She would not let you see it, but she had need of you tonight."

"I couldn't be in two places at once. I had to make a choice."

"You could have waited until tomorrow before going to see Skorsky."

"Mikhail, dammit, I told you—" Nicholas slowly shook his head in wonder. "What has Silver done to you?"

"Not what she has done to you." A faint smile touched Mikhail's lips. "But when one sees a wild bird soaring through the storm, it is only natural to wish it to reach a safe nesting place."

Nicholas smiled wryly. "I take it you consider me the storm and not the refuge?"

"I do not know. You have not been safe for a woman before, but Silver is not as other women."

Nicholas's hand tightened on the marble banister. "But she's still vulnerable and can be hurt, even broken unless we protect her."

Mikhail's eyes narrowed. "You found out something from Skorsky?"

"The circus is here, just outside St. Petersburg. They've been here for over three weeks. Skorsky says Monteith has set up his tents on the estate of Count Anton Peskov. The count has extended his patronage to Monteith and his troupe."

"Is that a problem?"

"Perhaps. I don't know yet. Peskov has considerable influence at court. If he chooses to protest our removal of the child, Etaine, from Monteith's so-called 'protection,' it could be awkward. I'm afraid it's not just a matter of riding in and taking Etaine any longer." He smiled crookedly. "We have to try diplomacy first."

"And if that does not work?"

Nicholas's dark eyes glinted with recklessness. "Why, then we ride in and take her, of course."

Mikhail's deep laughter boomed out. "Ah, that is good."

"But, my bloodthirsty friend, first we see if we can accomplish our ends without involving the tsar. I have no desire to be exiled to Siberia at this time."

Nicholas paused. "And we both know Silver isn't going to be pleased at the delay. I can't be with her every moment of the day. Will you stay by her side?"

The Cossack appeared suddenly uneasy. "I cannot promise you that I can prevent her from doing as she wills. She is a strong woman."

"I know that. I ask only that you try to keep her and the child safe. Will you do this?"

Mikhail nodded. "You show great concern about this Monteith. He is a dangerous man?"

"I met him only once, but I think he could be . . . anything." He turned and again started up the stairs. "Keep Silver away from him if you can. God knows it won't be easy."

Nicholas heard a sound from Mikhail that fell somewhere between a grunt and a sigh of resignation. It was followed by the click of Mikhail's boots on the polished parquet floor and then the slam of the door leading to the quarters the Cossack had chosen for himself near the stable.

The pale light streaming through the long windows of the upper hall cast a mellow glow on the portrait of his father on the wall at the head of the stairs. Nicholas's lips curved in a self-mocking smile as he paused a moment to stand before the portrait. How many times had he sworn he would not follow in the footsteps of his father? Yet here he was, caught in the same silken net that had destroyed Dimitri Savron as surely as the sword thrust had extinguished his life's breath.

Nicholas stared at the portrait, a slight frown wrinkling his brow. But he was not his father and Silver was not at all like his mother. There was no resemblance between the two women except for their strength. His mother was ice and Silver was flame. . . .

"Nicholas?"

He whirled to face the windowed alcove across

from the staircase, relaxing as he caught sight of the slender woman standing there. Silver was not flame at the moment but an ethereal creature, transformed by the opalescent light. She was dressed in a loose white robe, her long dark hair falling straight and shining down her back. Her face was in shadow, and he couldn't see her expression, but there was a charged tension emanating from her that caused him a thrill of concern. "For God's sake, what are you doing wandering around in the middle of the night? Are you ill? The child—"

"I'm not ill." She again turned her head to look out the window, and her profile was framed against the glowing pearl patch of the sky. "I couldn't sleep. After I wrote my guardian, Patrick, telling him we'd arrived safely and all was well with me, I just lay in bed and ... It's no real wonder I couldn't sleep. I knew Russia would be a very peculiar country, but I had no idea it would be so upside down." She added quickly, "However, I'm sure that I'll get used to it very soon. It's not as if it truly bothers me. I'm certain it was the long trip and then this peculiar night light. In a few days—"

"Hush." Nicholas crossed the space between them in long quick strides and pulled her into his arms. He knew instantly that it was a mistake. He had acted on impulse, unable to bear the poignant feelings that had assaulted him as he watched her struggling with her isolation and loneliness. He had wanted to comfort not seduce her, but his body was blind to motive. It responded only to her warm full breasts and the scent of her. He could feel the sharp edge of desire harden his loins and tighten the muscles of his belly. Comfort, he prayed desperately. Give to her, don't take. But comfort could be given only if he distanced himself physically. He drew a deep, ragged breath and reluctantly pushed her away from him.

He said lightly, "I humbly apologize for bringing you to my most peculiar land. Perhaps you'll be persuaded to forgive our little idiosyncrasies in time." He forced himself to drop his hands from her shoulders. "St. Petersburg has many attractions to balance against her faults."

She laughed. "You sound like Valentin. He couldn't stop talking about the wonders to be found here. He even hired four boatmen who sang to us as they rowed to the island. If they'd hit a wrong note, I believe he would have thought it dishonored his wonderful city and pushed them overboard."

"He believes no city is tolerable but this one. I'm not quite so enthusiastic. Every city loses some of its charm when one gets accustomed to it, and then boredom soon follows."

She stiffened. "Do you grow bored so easily, then?"

"Sometimes. Don't we all?"

"I don't." Her voice was suddenly fierce. "I think only dull, stupid people become bored. If one is intelligent and has imagination, one should be able to keep interest alive."

He inclined his head in a half-mocking bow. "I stand abased. Evidently I'm lacking in one or both of those qualities, as I find myself quite often in the doldrums. Though I admit that I haven't been so afflicted lately."

"No?" Her voice sounded breathless even to herself.

"Definitely not. Since you came into my life I've been hit on the head, forced to jump overboard to swim in that atrociously muddy Mississippi River, and been involved in the sinking of—"

"None of that was my fault," she interrupted. "It was entirely your own arrogant disregard of my rights that caused the trouble."

"Perhaps."

"No perhaps about it," she said indignantly, her eyes flashing. "You kidnapped me."

The air of vulnerability about Silver that had been troubling him was gone now, replaced by the blazing vitality that was her most salient characteristic. Just a bit more skillful maneuvering, Nicholas thought, and she would be fully herself again. He lowered his lids to veil his eyes. "It was necessary. You wouldn't tell me where Dominic Delaney was at the time. You're a very stubborn woman."

"Stubborn? You call it stubborn to defend myself from an arrogant jackass?"

He had goaded her enough. There was no longer a trace of the fragility that had made him want to cuddle Silver as if she were a child. She would be all right now. "Is that any way to talk to your lord and master?" he drawled. "Jackass, kidnapper. Gracious, I'm appalled."

"Lord and master," she sputtered. "You're not—" She stopped, frowning uncertainly. "You're laughing at me."

He shook his head. "I wouldn't dare. I was merely joking." He snapped his fingers. "I forgot you couldn't tell the difference. We must correct that." He pretended to think. "I have it. I will pull my left earlobe when I'm joking. Then you may respond with suitable wifely amusement." He shook his head morosely. "No, that wouldn't do. I'm too witty. By the end of the year my earlobe would be dragging my collar."

Silver laughed and Nicholas felt a river of pleasure run through him. He gently touched her lips with his index finger. "You weren't supposed to laugh at such a bad joke, my dear. I guess I'll just have to risk lengthening my earlobe."

"I thought it was funny." She gazed directly into his eyes. "And I'll laugh when I please."

"Probably at my humble self." He couldn't look

away from her. His senses were singing with the scent of her hair, the fragrant warmth emanating from her body. He could see the throbbing of her heart beneath the delicate golden skin of her temple. He had never known a more responsive woman ... and she was responding to him now. Her musky scent intensified, her breasts moved more quickly beneath the thin cotton of her robe, her eyes glowed. Her body was unconsciously readying itself for him, and he found the knowledge was wildly exciting. Heaven knew his own body was ready. He had never been more conscious of his body and its sexual purpose, its animal strength. His heart was slamming against the wall of his chest, and the hard length of his arousal pressed urgently against the material of his trousers.

This restraint was madness. He had always been more Cossack than gentleman, so why didn't he take what he wanted. Even as he asked himself the question, he knew the answer—the same answer he had arrived at that night on the *Mississippi Rose*. And it had caused him a damnable amount of discomfort for the last two months.

Christ, he didn't *want* to step back away from her. But reluctantly, slowly, he did.

Memories flooded back to him causing a wrenching, twisting hunger in his loins. She was looking at him in bewilderment. How long had he stood there in this haze of rutting hunger? Too long, and it must end or he would break.

He took another step back. "It's time you were in bed. It's nearly dawn."

"How can you tell?"

"I can tell. What room did Valentin give you?"

She gestured vaguely to a paneled door down the hall. "It's very grand. The bed is almost as big as the entire riverboat."

She had been given the master bedroom, Nicholas realized. Valentin knew very well Nicholas wasn't occupying Silver's bed. Giving Silver Nicholas's bedchamber could be either a result of Valentin's puckish humor or an attempt to spare Silver the servants' gossip. The motive didn't really matter at the moment. It was done now.

"At least the bed's firmly anchored to terra firma. That will be a change from the bunks you've occupied for the last weeks." He grabbed her hand and drew her quickly down the hall. "Come along. I'll show you how we 'peculiar' Russians cope with our white nights." He threw open the door and drew her across the room to the huge gilded canopy bed in the center of the chamber. "Ah, I thought so. The servants weren't called to draw the drapes. Climb into bed while I close them." He started toward the bank of windows on the north wall that reached almost from floor to ceiling.

"I don't want them drawn," Silver protested as she took off her robe, got into bed, and pulled up the crimson velvet coverlet. "I can't breathe. . . ."

He stopped and turned to look at her. Of course she couldn't breathe, he realized in a sudden wave of empathy. Silver required freedom as she did air, and she must have felt stifled in a room as heavy with tradition as it was with ornate furnishings. Poor little firebird.

"Then we'll leave them open. I don't like to draw them myself. Sometimes when I wake in the night from a bad dream it makes me feel better to see the light streaming into the room. It helps me forget that smothering darkness and go back to sleep."

"Forget your nightmares?"

He shrugged. "And something that happened a long time ago." He crossed the room and sat on the edge of the bed. "But if we leave the drapes open, you'll have to learn to contend with the light."

She closed her eyes. "It really wasn't the light that bothered me. I don't know what made me so uneasy."

"Don't you?" He knew very well what was troubling her. He had experienced that sense of isolation himself the first few weeks after he had left the Kuban. "Perhaps you were worried about your little friend, Etaine. Will it make you rest easier if I tell you I know where she is now?"

Her eyes flew open. "You do? How? Where is she?"

"I paid a visit to a gentleman by the name of Ivan Skorsky tonight. Skorsky's a hanger-on at court who makes himself popular by knowing everything going on in this fair city. Of course he could tell me exactly where a certain circus is performing."

She stared at him in surprise. "It seems too easy. I expected to have to search for them."

"Which should prove to you how useful it is to have me as your husband."

"But why did you go straight to Skorsky?"

He avoided her eyes as he tucked her coverlet carefully around her. "I thought you would rest easier."

"I will," she said haltingly. "Thank you."

"Thank me after I've plucked your little Etaine from beneath her fond papa's nose. I don't think that will be as easy as finding her."

"What do you mean?"

He stood up. "Tomorrow. You have enough to think about tonight. You may have trouble going to sleep now. I probably should have waited until morning, but I wanted you to know your Etaine is nearby."

"I don't care if I sleep. Nicholas, I want to know—"

"It will wait." He started for the door.

"You're the most exasperating man. I hate to wait for anything. I don't *want* to wait."

Heaven knew he didn't either. He had waited far too long already. He opened the door. "I've been told that anticipation is the most exotic of sauces."

"Your exotic sauce gives me a bellyache," she said crossly. "Nicholas, tell me—"

"No," he said firmly as he turned to face her.

She was silent a moment, and he waited, expecting an explosion. Then her expression suddenly altered. "You're not the same."

"In what way?"

"I don't know." Her gaze searched his face. "But you're not behaving the way you did on the ship."

He smiled faintly. "Perhaps I've sipped at that sauce for too long. I'm afraid I don't have the palate of a courtier. A Cossack doesn't taste, he devours."

The door closed behind him.

Silver forced herself not to gaze after him like a breathless ninny. He had been kind, gentle, almost brotherly. He had said little to indicate he was feeling the same hunger as she. Perhaps she was imagining the tension that crackled between them.

Her hands clenched nervously on the edge of the soft velvet coverlet. She was *not* imagining it. The maddening man wanted her. She knew he did. She had lain here looking up at him, seeing that pale light shine on his golden hair and the devil-angel beauty of his features, willing him to touch her.

And he had walked away. He had wanted her and he had walked away.

What kind of man *was* Nicholas Savron, for heaven's sake?

The question remained unanswered when she finally fell into a troubled sleep over an hour later.

"Patience." A gentle, almost loving smile touched Paul Monteith's well-shaped lips as he gazed down at the sleeping child on the cot. "You've had to wait only a few short weeks, Peskov, while I've been holding a watch for ten long years. It will happen soon."

"I'm not the only one who's impatient," the count

muttered. "There are others to whom I've made promises. You can't expect me to put them off indefinitely. You gave me your word, Monteith."

"And I shall keep it." Monteith turned away and moved gracefully toward the door of the tent. "When the time is right. You don't pick an apple until it blossoms." He stepped through the doorway and breathed in the cool air. Early morning mists enveloped the circus tents; an impressive manor house was just discernible through a stand of birches to the north of the encampment. "Go home," he said to the older man, stepping aside to let him pass. "And tell the others that it will be when I say or not at all. I will not be rushed."

"Are you sure it will work? What if she's not the correct . . ." Peskov faltered and then stopped as he met Monteith's gaze. He nervously gnawed at his lower lip. "Of course, I didn't mean to question you. I only wondered—"

"Then wonder no longer. I've tested her and she has proven true." Monteith's deep voice vibrated with certainty. "You're lucky that I'm allowing you and your friends to participate."

"We realize that." Peskov's tone was placating. "We're honored that you contacted us when you arrived in St. Petersburg."

Monteith shrugged. "It is the custom."

"And the gift of the child." Peskov smiled. "We are truly overwhelmed."

"It is not a gift. You presume too much." Monteith's tone was impatient. "I will merely allow you to draw the essence."

"There's another matter." Peskov hesitated. "The others wish me to convey their concern."

"Concern?"

"They're afraid the child may be damaged." Monteith's face held no expression, but Peskov found himself hurrying to finish. "You send her into the cage every night with those three lions. It's too dangerous."

"Is it?" Monteith's voice was silky. "Etaine's been doing this act since she was five years old. She has a way with animals. You saw her kneel there among those beasts like a maiden with her unicorn. Tell me, does it excite you to know that just one swipe of a lion's sharp claws could kill her?" Monteith smiled faintly. "Ah, I can see that it does. It excites me too. Even after all these years."

"But that swipe would also destroy your plans for her," Peskov reminded him.

Monteith shook his head. "She is nothing until she is honed. Each time she goes into the cage she becomes more finely drawn, her facets become more highly polished. I lose nothing if I lose her now."

"But we think—"

"Do you wish me to leave your fine city?" Monteith interrupted softly. "Perhaps I should take Etaine to benefit another of our groups?"

"I didn't say that," Peskov said hurriedly. "Naturally her preparation is at your discretion. We merely make a suggestion."

"And I merely ignore it." Monteith's smile was coolly contemptuous. "Good night, Peskov. I trust I'll see you at the performance this evening?"

"Of course," Peskov muttered. "I hope you're not offended, Paul."

Monteith didn't answer.

The count reluctantly turned away. "Good night." He started briskly toward the path that led through the stand of birches toward the manor house.

Paul Monteith watched him until the count was lost from view, the faint smile never leaving his lips. What a fool the man was. Peskov would never rise to be more than a bumbling acolyte no matter how hard he strove. Not that the count would strive very hard. He was far too fond of his fine house and stables and his position at court. He had not learned how little the trappings of wealth mattered when one was pursuing the ultimate experience. Peskov had actually been surprised when Monteith had refused his invitation to stay at the manor instead of remaining with his circus. The pompous idiot didn't realize how easily Monteith could have acquired what the count valued so highly. He understood greed and had even found it convenient to pretend to have that motivation in the past, but Peskov equated power with wealth and possessions. Monteith knew about power. Power could draw riches, but it could also draw more. . . .

Monteith turned away to gaze at the iridescent horizon. He had enjoyed the white nights but he was glad they would not last for much longer. He had always had a taste for the unusual, like these white nights, but he was bored with them now and wanted a change. Ah, but changes were coming, he thought. Wonderful, dazzling changes. He had known as soon as he set foot on this shore. Every instinct had quivered with certainty. After ten years of waiting he would soon know the satisfaction of seeing everything slide into motion just as it was meant to do.

He was still smiling with contentment as he opened the flap and entered his tent. Yes, he was very glad he had decided to bring Etaine to Russia.

2

S ilver hesitated on the top step of the grand staircase. Dear God, she had been too weary when they had arrived the night before even to take in the grandiosity of the foyer of the palace. She straightened her shoulders and sailed regally down the steps. "Nicholas, Mikhail, Valentin," she called imperiously, her voice echoing off the arches of the soaring ceiling. "Where are you?"

A servant dressed in dark green livery appeared at the curve of the staircase. "If it pleases your highness, Prince Nicholas and Master Kuzdief have gone into town. I am Rogoff. May I be of service?"

Silver stopped on the third step from the bottom. "Count Marinov?"

"In the breakfast room."

"Take me there."

She followed the servant from the foyer down a long gleaming corridor, her heels echoing loudly on the shining parquet floor. They passed two footmen standing rigidly at attention before Rogoff paused before a beautifully carved mahogany door. He threw it open with a little flourish and announced, "Her Highness, Princess Savron."

Valentin was seated at a rosewood table and hurriedly got to his feet, pushing back his brocade-cushioned chair. "Lord, Silver, I didn't think you'd be up for hours yet. Nicholas said he found you wandering around the halls in the middle of the night."

"I've slept long enough." She cast an uneasy glance at the servant, Rogoff, who had seemingly turned to the same motionless stone as the two men she had passed in the hall. "Is there something wrong with him?"

Valentin's eyes twinkled. "No, he's just being properly subservient. You'll get used to it."

"I doubt it. It seems very foolish to me." She glanced at the half-empty plate on the table before Valentin and announced, "I'm hungry."

"I expected as much." He gestured to the long sideboard against the wall on which there were several covered silver platters. "I took the liberty of ordering a mixed selection of English and Russian breakfast dishes from which you may choose."

"Good." She crossed the room and took a china plate from the sideboard. "And while I'm choosing, could you tell Rogoff to go be subservient somewhere else?"

Valentin chuckled before motioning for Rogoff to leave. "I believe you've hurt his feelings, Silver," he commented after the servant had majestically marched from the room.

"I'll hurt more than his feelings if he continues to bellow my name whenever I enter a room." She lifted one of the covers. "What's this black mush?"

"Caviar. Fish eggs."

She shrugged and spooned a little on her plate before moving to the next platter. "Where did Nicholas go?"

"He and Mikhail are paying a visit to court."

She looked at him inquiringly.

"The tsar's summer palace. He's hoping to contact Count Peskov there."

"Who's Count Peskov?"

"Your Mr. Monteith's patron for his circus. Ivan Peskov is a favorite of the tsar, and Nicky is trying to determine whether the count will be a problem to us when we take Etaine away from her father."

"I see." Silver frowned as she automatically made her way down the sideboard, heaping eggs and ham on her plate. "Would it matter if he did object?"

"Not if you don't mind seeing Nicky sent away from St. Petersburg to a place in the north that is less than pleasant," Valentin said dryly. "The tsar already finds him a little too reckless with his tongue on occasion. Our benevolent Tsar Alexander may believe in emancipation for the masses, but he keeps his boyars firmly under his thumb."

"How can Nicholas tolerate such oppression?"

"It's usually fairly easy to avoid his majesty when the guests at his balls number anywhere from two to five thousand."

"At one party?" Silver sat down opposite Valentin at the table. "How can he feed them all?"

Valentin's amused gaze rested on Silver's plate. "Thank God his guests don't all eat like you, or the treasury would be seriously depleted."

Silver smiled. "It would serve him right. Having five thousand guests at one time is a senseless extravagance. Our government would never tolerate it."

"Our?" Valentin lifted a brow. "I presume you're

referring to the United States. Didn't it occur to you that when you married Nicky, Russia became your country too?"

Her eyes widened at the thought. "It didn't. Arizona isn't a state yet, but I've always thought of myself as an American. I don't think I could ever belong anywhere but in America."

"Perhaps you'd better try." He added deliberately, "Your Highness."

She gazed at him uncertainly. "I don't know about all this, Valentin. It confuses me. Palaces and footmen who freeze into statues and tsars . . ." She shrugged. "Does Nicholas like being a prince?"

"I don't believe he thinks about it one way or the other. He was born into the position just as you were born—" He hesitated before finishing. "A Delaney."

Her lips twisted. "You mean a half-breed bastard. There's no real meeting ground between Nicholas and me."

"Evidently he found one. After all, he did marry you."

She looked down at her plate. "That doesn't mean anything. He couldn't help—" She broke off and picked up her fork. "It was sort of a marriage of convenience."

"Hmm." Valentin leaned back in his chair and gazed at her speculatively. "I admit I've been wondering about that, I'm accustomed to Nicky's impulsiveness, but I was a little surprised to come back to the *Rose* that night and find you two joined in connubial bliss." He made a face. "And I could get nothing from Nicholas but an icy stare when I had the audacity to question him. I don't suppose you'd care to tell—"

"No," she cut him off bluntly. She changed the subject. "These fish eggs aren't bad."

"I'm glad something Russian meets with your approval."

She suddenly favored him with a brilliant smile and reached across the table to cover his hand with her own. "I'm very fond of at least three things Russian. You, Mikhail . . ." She took another bite. "And caviar."

"And I'm excluded? What a blow to my self-esteem." Nicholas stood in the doorway, a faint smile on his face. "Good day, Silver." He came leisurely toward her. "I see you're in good appetite."

Silver withdrew her hand from Valentin's and after a quick glance at Nicholas was glad of the opportunity to lower her eyes to her plate. "Hello, Nicholas."

Nicholas's dark blue coat and matching trousers clung with sleek elegance to his tall muscular body, and he was everything that was both fashionable and assured. The brilliant sunlight streaming through the windows of the breakfast room seemed to become a part of him, tangling in the gold of his hair and caressing the deep bronze of his skin as if it loved him. She realized with a pang that Nicholas truly belonged in this great palace as she never would. She began eating her eggs. "What did you find out at court?"

"Nothing very promising. Peskov is quite protective of his new toy. It seems that the circus is the rage of everyone at court and it's become the thing to visit Peskov's estate at least once a week to see a performance." Nicholas's lips thinned. "Peskov is obviously lapping up the attention and wants no interference."

"Too bad." Silver frowned as she cut into the thick slice of ham on her plate. "When do we get Etaine?"

"Soon. I want to try something else first."

Valentin's gaze flew to Nicholas's face. "Natalya?"

Nicholas nodded. "I saw her briefly this afternoon. She had already heard that I'd brought home a bride."

Valentin grimaced. "How the devil did she find out so soon? We just arrived."

"You've forgotten how omniscient my dear mother can be." Nicholas's lips twisted. "She wants to meet Silver."

Valentin glanced swiftly at Silver. "Is that wise?"

"She has more power at court than Peskov. She might be persuaded to intercede if he makes a complaint when we take the child."

"What are the chances?"

Nicholas shrugged. "Probably not good."

Silver put down her fork. "Your mother wouldn't help you if you asked her?"

"My mother and I aren't on the best of terms."

Silver looked intently at Nicholas. He clearly didn't want to ask his mother this favor. Yet he was going to do it because of his promise about Etaine. "Will it help if I go to see her?"

"It may." His gaze met hers. "But you have to understand that my mother is . . ." He paused. "It won't be pleasant for you."

"I'm not afraid of her. If there's a chance that it will make our task easier, then I'll go to see her. What can she do to me?" She tossed her napkin on the table and rose to her feet. "I'm ready. Let's go."

Nicholas chuckled, the expression in his eyes suddenly warm. "We don't have to go this minute. My mother suggested that I bring you to the palace. There's a ball tonight."

"I'd rather get it over with."

Nicholas made a face. "Lord knows, so would I. But my sweet *maman* has other ideas. Besides, there's something else you have to do this afternoon."

"What is that?"

"I had another reason for going to town today. I brought a doctor back to examine you."

"Why? I feel fine."

"You haven't been examined by a physician since you conceived the child. I just want to assure myself that you're in good health."

"I'm as strong as a mountain pony."

He smiled with beguiling sweetness. "Humor me."

She felt suddenly breathless and she lowered her lids so he wouldn't see the glow of warmth produced in her by his smile. "All right."

"I had him shown to your chamber when we arrived. Dr. Rellings is English and very popular with the ladies of the court. I thought you'd prefer him to a Russian physician."

"I do. Though I've noticed everyone I've met here and at the docks spoke English."

"We have a great many English families in St. Petersburg," Valentin said. "Though the official language at the court is French, you'll find almost anyone you come in contact with speaks a little English."

"French?" Silver echoed warily. "I hope your mother understands English. Rising Star tried to teach me French, but I wasn't a very good pupil."

Nicholas's smile faded. "My mother can make herself very clearly understood whether she speaks the language or not." He turned away abruptly. "Escort Silver to her chamber and introduce her to Dr. Rellings, will you, Valentin? I want to see about sending someone to Madame Lemenov's to fetch a suitable gown for her."

"But I have all those gowns you got for me in New Orleans," Silver protested.

He glanced over his shoulder. "And you look quite charming in them, but tonight you need something special."

"Armor," Valentin suggested softly.

Nicholas nodded curtly. "Armor." He strode swiftly from the room.

Valentin got up. "Shall we go?"

Silver nodded absently as she moved toward the door. "You said that Nicholas's father renovated the palace for his wife. Why doesn't she live here?"

"She prefers life at court." Valentin's expression was grave as he fell in step with her. "You have to realize something about Natalya, Silver. She's eaten up by ambition. From the moment she married Nicholas's father, every thought, every action, has had only one aim—to make everyone who mattered to her forget that she was born the daughter of a serf. She's spent thirty years erasing that memory and building her influence at court."

Silver gave him a curious glance. "Are you warning me?"

"Yes," he said soberly. "I think I am."

"Thank you, but you needn't worry. I'm not afraid of her."

"I know, but perhaps you should be."

She gazed at him thoughtfully. "Nicholas has no love for her. Why is that?"

"His father was killed in a duel over her honor. Not that she had retained much honor by the time the duel occurred. Natalya was rumored to be sleeping not only with the gentleman in question but with half the noblemen at court."

Shock rippled through Silver and with it came the beginning of understanding. Nicholas had told her he had little trust in women, and it was no wonder, when his own mother behaved no better than a strumpet. "I can see why he didn't want to ask a favor of her."

"No, you can't." Valentin didn't look at her. "His father's death was only the beginning. Natalya has done some rather unspeakable things to Nicholas."

"What?"

He shook his head. "I've told you enough. Nicholas doesn't care to have his past discussed. Just be on your guard with Natalya."

"I will." A silence fell between them as they started to ascend the stairs. There was no reason for the uneasiness she was feeling, Silver told herself. What could the woman do to her? She was young and strong and Natalya Savron would soon be an old woman.

No, there was nothing to fear from a meeting with Nicholas's mother.

The woman who rushed up to Nicholas as soon as they entered the ballroom was definitely not his mother.

"Nicholas, how splendid to see you again." The small red-haired woman moved closer, brushing her satin-covered bosom against Nicholas's sleeve and smiling with unmistakable intimacy. "I've missed you."

No, this woman had no maternal feelings for Nicholas, Silver thought crossly. Though she was no longer in her first youth, her attitude toward Nicholas was both lustful and possessive.

Nicholas bowed politely. "Katya. May I present my wife, Silver? Silver, the Countess Katya Razskolsky, an old friend."

The countess gave Silver a fleeting glance and then turned back to Nicholas. "Natalya told me you had married. I was happy to hear it. Marriage can be a great convenience." Her gloved hand reached up to caress his cheek. "Do call on me soon." Then she was gone, lost in the crowd.

"An old friend?" Silver muttered. "Very old. She has crow's-feet around her eyes."

"How unkind of you to notice." Nicholas looked

around the room. Suddenly he stiffened. "There's my mother."

Natalya Savron's beauty shone as radiantly as that of her son, Nicholas. Her golden hair was a few shades lighter, her eyes a velvet brown instead of Nicholas's darker ebony. A low-necked sapphire gown clung to a figure that was still firm and voluptuous and, from where Silver and Nicholas stood in the doorway of the ballroom, Natalya looked not a day over thirty. She was talking to a dark-haired young man who was gazing at her with besotted devotion.

"She's very beautiful," Silver whispered to Nicholas. She knew the words were pitifully inadequate. Natalya Savron had more than beauty; she exerted the same sensual magnetism that Nicholas possessed.

"Yes." Nicholas's voice was totally expressionless. He took Silver's elbow and began to propel her through the crowd toward his mother. "But so are you. That gown is most becoming."

Silver glanced down at the exquisite rose silk gown she was wearing. For the first time she began to understand why Valentin had used the word armor. Nicholas had produced not only this lovely gown but a young housemaid, who had curled and combed Silver's hair into a high chignon that she had assured her was the current fashion at court. And now Nicholas's hand on her arm was blatantly protective. All to prepare her to meet this beautiful woman who had shifted her gaze from the young man murmuring eagerly in her ear to watch them walk across the ballroom toward her.

Natalya Savron smiled brilliantly. There was no warmth, no emotion in her gleaming smile, and Silver suddenly shivered as a memory of her childhood returned to her. *Old Snaggle-Tooth.*

"Nicholas." Natalya languidly held out a gloved

hand in greeting. "I was hoping you would decide to come." She gestured to the young man next to her. "You know Count Denis Stepvan."

Nicholas touched his mother's hand perfunctorily and nodded to the man next to her. "Stepvan. My wife, Silver."

The young count murmured a greeting, his gaze openly admiring as it lingered on Silver.

"Oh, yes, Silver . . ." Natalya's voice held the tart sweetness of elderberry wine. Her gaze rested on Silver's face for a long moment before shifting back to Nicholas. "Why don't you and Count Stepvan sample the punch bowl, *chéri*. I wish to become better acquainted with your little bride."

"I'm not thirsty." Nicholas's grip tightened on Silver's elbow.

"Nicholas, must I plead with you?" Natalya turned to the young count. "He is such a wicked boy. Take him away, won't you Denis?"

The count seemed intimidated by the prospect of trying to take Nicholas anywhere he didn't wish to go. "I'm sure your son is happy to oblige you."

"Oh, no, he isn't," Nicholas said flatly.

"Go away, Nicholas," Silver said, not looking away from his mother. "And don't come back. I'll find you when your mother and I have had our talk."

Nicholas frowned. "Dammit, Silver, I'm not—"

"Go. Nothing will be accomplished by you hovering."

He hesitated uncertainly before inclining his head. "As you like, my love. If you decide you require my 'hovering' presence, you need only to call."

Silver watched Nicholas and Count Stepvan start across the ballroom and then turned to Natalya Savron. "Now we're alone. Begin."

A flicker of surprise touched the other woman's face. "You handled Nicholas very badly, you know. A man must be guided subtly in the way you wish him to go."

"With lies and deceit?" Silver shook her head. "That's not my way." She squarely met Natalya's gaze. "Though I think it may be yours. However, you will not use them on me."

"Will I not?" Natalya smiled faintly. "You seem very sure."

"I have known a woman like you before. There was an old hag in our village who was very good at torturing captives. She was called Snaggle-Tooth. She would smile"—Silver paused, remembering—"as you smile. Sweetly. The man tied to the stake would think she meant only kindness toward him. Then she would insert the first burning splinter beneath his fingernail."

Natalya's eyes widened in surprise. "Are you comparing me to a savage? I'm hardly an old hag, my dear Silver." Her smile was a mere baring of gleaming teeth. "Nor am I a dirty Apache squaw."

"How did you know that I'm Apache?"

"Naturally I was interested in the woman Nicholas had chosen, so I sent someone down to the docks to make a few inquiries." A sudden harshness edged Natalya's voice. "You made no effort to hide anything about yourself from the captain and the crew of the ship on which you arrived here. You evidently spoke of your mongrel heritage quite openly. I would have thought you'd seize the opportunity to try to disguise your unsavory origin."

"I'm not ashamed of what I am." Silver raised her chin. "Is this why you wanted to see me? Did you wish to tell me I must cringe and hide because I'm a half-breed?"

"I will not permit—"

"Do you think I care what you will or will not permit?" Silver's eyes were blazing.

Natalya drew a deep breath. "I've spent many years making sure no one remembers that I was not born of the nobility. Do you think I will let you flaunt your birth and remind everyone that our blood is tainted? I cannot believe Nicholas would be so stupid as to marry you."

Silver flinched. "Perhaps he doesn't care if I'm a half-breed."

Natalya's eyes narrowed on Silver's face. "Oh, he cares. Have him tell you how he was treated at court as a child. He's felt the sting of contempt just as I have. Now that he's seen fit to take you as a wife, he'll feel it even more."

Silver felt a jab of pain and struggled to keep her face expressionless. The first burning splinter had been inserted, and Natalya was eagerly searching for signs of agony.

"You don't know that. Nicholas is not you."

"Who knows a man better than his mother?" Natalya asked silkily. "If you care anything for him, you will go away. I'm sure he would not be lacking in generosity. However, I would be pleased to buy your passage back to America, where you're accepted."

Accepted? Where had she ever been accepted, Silver wondered bitterly. "I won't leave. I have a reason for being here."

Natalya's lips curled. "I'm sure you do. The dirty little savage is now a princess. A few words spoken by a priest doesn't make a princess, Indian."

"And neither do thirty years of clawing and lies."

The older woman's face hardened. "Leave St. Petersburg. I won't tell you again."

Silver gazed steadily at her, suppressing shivers of apprehension. She refused to be afraid of this virago. Nicholas's mother would feed on fear just as old Snaggle-Tooth had. Silver smiled sweetly. "I cannot leave. You see, I am with child."

Natalya inhaled sharply. "You can't be."

"But I am. Dr. Relling said that I'm in wonderfully good health and will have a fine strong babe." Her smile broadened. "A babe with my tainted blood and your name to remind everyone that you have neither lineage nor youth." She paused. "I'm sure you can hardly wait for the happy time when you'll become a grandmother."

Natalya's cheeks were flushed, and she seemed to be struggling to speak.

Silver sketched a curtsy. "I believe our conversation is finished. Good evening, Your Highness." She turned to leave. "I'll send Count Stepvan to you. It must be gratifying to receive a young man's adoration at your advanced age. Enjoy it while you may. The years pass so quickly, don't they? Perhaps he will—"

"One moment." Natalya's whisper was quivering with fury. "Have you thought how this 'tainted' child will be received by Nicholas?"

Silver froze and then repeated Valentin's words of reassurance. "Every man wants an heir to carry on his name."

Natalya smiled coldly. "Has he told you he will welcome a baby with mixed blood?"

Another splinter, well placed and agonizingly sharp.

Silver averted her eyes. "He didn't have to tell me." She heard Natalya's soft laughter behind her as she walked quickly toward the long damask-covered banquet table across the room, where Nicholas and Count Stepvan were standing.

"You can go back to her now," she told the young count curtly.

Stepvan smiled tentatively before hurrying across the room toward Natayla Savron.

Nicholas's gaze searched Silver's face has he handed her a crystal cup full of punch. "Are you all right?"

"Of course." Silver forced herself to smile. "I counted more coups than your sweet mother, I think." She took a sip of the punch. "But I doubt if she'll be persuaded to use her influence at court, unless it's to have me beheaded."

Nicholas smiled faintly. "Even my mother doesn't have the power to have a princess executed."

She put the cup down on the table. "Well, that's a relief. Can we go now?"

"It's considered rude to leave before the appearance of the tsar. Don't you—" He stopped as he noticed the faint lines of tension around Silver's mouth. "Yes, we can go." A reckless smile touched his lips. "Who knows? The tsar might even be disappointed if I obeyed protocol for once." He took her arm and urged her toward the arched doorway across the room.

Count Stepvan's gaze followed Silver and Nicholas as they moved across the ballroom. "Your son's wife is very beautiful."

Natalya's lips thinned as she languidly moved her bejeweled fan back and forth. "You think so? I find her quite ordinary."

The count's gaze was on Silver Savron and he failed to notice his lady's displeasure. "She has a certain . . ." He tilted his head, searching for the right word to describe the tempestuous appeal of Nicholas Savron's wife. "Fire. She may well become the rage, you know."

Natalya's grip tightened on her fan as her gaze followed Stepvan's. The impudent bitch *was* beautiful and her audacity might prove refreshing to a jaded court where anything different was considered exciting and seized upon with enthusiasm. If Silver Savron did become the rage, she would bask in a notoriety that would inevitably include Natalya. And when society grew tired of their new toy, they would throw Silver aside but the glare of notoriety would remain and wouldn't be easily forgotten. After that damnable duel, Natalya had been forced to fight a hellish battle to prevent herself from being exiled from court. She wasn't about to go through the humiliating experience of being an outcast again.

Natalya turned and smiled with enchanting sweetness at Stepvan. "I have a favor to ask, *chéri*. Would you be an angel and find Count Peskov in this mad crush? I really must speak to him before the tsar arrives."

"What did she say to you?" Nicholas asked quietly.

Silver didn't answer. The only sound was the creak of the carriage and the sharp clip of the horses hooves on the cobbled street.

"I want to know, Silver."

Silver shrugged. "Whatever she thought would hurt me. She's a very clever woman, your mother." Silver looked out the window. "She says she knows you well. Is that true?"

"As you say, she's a clever woman. We've come to understand each other over the years." She could feel his gaze on her face. "Why do you ask?"

"No reason." She continued to look out the window. "She wasn't pleased about the child."

He chuckled. "You told her? No wonder she looked like she was about to explode. My beautiful *maman* has no desire to appear other than perpetually young."

"I thought she wouldn't like it." There was a thread of defiance in Silver's voice. "That's why I told her. Do you mind?"

"Look at me, Silver." When she didn't obey, he reached out and turned her face so that she was forced to meet his eyes. "Now, listen carefully. I know exactly what my mother is and how cruel she can be. I'll never blame you for striking out to defend yourself."

"She's your mother," Silver whispered. "Do you have . . . affection for her?"

He was silent for a moment. "I don't know. When I was a boy I loved her. Later, I hated her. We're bound together by the ties of blood and experience, but affection?" He shrugged. "Over the years the boundaries of hate and love tend to blur."

"Do they? I never knew my mother."

"But you had Rising Star."

"Yes, but there was never any doubt about how I felt about my aunt. I loved Rising Star."

"I know." Nicholas suddenly felt very old and world-weary. Everything was so simple for Silver. She saw things with a clear, shining honesty that would never become muddled with time or jaded with experience. "You were both very lucky."

He wanted to draw nearer, not in passion, but to share the tenderness he felt for her. Yet if he did, he knew passion would soon follow. His fingers dropped away from her chin and he moved away. "Did you like Dr. Rellings?"

She drew a deep breath and looked away from him again. "He appears competent enough, but I don't think I'd trust him if anything went wrong. He reminds me of a doctor I knew who practiced in Hell's Bluff. That old sot would go off on a drunken spree at the wink of an eye."

"If you don't trust him, then we'll get someone else."

"He'll do as well as anyone." Her brow wrinkled in thought. "I might decide to deliver my baby myself. I've helped with other births, and it shouldn't be difficult."

"No," Nicholas said firmly. "We'll keep Dr. Rellings.

You may not be worried, but I'd feel a great deal more secure if there were a physician attending you."

"Would you?" She tried to hide the burst of happiness that spiraled through her. "Then we'll keep him on. It doesn't really matter."

"I think it matters very much."

Nicholas actually cared that she was safe and well. She mustn't become so excited; she mustn't let it mean so much to her. She moistened her lips with her tongue, her gloved fingers tightly clutching her small beaded purse. "What are we going to do about Etaine?"

"I was wondering when you were going to bring that up. We can obviously expect no help if Peskov decides to cause trouble."

"I can go after Etaine myself," she said haltingly. "This isn't even your responsibility. I'm the one who promised Etaine—"

"And I'm the one who promised *you* that I'd see that Etaine was taken from her father. I'll keep that promise." He smiled. "Tomorrow night, Silver."

Her eyes lit with excitement. "Truly? How? When will we—"

"*We* are not going to do anything. *You* are going to stay safely home on Crystal Island."

She frowned mutinously. "I'm going with you."

"Silver, I won't permit it."

"Permit?" Silver asked with ominous softness. "Your mother used that word with me. I like it no better from you."

Nicholas gazed at her in exasperation. Silver's gray eyes were bright with anger and her jaw was set in determination. He could see that persuading her to stay at home was going to be a hellishly difficult task. He had a fleeting memory of the night of their marriage on the *Rose*, when he had told himself how easy his firebird was going to be to tame. Good Lord, he must have been mad.

He leaned forward and began to speak quickly and persuasively. Then, as she merely stared blankly at him, he spoke more harshly, more authoritatively, ending with, "So you will not go."

"You're not being sensible. I have friends with the circus who will be able to help us if we have need of them. It's settled. I'm going with you, Nicholas."

"It is *not* settled, Silver," Nicholas said firmly, and experienced a sinking sensation even as he braced himself to resume his arguments.

3

Silver dodged agilely through the throng milling around the circus grounds and stopped to catch a quick breath as she reached Nicholas, Mikhail, and Valentin. "I know where she is! I just spoke to my friend, Sebastien, the knife thrower, and he said Etaine is performing in the big tent right now." Silver looked at the crowd, then sighed with relief "I don't see Monteith. Perhaps he's not here to—" She broke off as she caught sight of the elegant gray-clad figure of Monteith leaning idly against the platform of the freak-show tent. Her heart gave a leap of sheer terror, and she drew a deep breath to try to steady herself. It was stupid to be so afraid of Monteith. He was only a man. Why did she always have this reaction when she was in his presence? "No, there he is, talking with that plump man wearing the yellow cravat."

"Peskov," Nicholas murmured. "Which means the situation may become a bit dicey. I don't suppose I could persuade you to go back to the carriage?"

She shook her head emphatically. "I don't know why you're so worried. We outnumber him." She gestured to Mikhail and Valentin on either side of Nicholas. "All we have to do is to wait until Etaine comes out of the cage and march in and take her."

Silver wasn't aware of the bravado in her tone, but Nicholas recognized it as the same uneasiness that was besetting him. There was something about Monteith that made him tense and arch like a cat in the graveyard sensing . . . What, for God's sake? He had never been one to waste time caviling before phantoms that didn't exist. With barely contained impatience, he turned toward the big tent. "Then let's go take her."

Paul Monteith glanced up and saw them. For an instant he appeared startled and then, curiously, he smiled with genuine pleasure. He straightened and bowed politely.

Silver clutched Nicholas's arm. "Yes, let's go."

"Our villain doesn't seem to be apprehensive," Valentin commented to Silver as he fell into step with them. "I expected the man to be a demon incarnate from your description of him. He's actually quite a handsome fellow."

"He is *not* handsome," Silver said harshly. "Not on the inside. He's ugly and slimy and—"

"I think Valentin gets the gist of your meaning," Nicholas said as they entered the big tent. He wrinkled his nose at the distasteful odor of sawdust, sweat, and perfume. The tiers of benches were packed with a motley collection of humanity. Peasants garbed in coarse homespun contrasted sharply with elegantly dressed gentlemen and satin-gowned women. The audience in the tent had only one common denominator, their breathless, almost hungry fascination with what was happening in the cage in the center ring. Nicholas found himself swept up in the same mesmerizing horror. "Good Lord," he whispered. "Is that your Etaine?"

Silver nodded. "The act's almost over. There's just the last bit that's called 'The Sacrifice.'" She swallowed to ease the painful tightness of her throat. "It's terrible. I hate to watch it."

But she knew she would watch the rest of Etaine's act. She always had been compelled to despite—or perhaps because of—the sick terror she felt for the child.

"This is wickedness," Mikhail said slowly, his gaze on Etaine's small figure in the cage.

Silver was surprised to see Mikhail's enormous hands clench into fists at his sides. Mikhail so seldom showed ferocity that it jarred her out of her thrall of horror. "Yes, it is."

Etaine's silver-white curls shone brightly beneath the harsh light as she slowly crawled up onto a black marble slab resembling an altar. Two pedestals were positioned about a foot from the edge on either side and a third was set even closer to the head of the marble slab.

Etaine clapped her hands and the two male lions bounded across the cage and leapt onto the pedestals. Then she clapped her hands again and the female lion pranced more slowly to the pedestal at the head of the altar. The lioness snarled, her yellow eyes blazing defiance as she lifted a paw to claw at the air. It took another command from Etaine to get her to leap onto the pedestal.

Then slowly, deliberately, the child stretched out on the altar on her back.

"My God," Valentin said. "Those lions are only inches from her."

Etaine waited another moment and then scooted to the end of the altar so that her slender neck hung off the slab; it was suspended directly below the bared teeth of the lioness.

"They will kill her. Why do we not stop it?" Mikhail said through clenched teeth.

Silver shook her head. "No, if we try to interfere now, it will startle them and Etaine will lose control."

"She doesn't look as if she has much control now," Nicholas said grimly.

The child looked totally helpless and infinitely fragile in her pink tights and tutu as she slowly threw out her arms as if to embrace the death that surrounded her.

Silver moistened her dry lips. "She has control. Etaine is magical with animals." Silver was reassuring herself as well as them. "She'll be finished soon."

Etaine stayed frozen in that position for another half minute, before carefully folding her arms across her chest and closing her eyes. This was always the worst moment of the performance for Silver. Etaine looked like the effigy on a tomb, reminding everyone in the audience just how close death was to her.

Then it was over. Silver breathed a sigh that quivered through every nerve of her body as Etaine opened her eyes and slowly, cautiously, sat up. The audience gave a communal gasp as Etaine's soft curls brushed the lioness's sharp yellow teeth.

In another moment the child had slid to the other end of the altar, gotten down, and turned to face the lions.

The lioness snarled before gliding down onto the black marble slab Etaine had just vacated.

"Merde!" Mikhail took an impulsive step forward.

But the lioness went no farther. She only stood and watched with hungry golden eyes as Etaine backed step by step across the cage toward the door.

"If you'll excuse me."

Silver turned to see Paul Monteith standing behind her in the aisle. "How delightful to see you again, Silver. I'd love to stay and chat, but I must go unlock the cage. Sultana appears a trifle distraught tonight, doesn't she? We wouldn't want Etaine to experience any . . . difficulty."

Nicholas watched Monteith walk slowly down the aisle toward the ring. "He *locks* Etaine in that cage?"

Silver nodded. "With great ceremony at the beginning of every act. He says it adds to the excitement for the audience to know that Etaine can't get out of the cage."

"I think I will break his bones," Mikhail said.

Nicholas began to swear softly under his breath.

Paul Monteith had reached the door of the cage and held up the key for the audience to see. Then he paused, his gaze holding Etaine's through the bars of the cage. The lions were moving restlessly behind the child, but she didn't seem to be aware of them. Her entire attention was focused on her father and the key in his hand.

Monteith inserted the key, unlocked the door, and grabbed Etaine's wrist, drawing her out of the cage.

The audience exploded into applause, shouting, screaming, clapping.

Paul Monteith stepped aside and watched with a slight smile as Etaine took her bows.

"Now," Mikhail said. "We wait no longer." He strode swiftly down the isle toward the center ring with Silver, Nicholas, and Valentin in his wake.

Silver felt a rush of surprise. She had never seen Mikhail take the initiative as he was doing tonight. He had always seemed to prefer to fade into the background. Now he was very much in the forefront as he brushed everyone from his path and strode into the ring.

Etaine's eyes showed her surprise as she looked up to see the mountain of a man striding across the ring, the light of the lanterns blazing on his mop of red hair.

The audience suddenly fell silent as Mikhail knelt in front of Etaine. He smiled gently. "I am Mikhail Kuzdief. I have come to take you away. You will be safe with me. Will you trust me and come?"

Etaine gazed at him in wonder before shooting an apprehensive glance at her father.

Paul Monteith merely stood watching them both, an amused smile on his lips.

Silver had finally reached the ring. "Go with Mikhail, Etaine. We'll join you in a moment."

A brilliant smile lit Etaine's face. "Silver, you're *here*!" She ran across the few yards separating them and threw herself into Silver's arms. "I thought I'd never see you again."

Silver's arms tightened around Etaine's thin body. "Did you think I lied, then?" she asked teasingly. "I promised you we'd be together."

"But Russia was so far." The child cast another glance at her father.

"Go to your tent, Etaine," Monteith said. "Now."

Etaine shivered but then turned to look defiantly at her father. "No." Her voice was a mere breath of sound, but her deep blue eyes were blazing in her pale face. "I won't obey you. Not any longer. I'm going with Silver."

Monteith went still, his gaze searching Etaine's face. "Are you, indeed? How interesting," he commented lightly.

Nicholas stepped in front of Monteith. "Take her to the carriage, Mikhail." He stared at Monteith. "You're not going to stop us, Monteith."

"Am I attempting to do so?" Monteith watched as Mikhail gathered Etaine in his arms and strode down the aisle and out of the tent with Valentin following closely behind. "I have no objections at the moment. In fact, I approve."

Silver gasped in disbelief. Whatever reaction she

expected from Etaine's father, it was not this one. "We're not going to give Etaine up either now or later, you know."

Monteith's narrow-eyed gaze shifted to Silver. "No, I don't suppose you will. You always were an obstinate young woman. But that won't be a real problem. When I want Etaine back, I'll simply take her. Until that time, I'll permit you to keep her. I think you'll be good for Etaine during this period." He smiled gently. "And a fond father always wants what's best for his child, of course."

Silver didn't know what to say. She gazed at him in bewilderment before turning on her heel and hurrying down the aisle.

Nicholas hesitated. He could understand Silver's confusion; this had all been too easy. "Don't come after us, Monteith. It would be exceptionally bad for your health." He waited, but Monteith's only response was that same faint smile.

As Nicholas left the tent, there was a rush of sound when the crowd in the tiers seemed to move as one, restless now on the hard benches. Monteith didn't move from the center of the ring. He stood straight and majestic beneath the harsh light of the lanterns that painted shadows of darkness on his fine-boned features.

Etaine was cuddled close against Silver when Nicholas entered the carriage and sat down opposite them next to Valentin.

Mikhail scarcely waited until the door was closed to whip the horses into a brisk trot.

"Well, that was no problem," Valentin said. "I confess I'm a little disappointed. I expected more excitement."

"It's not over." A frown wrinkled Nicholas's brow. "Monteith was entirely too accommodating. I don't like it."

"Neither do I." Silver's arm tightened around Etaine. "He seemed to want us to take her. Do you think he means to ask Peskov to intercede to have her returned to him?"

"We'll know tomorrow." Nicholas's eyes shifted to the child next to her. "You haven't introduced us, Silver." He smiled at Etaine with heart-stopping charm. "Your servant, Mademoiselle Etaine. My name is Nicholas Savron, and I have the honor of being the husband of your friend Silver."

Etaine's gaze flew to Silver's face. "Truly? I didn't even know you were affianced. You didn't tell me—"

Silver was laughing as she hugged Etaine. "What you mean is that you thought no sane man would risk marrying a virago like me. Perhaps Nicholas is not as sane as most men."

"Stung again. Someday you're going to find one sterling quality in my iniquitous character," Nicholas murmured, his gaze lingering on Silver's face before shifting back to Etaine. "At any rate, since our fates seem to be entwined through Silver, I hope we can be friends."

Etaine studied him for a moment, and Nicholas became aware of how keen and unchildlike was her regard. Then Etaine smiled and he felt as if he had been given a very rare and special gift. "I would like that very much . . . Nicholas."

"It's my custom to protect my friends. And I'd like to protect you, Etaine, but I need your help. Do you know why your father let you go so easily tonight?"

Etaine shook her head.

"He's a most unusual man," Nicholas murmured. "I don't understand him."

"No one does," Etaine said simply. "But he won't give up. He never gives up."

Nicholas smiled gently. "Well, neither will we." He turned to Valentin. "I think we should find out more about Paul Monteith. Will you speak to my attorneys tomorrow and have them make inquiries into Monteith's background?" He paused significantly. "And make sure they hire more competent investigators than the ones they employed to find Dominic Delaney."

"Where shall I tell them to start?" Valentin asked. "St. Louis?"

"No. Monteith's accent is very clipped, very British." He looked at Etaine inquiringly. "However, you have an entirely different accent. Were you born in America?"

"I don't think so. Khadil says she thinks I was born in Yorkshire, but I remember only London and Liverpool. We were in America for . . ." She gestured vaguely. "I can't remember. It seems like a long time."

Nicholas smiled at the child. "Tell them to start in Yorkshire, Valentin. Perhaps you've heard that knowledge is power, Etaine. We're going to see if we can acquire a bit of that commodity to use as a weapon against your father and keep you safe."

She gazed at him in wonder. "You're not afraid of him, are you?"

"Should I be?"

"Yes," Etaine said gravely, then settled once more against Silver.

Nicholas was conscious that the child's gaze dwelt thoughtfully on him many times during their ride to the quay.

"Etaine went right off to sleep. I was afraid she'd be so excited she'd have another attack, but thank heaven she seems to be growing out of them." Silver looked immensely relieved as she closed the door of the study and crossed the room to where Nicholas and Valentin stood by the open French doors. "She told me she'd had only one attack since she left America. She must be getting stronger."

Nicholas raised a brow. "She struck me as being quite strong already. Your Etaine is ... extraordinary."

"She's had to be to survive." Silver's lips tightened. "I understand she's had this affliction of the lungs since she was born and with Monteith as a father ..."

"I can see how she'd have difficulties," Valentin said. "She is only ten years of age? She appears much older and very intelligent."

Silver nodded eagerly. "Etaine's very bright and she loves to learn new things. She's never been to school, but the people in the circus have taught her many things. Khadil taught her to cipher; she learned to read from Sebastien; she can speak French, Spanish, and Italian. She even knows—"

"How to tame ferocious lions," Nicholas interrupted. He smiled indulgently. "You don't have to defend Etaine to me, Silver. As I said, I think she's extraordinary."

"But she's more than intelligent, she's sweet and loving and she cares about people. I know that taking her from her father may cause you a great deal of trouble and I'll be sorry if your tsar becomes angry with you." She lifted her chin. "But saving Etaine is worth it."

"I'll try to remember that as I trudge through the snow in Siberia," Nicholas said dryly.

Silver frowned uncertainly. "Would he really send you there? Perhaps if I went to see him and explained ..."

Valentin chuckled. "It's a trifle difficult to sit down and have a cozy chat with his imperial majesty, you know."

"No, I don't know. I don't know anything about

the tsar or your customs." Silver's gaze was fastened on Nicholas's face. "Then I won't chat with him. I'll just tell him to send me to Siberia instead of you."

Nicholas went still. "You'd do that?"

She looked at him in surprise. "Of course. It was for my sake that you took Etaine away from that bastard. If someone has to be punished, it's only fair that it be me."

Nicholas's expression was a curious blend of shock and tenderness as he stepped a pace closer and took her hand. "You never cease to amaze me, Silver." He lifted her hand to his lips and pressed a gentle kiss on the center of her palm. "I confess I'm not accustomed to dealing with a woman with such a profound sense of justice. I'm quite touched."

"Are you laughing at me?"

"Oh, no." His eyes met her own. "I'm not laughing. I've never felt less like laughing in my life."

Neither did Silver, but still she found herself laughing tremulously. "I think it very sensible for me to go to Siberia in your place. After all, I'm accustomed to living on the land, and my life has been rougher than yours. I'd probably even enjoy it. I have no liking for stuffy palaces and footmen and . . ." She trailed off and, bemused, simply gazed at him. Sweet heaven, he was beautiful. His dark eyes were sparkling with a thousand secrets and his lips were turned up in a smile so tender that it sent tingles of warmth through her every vein. It wasn't fair for a man to look like this. Men were supposed to be hard and rough-edged, not glowing like a flame, burnishing everything around them with a shimmering luster.

His eyes were twinkling now. "You make Siberia sound almost inviting." He turned her hand over and brushed her knuckles with his lips. "So inviting that I find it impossible to let you take my place there. I can hardly wait to taste the joys of—"

"You're both mad," Valentin observed, his bright blue eyes darting from Silver to Nicholas and then back again. "Exile is no joke."

Nicholas's gaze never left Silver. "Silver would never make that mistake. She doesn't understand jokes, Valentin." He smiled gently as he released her hand and stepped back. "But I'm working on it."

"Why do I suddenly feel *de trop*?" Valentin asked.

Silver tore her gaze away from Nicholas's. "No, I only came to . . ." Why had she come? Etaine. She had come to tell him she was grateful about Etaine. "I came only to thank you for helping Etaine."

"And to tell me you'll suffer Siberia in my place," Nicholas said. "We'll cross our Siberian bridge if we ever get to it." Then something flickered in the depths of his eyes. "However, if you're feeling grateful, I may as well take advantage of it."

"What do you mean?"

"I think it only fair that you stay by my side until we see what the outcome of tonight's events are going to be." He bowed mockingly. "Like a proper wife."

"I've never been a proper anything," Silver said absently, her gaze searching his face. "You truly want me to stay?"

"I *do* believe it's time I bid you both a good night," Valentin said.

Nicholas ignored him and nodded solemnly at Silver. "I just might decide to accept your offer. Tsar Alexander can be very intimidating when he's—" He broke off as he saw a worried frown come to her face. He sighed ruefully and deliberately reached up and tugged his left earlobe.

Silver burst out laughing.

Nicholas nodded in satisfaction. "That's right. You did that very well, Silver. In no time at all I'll have you trained."

"I think not, Your Highness. I'm not easily trained."

She lowered her gaze to veil the joy that was bubbling through her. He *wanted* her to stay. She turned away with a careless shrug. "But if you wish me to remain for a while, I'm willing to do as you ask. I have no urgent desire to get on another ship so soon." She moved toward the door. "I grew very bored with the ocean by the time we arrived here."

"We'll strive to keep you from suffering a similar ennui on Crystal Island."

Silver opened the door. "Oh, I don't think I'll be bored."

"No?" Nicholas's tone was softly seductive.

"After all, Etaine is here now."

Nicholas gazed blankly at the door Silver had just closed behind her.

Valentin made a sound that fell somewhere between a snort and a chuckle.

"I see nothing amusing," Nicholas said sourly.

"Then why am I amused?"

"God knows."

"It could be that I find Silver very refreshing."

"Or it could be you enjoy seeing my self-esteem in the dust."

Valentin grinned. "Is that what she did? I really didn't notice."

Valentin was enjoying Silver's putdown enormously, Nicholas realized. Well, let him have his pleasure. She had agreed to stay, and even though it was only a first concession, he was content for now.

Firebirds seldom made any concessions at all.

"They took her." Ivan Peskov's voice was trembling with anger as he stormed into Monteith's tent. "You let them take her."

Monteith nodded. "I thought it best."

"How can you say that? They *took* her." Peskov pulled a fine linen handkerchief from his pocket and wiped the perspiration from his neck. "It's all very well for you to be so calm, but how do I explain to—"

"You will say I chose to give her to Savron for reasons of my own." Monteith smiled. "Don't worry. This move may bring Etaine to the level I wish more swiftly than I had hoped. Silver Delaney seems to have the same honing effect as the cats on my sweet daughter. Etaine's defiance tonight was very promising."

"I don't know what you're talking about," Peskov said with exasperation.

"I know you don't." Monteith's smile deepened with contempt. "You don't have to know. Your part is only to make sure Savron and his mistress remain in Russia. All will be well if the Delaney woman doesn't take it into her head to set sail with Etaine."

"She's not his mistress, she's Nicholas Savron's wife."

Monteith lifted a brow. "He married her? Then there should be no problem."

"There is a very great problem in Natalya's eyes." Peskov wiped his upper lip. "I've never seen her so fierce. She said I had to do something. What in Hades *can* I do?" His dark eyes glinted with sudden cunning. "But since Savron's bride appears to figure prominently in your plans, perhaps you'll be able to think of something that will satisfy both your own and Natalya's requirements."

"Perhaps." Monteith's gaze narrowed on Peskov's face. "Suppose you tell me what our dear Natalya wants of you."

4

"**I**'ve brought your tea." Etaine made a face. "It smells terrible, but Nicholas told me to make sure you drank every drop." She handed Silver the delicate china cup and saucer and plopped down beside her on the marble bench with a sigh of contentment. "I love this garden. The hanging gardens of Babylon couldn't have been prettier."

Silver slowly sipped the sassafras tea as she followed Etaine's gaze over the shrubs and flowers and then to the magnificent fountain located in the exact center of the garden. "It's very lovely," she agreed. "Though it's a little too orderly for me. I like to be surprised."

Etaine turned to look at her. "Yet I think you're happy here." She tilted her head, studying Silver consideringly. "You've changed, you know."

Silver shook her head. "I'm the same as I've always been."

"No, there's something different." Etaine hesitated. "I believe you're . . . softer."

"Did you find me hard before?"

"Not exactly." Etaine frowned. "You know I love you, no matter—" She broke off. "But I think you sometimes appeared hard to people who didn't know you. You kept yourself surrounded by walls to keep people away."

Silver laughed. "And now the walls are gone?"

"Not all of them, but enough so that people can see what you are."

"And what am I?"

"Beautiful."

Silver shook her head. "You're wrong, I'm not beautiful inside. I'm still too full of anger and rebellion." She paused, thinking about Etaine's words. "Perhaps what you see is my baby. I think my child must be beautiful. Rising Star used to tell me that if a baby is loved, it casts a glow on everything around it." She gazed unseeingly at the fountain. "I believed her because she shone like a candle in that darkness at Killara while she was with child. I never thought I'd be like her, but sometimes I can feel that shining within me." She smiled. "All my life I've been alone and now I have the child. It fills me with wonder."

A silence fell between them as they sat there enjoying the sunlit garden. The only sounds that broke the stillness were the singing summer harmonies of a breeze ruffling through the branches of the birch trees and the humming of the bees around the flowers.

"I'm glad you married Nicholas," Etaine said suddenly. "I like him. He makes me feel safe."

It was strange how differently people perceived one another, Silver thought. *Safe* would never be a word she would have associated with Nicholas. She herself saw him as exciting, maddening, sensual, but never safe. "You *are* safe here, Etaine. It's been four days since we brought you to the island, and Nicholas says that if Peskov hasn't made a move by this time, he must have no intention of doing so. And without the tsar's intervention, there's really nothing to worry about. The island is well guarded, and no strangers are permitted to come here. Your father would be a fool to try to take you away from us."

"He'll try," Etaine said quietly. "When he's ready, he'll come for me. What's between us hasn't ended yet." She smiled. "But that's in the future. Now I have fine new clothes and flowers and sunlight and friends like you and Nicholas and—"

"One of those friends is coming down the path right now," Silver said. "I wondered when he would show up. He's scarcely let you out of his sight since we brought you here."

Etaine's gaze followed Silver's to the tall red-haired Cossack striding toward them. "Mikhail." She smiled affectionately. "Yes, Mikhail's my friend, but it's really you that he tries to be near. It's just that I'm often in your company."

Silver wasn't at all sure that was true. The bond between Mikhail and the child had grown steadily during the last four days. The camaraderie between them was unusual, not only because it existed in a man close to thirty and a child of ten but because of the nature of that friendship. They both exhibited a supreme naturalness in each other's presence. It was as if they had been companions since the moment of their births.

"Come and sit with us, Mikhail," Silver called as he approached. She held out her cup with a teasing smile. "Have some sassafras tea."

"I am not with child." Mikhail pulled a face as he dropped to the ground on a patch of grass near the bench and crossed his legs tailor fashion. "That brew may be healthy but it tastes bitter as bile. I think you are very brave to drink it twice a day."

Silver shrugged. "Dr. Rellings sent it to Nicholas

to strengthen my blood. I'm not sure it does any good but it can't do harm." She gritted her teeth and took another sip. "Except to my disposition. After the second cup I'm usually bad-tempered enough to scalp someone."

Mikhail's eyes twinkled. "I will be sure I am not the one who serves you that second cup. I have had experience with your temper."

"It was only a pinprick of a wound," Silver protested. "And you shouldn't have let Nicholas persuade you into doing something so foolish. I had to defend myself, didn't I?"

Mikhail nodded. "I hold no ill will." His brow wrinkled in a frown. "But I told you that Nicholas did not try to persuade me. He wanted it done, but he did not ask me to bring you to him."

"Do you always do what Nicholas wants you to?" Silver asked curiously. "You told me once that your loyalty would always be to him. I find it strange that you set no boundaries."

"Nicholas set no boundaries when he gave me his help," Mikhail said simply. "He gave up what he would have given his soul to keep. It is only right that in return I try to give him whatever will make his life tolerable."

"If that includes abducting women, I believe you will soon find *your* life intolerable."

Mikhail only smiled.

"What would Nicholas have given his soul to keep?"

"Freedom."

Silver gazed at him thoughtfully. It wasn't the answer she had expected, and it only demonstrated how little she really knew about Nicholas. "Freedom is a great gift."

Etaine shivered. "It's more than that. It's life itself. Every time I heard the key turn in the lock of the cage and knew there was no escape—"

"Don't think about it." Silver's arm slid quickly around the child's shoulders.

"She has to think about it." Mikhail's voice was gentle as his gaze rested on Etaine's face. "It's a part of her. It will always be a part of her. We are what life makes us."

Etaine's eyes met Mikhail's with complete understanding and that odd sense of kinship. "Yes, that's true."

"But there's no reason we can't enjoy what we have in the present," he said gravely. "There are many pleasures. The sunlight, the flowers . . ."

They were almost the same words Etaine had used before Mikhail had joined them. Why, they were really very much alike, Silver realized suddenly. They both possessed a shining simplicity of spirit, a belief that each minute must be treasured and filled with as much delight as possible. No wonder they had instantly recognized each other as kindred spirits. How wonderful it must be, she thought wistfully, to know a perfect meeting of the spirit would banish loneliness forever. Perhaps when her child was born she would have someone to belong to and to share moments like these.

She took one last sip of her sassafras tea and set the cup and saucer down on the bench beside her. She stood up and briskly smoothed the skirts of her gown. "Well, I've had enough of sunlight and flowers. Doing nothing every day is driving me mad. I'm going to see if I can find something interesting to read in the library."

Mikhail unwound his powerful limbs and rose to his feet. "I will go with you."

"You don't have to stay at my side all the time." She gazed at him in exasperation. "I don't need an escort to curl up in a chair with a book."

"I promised Nicholas that when he was not with you, I would be near."

And Nicholas chose to not be with her an amazingly large part of every day, she thought with a wrenching pang. "I don't want you. I can amuse myself," she said with sudden fierceness. "I need no one near to—"

"I think I'll go inside too." Etaine jumped up and slipped her hand in Silver's. "Come along, Silver. Are there any books about tsars, do you suppose? Mikhail told me about Tsar Peter and how he built this city out of marshland." She was pulling Silver swiftly down the path toward the terrace, chattering brightly. "And he moved the capital from Moscow to here and made all his nobles follow him. I think that's interesting, don't you?"

"Very interesting." A faint smile tugged at Silver's lips as she allowed Etaine to lead her down the path toward the distant palace. "And you don't have to try to distract me any longer. Your precious Mikhail isn't in any danger of being scalped at the moment."

"What a relief," Mikhail murmured. "I understand red hair is very much prized among your people."

Etaine grinned as she slowed her pace to a walk. "It wasn't only for Mikhail. You're not happy when you're annoyed, Silver. I wanted only to—"

Silver began to laugh as she held up her hand. "I know exactly what you wanted to do, Etaine. Sunlight and flowers. Am I right?"

Etaine nodded. "I'm sure it's much better for you and the baby not to be troubled."

Silver's hand went protectively to her abdomen. The baby . . . Was it really bad for the baby for her to be upset? And, if it *was* bad, how did someone with her uncertain temperament keep from exploding occasionally? There was more to this matter of having a baby than she had dreamed.

"What's beyond the wall?" Etaine was pointing to the high brick wall that bordered the western perimeter of the garden. "Another distraction?"

Silver shook her head. "I have no idea. I've never been curious enough to inquire."

"No, truly. I've been wondering about it ever since I came here." Etaine turned to Mikhail. "Do you know? Yesterday I tried the door in the wall but it was locked."

"It is the bathhouse garden and only Nicholas has the key."

"The bathhouse?" Silver frowned in puzzlement. "But a hip bath is brought to my room every morning."

"That is because it is summer. The bathhouse is used only in the winter."

"But that doesn't make sense. I've heard it becomes terribly cold here in the winter. Why should anyone trek down from the house in the freezing—"

Pain!

Silver stopped dead in the center of the path, swaying, breathless.

"Silver . . ." Etaine's face was suddenly pale and frightened as she peered up at her. "Silver, what's wrong? You look so—"

A scream issued from Silver's throat as jagged pain ripped through her belly. She bent over, clutching her abdomen. The garden shimmered around her as wave after wave of agony struck through her. "No! Dear God, I won't *have* it!"

"Let me help." Mikhail was lifting her easily, his rough-hewn features above her taut with concern. "It is all right, Silver. I will get you to Nicholas."

"Hurt . . ." Tears were running down her cheeks, she realized dimly. She should have had more courage than to weep like a babe in a papoose, but the suddenness of the pain had surprised her. Another spasm shuddered through her and she gasped, trying to draw up her knees.

"I know you hurt." Mikhail walked swiftly toward the terrace, his gaze fixed straight ahead. "It will soon be over."

She had never seen Mikhail look so grim, she thought hazily. "Mikhail . . ." Then another convulsion of agony caused her to clutch his arms, digging her nails into his flesh.

"Don't be frightened, Silver." Etaine's voice was urgent, frantic. "We'll take care of you."

She would not be all right, Silver knew with sudden dismal clarity. Nothing would ever be all right again. There was only loneliness and sadness and pain in the world. Once there had been a hope for something else for her, but it was gone. "Nicholas," she whispered. "Nicholas, help me!"

Then the darkness began.

"She's lost the child," Matthew Rellings said. "She's very young and no doubt the journey from America was too much in her frail condition."

Nicholas's hands closed into fists at his sides. Lord, the man was a fool. "She's *not* frail. She's strong and healthy and this shouldn't have happened. You shouldn't have permitted it to happen. What kind of doctor are you, anyway? If there was a problem, you should have seen it coming."

"I'm only a physician not a seer," Dr. Rellings said ponderously. "I know you're upset, Your Highness, but you mustn't be unreasonable. Sometimes these things are guided by a higher power than our humble selves and—"

"Get out of my sight." Nicholas's voice cracked like a whiplash across Dr. Relling's sentence. "I never want to see your face again."

Dr. Rellings sidled quickly toward the door of the

study. "You're being most unfair," he whined, glancing apprehensively at Nicholas and then to the corner of the room where Mikhail loomed intimidatingly. "Her Highness had lost the child before I ever set foot inside your front door. It's not my fault—"

"I don't feel like being fair," Nicholas said savagely. "I feel like throttling someone, and if you don't get out of here, it may be you."

Dr. Rellings opened the door. "I'm sure you'll realize how inevitable this tragedy was when you become calmer. Do call on me at any time. I've given my instructions to Count Marinov regarding the care of your poor lady." He smiled tentatively over his shoulder. "You'll be happy to know it was only a girl child, Prince Savron. No heir for you. Perhaps next time you'll be more fortunate. I've left an elixir for Her Highness that may help her to conceive a fine, healthy boy to—"

"*Get out!*"

The door shut quickly behind Dr. Rellings.

"Only a girl child," Nicholas repeated bitterly. "I *should* have strangled the idiot. What do I tell her? 'It doesn't matter that your child is dead, Silver, it was only a female. Not really important.' "

"As you say, the man is a fool." Mikhail moved out of the shadows to stand beside the desk. "He does not realize you would have valued the child even though she would not have carried on your name." His gaze searched Nicholas's face. "The child *did* have value for you?"

Nicholas whirled toward him. "Of course the child had value for me. Why do you ask?"

Mikhail's expression became shattered. "One does not learn unless one inquires. Are you going to her now?"

Nicholas nodded jerkily as he strode toward the

door. "I want to be there when she wakes. Though God knows how I'm going to tell her about the child."

The door closed behind him.

Mikhail gazed after him for a moment, his broad forehead creased in thought. Then he turned and moved slowly toward the French doors that led to the terrace.

"You can leave now, Valentin. I'll stay with her."

Nicholas moved across the bedchamber to look down at Silver's drawn face. God, she looked so damned weak and helpless in the candlelight. Maybe Rellings wasn't such a fool as he had thought. Perhaps Silver really wasn't as strong as he had believed and should never have conceived the child. She seemed little more than a child herself at the moment, a child whose body he had taken and plundered for his own pleasure. "How long did Rellings say she would sleep?"

"He gave her laudanum for the pain." Valentin rose from the chair beside the bed. "He said she might sleep through the night." He nodded to the small bottle on the bedside table. "He left more laudanum if she needs it." He hesitated, his gaze on Nicholas's ravaged face. "Would you like me to stay with you?"

Nicholas shook his head as he dropped down into the chair Valentin had just vacated. "Go to bed. Thank you for staying with her."

"Silver is my friend." Valentin smiled wearily. "And someone had to keep you from mutilating Rellings. You were like a madman when he told you she might have lost the child."

"He should have been able to save it." Nicholas's hands clenched on the brocade arms of the chair. "And Silver was *crying*, dammit. You know Silver never weeps like other women. And that idiot Rellings just stood there with a sanctimonius look on his face shaking his head. He should have done something to make her stop crying."

"He appeared to do everything he could for her."

"Perhaps." Nicholas's gaze was fastened on Silver's face. "I still never want to see that bastard again. Send for another doctor to tend her."

Valentin nodded. "First thing in the morning. Call me if you need me."

Nicholas stared unwaveringly at Silver. Why didn't she wake? He didn't want to sit there all night dreading the look on her face when he told her there would be no child. Even the thought sent an ache surging through him. He wanted it over.

He seemed destined to hold vigils beside her, watching helplessly as she suffered because of his own self-indulgence. Sitting there was entirely too reminiscent of that night on the *Mississippi Rose* after Bassinger had beaten Silver unmercifully. Yet there he sat, wondering how he could ease a pain that was far greater than the whipping she had endured on the *Mary L.*

Damn, he had never felt so guilty in his life. Why must Silver hurt because he had lost all control since the moment he had met her. He was little more than a rutting animal when he was near her. There was no justice for women in this world. It appeared even God was unfair to them.

His lips twisted in a bittersweet smile. Lord, how he had changed since Silver had come into his life. He had always believed it was the man who was the eventual victim in any relationship with the fair sex, and his cynicism and wariness had become legend in his circle. In the early days of their relationship he had wondered how a woman as strong and demanding as Silver had managed to earn his trust. Now he knew it was because Silver's strength was her own, not sucked from her victims, and he cherished her honesty and lust for life as much as he did her beauty and sensuality.

He leaned forward to carefully tuck the coverlet around her shoulders. Tenderness swept through him and he had to swallow to ease the tightness of his throat. He had hoped she would lose a little of her wariness of him as they shared the coming of their child, but that was not to be. He would have to find another way to gain her trust in the future. Now he must wait and help Silver through the agony to come. Dear God, how was he going to tell her?

Nicholas was sitting in the chair by the bed when Silver opened her eyes. He looked tired, she thought drowsily, and terribly, terribly sad. Poor Nicholas, why was he so upset? She instinctively reached out a hand to comfort him but found it too heavy to move. Strange, her head felt heavy too. She must be ill. She rejected the thought immediately. Nonsense, she was never ill. Then why was she lying there . . .

The baby!

"Nicholas. The child. Is my child safe?" Her words were slurred and she barely had been able to form them.

He slowly shook his head as he reached out and covered her hand with his own. "No," he said gently. "Our little girl is gone, Silver."

Emptiness. Somehow she had known she was alone again. She had always been alone, but not like this. Not with this echoing hollowness, not with this void of desolation. "It was a girl?"

"Yes." Nicholas tightened his hand on her own. "The doctor says you'll be fine in a few weeks."

The doctor was wrong. How could she be fine when the world had turned to ice? "Why?" she whispered.

"Why did she have to die? Why couldn't I keep my baby?"

A flicker of pain crossed his face. "Christ, I don't know, Silver. The doctor says it was God's will."

"But how could that be?" Her tone held a childlike wonder. "I've never had anyone of my own. Why would God take my baby too? It's not fair, Nicholas."

"No, it's not fair," he said huskily. "But you will have children."

How could she have children when there was only loneliness and isolation left in the world? She slowly shook her head and closed her eyes. Darkness. It was better in the darkness, where she could not see Nicholas's face. He was trying to be kind, attempting to comfort her for the loss of the child he had never wanted. In a tiny compartment of her mind she realized she should be grateful, but his kindness only reminded her of her pain and she must *not* remember that pain. She would stay in the darkness and the ice, freezing out all the memories and the loneliness.

"Silver . . ." Nicholas's voice held agonizing sympathy. She should answer him, she thought. But if she did, the ice might go away and that couldn't happen.

She withdrew her hand and deliberately turned away from him. Her hand felt strange, severed from Nicholas, severed from life. She would soon become accustomed to it, she assured herself. She was strong and would build a fine wall of ice that would hold out all the pain and loneliness.

"Silver, for God's sake, let me *help* you."

"Go away, Nicholas."

"The hell I will. I'm not letting you go through this alone."

But she was always alone. Didn't Nicholas know that? If he wouldn't go away, then she'd have to go away from him. It wouldn't be difficult; even now she was building the high wall of ice.

She kept her eyes tightly closed. "Then stay," she whispered. "It doesn't really matter."

The cup and saucer were still on the bench where Silver had placed them.

Mikhail stood looking down at them, his blunt features oddly stern in the moonlight. He bent slowly and picked up the cup. The china possessed an egg-shell delicacy in his big hands and he held the cup very carefully as he lifted it to his nose. There was still a residue of tea at the bottom of the cup and the strong odor of sassafras assaulted his nostrils. He breathed deeply, closing his eyes, trying to attune his senses to probing sharpness. It had been so long.

But not too long, he realized grimly. He still re-membered that night in the Kuban and everything connected with it. The events that had transpired were now being brought back to him with stunning force. Sweet Mary, he had hoped he was wrong, but he couldn't deny that what he smelled was—

"Mikhail."

He almost dropped the cup as he whirled around at the sound of his name.

Etaine, specterlike in her white nightgown and robe, stood on the path behind him, her short fair curls shining as if they were the moonlight itself.

He relaxed and casually replaced the cup on the bench. "You startled me. You should be in bed, Etaine. It is far too late for children to be running around in the garden."

"I couldn't sleep." She came closer. "I was worried about Silver and I was standing at the window when I saw you walking down the path." Her gaze went to the cup on the bench. "I'm surprised one of the servants didn't collect that. I guess there was too much confusion when Silver became ill."

Mikhail nodded silently.

Etaine's face became sad. "How quickly things change. Silver was so happy when I brought her that cup of tea and then later—"

"*You* brought her the tea?"

Etaine looked at him, surprised by the sharpness of his tone. "Why, yes. Nicholas asked me to do it. I was going to join Silver in the garden anyway. What difference does it make? None of that is important now. Silver's lost her baby, hasn't she, Mikhail?"

"Yes. Did no one tell you?"

"Nicholas sent Valentin to tell me that Silver was going to be all right but people don't talk to children about babies." Etaine wrinkled her nose. "I guess it's considered indelicate."

"I did not realize." Mikhail frowned. "It is not so among my people. Children are expected to face the harsh as well as the smooth." His gaze searched her face. "But you are not truly a child. You know too much; you have suffered too long."

She smiled faintly. "No, I'm not a child. I'm glad you see that, Mikhail."

He sat down on the bench gazing gravely out over the garden. "Sometimes I feel I do not see enough and at other times that I see too much. It is not comfortable to see what you do not want to see." He looked down at his big hands resting on his knees. "You have known Silver for a long time. Tell me, do you know her heart?"

"It's easy to know Silver. She never tries to hide anything."

"I did not think so either." He did not look at Etaine. "Did she ever speak to you of the child?"

"Yes."

"Was it . . . Did she want the child?"

"Oh, yes," Etaine said softly. "Silver has always been alone. The child would have made her so happy."

"She told you this?"

"Yes, she told me. Why do you ask?"

"No reason." His brawny shoulders shifted as if he were shrugging off a heavy burden. "I only wondered. Some women do not want a child. I knew such a woman many years ago."

She gazed at him shrewdly. "There *was* a reason, but you have no intention of telling me what it is."

Mikhail turned to look at her. "That is true."

She sighed. "I thought your people believed children should be able to face anything."

He smiled slowly. "Perhaps I have been away from the Kuban too long. I do not wish to burden you with something I am not certain of myself." His smile faded. "But I will be certain in time. There must be a way to find out. . . ." He trailed off, once again lost in thought.

Etaine tugged impatiently at the sleeve of his tunic. "Certain of what?"

He got abruptly to his feet. "The only thing I am certain about right now is that you should be in bed." He lifted her easily in his arms and started down the path. "Silver will need you tomorrow when she wakes. You will not want to be caught lying like a slug on your bed."

"Mikhail, won't you please tell me?"

"No."

"You're as stubborn as my lioness, Sultana, when she has a toothache." She made a face at him before sliding her slender arms trustingly around the Cossack's broad shoulders. "At least promise me that you'll tell me what's bothering you when you are certain."

"I promise that you will know someday."

It was the only answer she was going to wrest from

him and she would have to be satisfied with it, Etaine realized. Well, she could wait. Her life had taught her both patience and an acceptance of the things she couldn't change. It was only lately that she had begun to feel the first stirrings of defiance within herself. But there was no need for resistance or defiance here with Silver and her friends. Certainly not with Mikhail, who gave her not only friendship but a greater understanding than she had ever known. Yes, she could once again afford patience.

Still, Mikhail's words had been very curious.

5

"Where are you going, Silver?" Nicholas asked gently. He quickly crossed the parlor to stand beside her at the French doors. "It's starting to snow and the wind is sharp. You don't want to go out into the garden today."

Silver turned to look at him, her expression blank. "I have a cloak." She touched the marten fur trimming her black cloak. "I won't be long."

Nicholas shook his head. "I think it would be wise to skip your walk this afternoon. Yesterday you forgot the time and were quite chilled by the time Etaine found you. Wait until tomorrow."

She stared at him a moment, her gaze as chillingly remote as the leaden sky beyond the French doors. "Perhaps it will be even worse then." She turned away and moved toward the door leading to the hall. "But very well, it doesn't matter." Her voice held nothing but indifference. "I'll go back to my room."

"No, I didn't mean—" Nicholas stopped. Silver was already gone, flitting like a ghost from the room.

Nicholas's hands slowly closed at his sides. "Dammit, Mikhail, I can't stand much more of this. I want to *break* something."

"Silver?" Mikhail leaned his elbow on the marble mantel, his gaze fixed soberly on Nicholas's face. "She has angered you?"

Pain replaced the helpless frustration on Nicholas's face, and then only weariness remained. "No, I don't want to break Silver. Though Lord knows it would be easy enough to do. She's as brittle as an ice statue." He whirled away from the French doors with barely controlled violence. "Did you see her just now? She didn't even argue with me, for God's sake. She *obeyed* me." He began prowling back and forth. "And she scarcely eats a bite at meals these days."

For an instant the corners of Mikhail's lips quirked as he realized this latter circumstance was the ultimate proof of the seriousness of Silver's condition in Nicholas's eyes. The smile was never realized. There was too much suffering in Nicholas's face for Mikhail to permit himself levity. "She is not herself," he agreed. "Perhaps if you give her a little more time—"

"Time?" Nicholas interrupted harshly. "How much time is it going to take? It's been three and a half months. She lost the baby in July. It's November now."

"She grieves."

"Do you think I don't know that?" Nicholas's dark eyes were blazing in his taut face. "A blind man could see how she's hurting. I try to help her but she won't let me. She looks at me with those blank eyes and—"

"She won't let anyone near enough to soothe her sorrow," Mikhail said gently. "Etaine also grieves for her, but she cannot help either."

"Well, someone's got to help her. This can't go on. She's like a sleepwalker." Nicholas threw himself into the high-backed chair by the fireplace. "We've got to find a way to wake her up. I never thought Silver would react like this. I expected . . ." He ran his fingers wearily through his hair. "Whatever I expected, it wasn't this damnable melancholy."

"Silver is not the wild child she was when we first met her," Mikhail said slowly. "She has suffered much since then and it is natural she would change."

Nicholas flinched. "Thanks to my intervention in her life, you mean. I suppose you believe I should send her home?"

"Perhaps. Would you?"

"No." Nicholas gazed broodingly into the fire. "I won't let her go. But I can't stand to see her like this. I have to find a way to jar her out of her godawful trance. It's getting worse every day, and soon I won't be able to reach her at all."

"You are right, she is not becoming better. Still, I thought if we waited—" Mikhail paused. "I think I know a way to make her come awake."

Nicholas's gaze flew to his face. "Then why the hell haven't you done it?"

"Because I am not sure it is a good way. She is not of a calm temperament, and it is possible that she will . . ." He shrugged. "But at least she would no longer be a sleepwalker."

"What the devil are you talking about?"

"I cannot tell you. I will speak to Silver, but I will not tell you what I will say to her."

Nicholas's eyes widened in surprise. "My god, when have there ever been secrets between us, Mikhail?"

"Not until this moment," Mikhail said sadly. "I am sorry, my friend, but it must be this way."

"But dammit, I won't—" Nicholas broke off in exasperation as he saw the determination in Mikhail's face. "*Merde*, Mikhail, now isn't the time for you to turn obstinate."

Mikhail did not reply.

Nicholas gazed intently at the Cossack. "You truly believe you can bring Silver back to us?"

"I do."

"Then do it."

"You are sure?"

"I'm sure of nothing except that Silver has to be freed from this hellish prison she's locked herself into." Nicholas shook his head wearily. "Keep your secrets if you must. But for God's sake, *help* her."

Mikhail straightened slowly, his arm dropping from the mantel. "Now?"

"As soon as possible."

Mikhail nodded and spun on his heel, crossing the room in several long strides. The door closed softly behind him.

Nicholas stared into the depths of the fire. Why must Mikhail be so damned mysterious? He had never been anything but open through all the years they had been friends. It was Silver. Silver was the answer to all the changes that had taken place around and within him in the past months. But why should Mikhail be permitted to help her when he could not?

God, he was actually consumed with jealousy of Mikhail. How petty when the only thing of importance was that someone help Silver to become well and whole again. Mikhail had called Silver a wild child, but perhaps it was he, Nicholas, who deserved the description. He certainly felt wild at the moment, wild with despair and frustration, wild with worry and desire.

Desire? How had that word intruded into his consciousness when he had so carefully avoided admitting even to himself how much he wanted Silver.

What a selfish bastard he was, he thought in disgust. She had lost their child just a little over three months before. If he had been a more civilized man, he would have been able to deny his hunger for her. It had been beyond his capability to banish the carnal feelings he experienced when he looked at her, but he prayed God that he had hidden them well. She was carrying a heavy enough burden without being forced to accept a man who wanted to rip off her clothes and bury himself in the silken heat between her thighs.

The muscles of his stomach clenched at the thought, and he was aware of the familiar response in his groin. No, he must not feel this. . . .

He leaned back in the chair and forced himself to relax. He closed his eyes, trying to also close his mind and memory to the erotic thoughts that persisted in insinuating themselves among the tenderness and aching sympathy he felt toward Silver.

He must forget passion. Perhaps for a long, long time. Maybe forever, if Mikhail couldn't manage to rouse Silver to some semblance of normalcy.

But Mikhail couldn't fail in that task. Dear God, he *had* to rouse her.

What in heaven or hell was Mikhail saying to her?

"Come in."

Silver's voice was subdued, totally lackluster as she responded to Mikhail's knock. When he entered the bedchamber she didn't turn away from the window where she was standing watching the slowly falling snow.

Nicholas was right, Silver had lost weight these last few months, Mikhail thought sympathetically. In her high-necked green wool gown she appeared almost fragile, and that was a word he would never have thought he'd use to describe Silver.

He closed the door behind him. "I must talk to you."

"Yes?" Her tone was without interest. "If you like."

"I do not like." Mikhail made a face. "I only hope I will do no real harm in this. Will you look at me, Silver?"

She obediently turned to face him. Her expression was unmarked by any emotion whatever. "Of course. Has Nicholas changed his mind about letting me walk in the garden?"

"No." Mikhail hesitated, wondering how to begin. It would come as a shock . . . But a shock was what Silver needed to pierce through the barrier she had built around her emotion. "I have something to tell you."

She gazed at him blankly.

He took a deep breath. "I believe your child was murdered."

Something flickered in the depths of her eyes. "What did you say?"

"Murder," he said bluntly. "You were given something in the sassafras tea you drank that afternoon to cause you to miscarry your child. It was a potion made from rye grass."

She gazed at him incredulously. "It isn't possible. Who would want my child dead?"

"I do not know. That is for you to discover. If you choose to do so."

"If I choose—" She broke off and turned back to the window. "How could you know this is true?"

"The potion has a fragrance I know well. Even masked by the sassafras, that scent still lingered in the cup when I returned to the garden after you had lost your child. I suspected that there was something not right when the pain started so suddenly. I had gone through it before, you see. My wife found an old woman in our village who knew of the potion and persuaded her to give it to her. My wife was not clever about herbs and potions and took too much. She killed not only the child but herself. I found her

too late and she bled to death." He repeated, "I know
that scent well. It is something I cannot forget."

"Why did she—" Silver stopped. She knew she
should be shocked and sympathetic at the tragedy
Mikhail had suffered. Somewhere deep within her
she did feel sympathy but she couldn't seem to get
past the stunning realization of her own loss. The
wall of ice she had carefully erected and tended for
so long was melting, leaving jagged edges that seemed
to draw fresh blood with every passing second. "You're
sure I was given this herb, Mikhail?"

"I am sure."

"But who? I can't think of anyone who would want
to do such a monstrous thing. I've done no harm to
anyone here. I don't even know anyone in St. Petersburg except the people who live in this house."

"There are a few others you have met here. Monteith, Dr. Rellings . . . During the week after you lost
the child I paid a visit to court and asked a few
questions." He shrugged. "I could find out very little.
I do not belong to their world because I am neither a
servant nor a master. However, there are rumors
that the English doctor was a great favorite of the
married ladies of the court. It is said he was very
obliging about removing the awkward consequences
of their indiscretions. It could be that the potion was
already ground into the sassafras when he gave it to
Nicholas."

"Why would he do such a thing?"

"Rubles. Men can be bought."

Silver's palms touched and then spread on the cold
panes of the window. She needed that coolness. The
ice was gone, leaving only a parched, burning desert
in its place. "You believe he did this horrible thing to
my child?"

"It is a possibility. Or the potion could have been

added as the tea was brewed here on the island. Nicholas's servants are loyal, but again—"

"Rubles," Silver finished bitterly. "I can't believe that anyone could hate me so much. To kill my baby . . ." Her hands pressing against the glass slowly curled into fists. "You swear that you aren't lying to me, Mikhail?"

"I swear, Silver. Your baby was taken from you."

"Butchered," she whispered. She closed her eyes and leaned her head against the window. "My little girl. Monstrous."

"Yes," Mikhail agreed quietly.

There was no sound in the room, yet Mikhail was aware of a clarion call of rage and hurt vibrating from the woman by the window. Then Silver slowly straightened and turned to face him. Her eyes were dry, glittering crystal in the dimness of the chamber.

"Why didn't Nicholas tell me?"

Mikhail hesitated.

"Why?" The question snapped like a quirt between them.

"I did not tell him of the potion in your tea."

"Why not?"

"I thought it best." His gaze shifted away from her face to the snow falling beyond the panes of glass. "Nicholas would—" He broke off and turned away. "I have told you and that should be enough. I will be downstairs in the study if you have need of me."

"Wait, Mikhail. I need an answer."

"No more."

"Just tell me if you questioned Dr. Rellings."

"Dr. Rellings is no longer at court. Two days after you lost the child a note was found in his lodgings saying that he had returned to England."

Despair and rage flowed through her in a wild tide. "Did you find out nothing else at court? Do you have no clue as to who did this?"

Silver saw the muscles of Mikhail's broad back stiffen with sudden tension. He didn't look at her as he opened the door. "I told you that no one would talk to me." He closed the door behind him.

Silver stood in the center of the room, every muscle of her body rigid, her fingernails biting into her palms. It wasn't enough. Mikhail knew or suspected more than he was telling her. She could *feel* it. For some reason he was choosing not to tell her everything he had found out. Well, she would find out for herself. Someone had killed her child, and by heaven, she would find a way to exact vengeance. First, she must tell Nicholas and then . . .

Nicholas.

It had been Nicholas who had given Etaine the cup of sassafras tea to give to her with instructions to make Silver drink every drop.

Nicholas's mother had told her Nicholas would despise a child born of Silver's heritage.

Nicholas had never actually said he wanted the child.

Why should he want either Silver or her child? She had forced him at gunpoint into marriage and he had shunned her bed from that moment.

"No," she whispered. It couldn't be Nicholas who had done this. She had learned many things about him in the past months and she could have sworn he would never commit this hideously evil act even if he hadn't wanted her child. It had to be someone else. But who? Nicholas's mother had not been pleased that she was with child, but would any sane woman kill a child just because it had a half-breed's blood? Surely not.

And Mikhail had not told Nicholas. Was it because he knew his friend Nicholas already knew of the potion?

No, she could not tell Nicholas either. She must

know she could trust him before she confided in him, and there was no trust in her heart now.

Not for anyone.

She must think. Mikhail had gone to court to seek out the answers and so the truth must lie there. He had said he didn't belong to that world and therefore no one at court would speak readily to him. Well, she didn't belong to their world either. She knew nothing about the court or those fine noblemen and women, but she would learn. She would study their ways and make them her own until she had wrested from them the information she needed. She would find out who was behind the killing of her baby.

And then she would plunge her knife into the black heart of the murdering son of a bitch.

"I want to talk to Valentin," Silver announced as she stood in the doorway of the study. "Have you seen him this morning, Mikhail?"

Mikhail nodded. "As I came downstairs he was going into the parlor to join Nicholas."

"Good." Silver turned on her heel. "I want to talk to Nicholas too." The click of her heels echoed on the parquet floor as she strode briskly from the study and across the foyer to the parlor.

Mikhail hesitated and then slowly rose from his chair and followed her. He was in time to see her throw open the door of the parlor and sweep into the room like a storm wind across the steppes.

Valentin and Nicholas were sitting by the fire and looked up, startled, as Silver marched across the room to stand before them.

"I'm going to court," she announced tersely. "I'll need your help. Will you give it to me?"

Nicholas gazed at her and the surprise on his face was replaced by a brilliant smile. He rose slowly to his feet. "Silver ..." His glance traveled lingeringly over her flushed cheeks, taking in the blazing vitality that emanated from her. "You're looking well."

"Of course I'm looking well," she said with a shrug. "I haven't been ill for months. You know that, Nicholas."

"Do I?" His smile was faintly bemused. "Oh, yes, I guess I forgot."

Silver turned to Valentin, whose expression reflected a bewilderment similar to Nicholas's. "I've been thinking and I believe you may be the one to guide me, Valentin. Nicholas seems to have no liking or understanding of the people of the court, while you appear to know how they—" She broke off, gesturing impatiently with one hand as she tried to convey her meaning. "You can read the signs."

"Nicholas can also read the signs," Valentin said. "In many ways he's far more experienced at anticipating their reactions than I am." He paused. "Just what are you asking me to do, Silver?"

"I want to be accepted by all those people I saw when Nicholas took me to meet his mother. I want them to think of me as one of them. Can you help me learn to do this?"

Valentin glanced uneasily at Nicholas. "I'm not sure."

"Why?" Nicholas's smile had vanished and his face was totally expressionless. "Why is this important to you?"

"Because I *want* it." Silver met his gaze with defiance. "Do you find it odd that a half-breed would want to show your fine friends she can be as civilized as any of them?"

"No, I don't find that at all odd." Nicholas's smile was bittersweet. "My dear *maman* has held that particular ambition before my eyes since the moment of my birth."

"But I'm not like your mother," Silver said fiercely. "I don't care—" She fell silent.

Nicholas's gaze narrowed on her face. "You don't care about what?"

"It doesn't matter." She turned back to Valentin. "Will you help me?"

Valentin shrugged. "It will be difficult. St. Petersburg society doesn't welcome newcomers readily, and we'd have to find a way to lure them to come to you. We'd have to make you . . . unique."

"She's already unique," Nicholas said dryly. "You'd merely have to make them aware of the fact."

A glimmer of interest lit Valentin's face. "You know, it would be rather a challenge to turn a sow's ear into a silk purse." Then he grimaced sheepishly. "*Merde*, I'm sorry, Silver. I didn't mean you were a sow's ear. I meant only—"

"I don't care what you call me as long as you do what I've asked. Now, how do we go about it?"

"Rubles, style, and boldness," Valentin answered. "Quantities of all three. I'd say we'd have no trouble with the latter two." His gaze shifted inquiringly to Nicholas. "Rubles, Nicholas?"

Nicholas didn't reply for a moment, his gaze fastened on Silver's face. "I'll give orders to my man of business that she have whatever she wants."

Silver turned to him, the color burning brightly beneath the dusky gold of her cheeks. "I . . . thank you." Her words were halting. "When this is over, I will try to pay you back."

"Over? That's a rather peculiar word," Nicholas said slowly. "Would you care to elaborate?"

She took an impulsive step forward. "Nicholas, there's something I want—" She stopped suddenly and her eagerness was replaced by wariness. She shook her head. "Not now."

Nicholas's gaze moved from her face to Mikhail's.

The Cossack stood just inside the doorway across the room. "How mysterious. I suppose I must resign myself to learning patience." His glance shifted to Valentin. "Guard her well. There are wolves with very sharp teeth in the gardens of the Winter Palace."

"You'll have to show your support. They won't accept her without it."

"Oh, I'll be in attendance." Nicholas smiled crookedly. "I wouldn't miss one second of Silver's rise to the heights of that dung heap. However, it seems she's relegated me to the background for the present. Isn't that right, Silver?"

Silver's eyes were glittering in the firelight, and for an instant they reflected a curious torment as she looked at him. Then she glanced away and nodded jerkily. "Valentin can help me more now. I don't need you."

"But you do need my money. How fortunate that I have something you want." He turned his back on her to stare down into the fire. "Well, what are you waiting for, Valentin? I'm sure Silver is impatient to begin. Get the hell out of here and make your goddamn plans."

Valentin frowned in concern. "Nicholas, are you sure this is what you want?"

Nicholas didn't answer.

After a moment Valentin shrugged and turned to Silver. "He's right, you know. We have a lot to do. We'll have to go to the best seamstress to outfit you with a wardrobe that will dazzle the court. Do you dance?"

"They tried to teach me the waltz at school, but I didn't pay much attention to the dancing master. I saw no sense in learning something so useless."

Valentin shook his head. "We'll have to correct that immediately. Come along to the ballroom and we'll begin your lessons." He grasped her elbow and propelled her toward the door. "Of course, the first dance you must learn is the polonaise. It's more of a formal march than a dance, on the order of a minuet. Every imperial ball is opened with the polonaise."

"Then I'll learn it," Silver said. "It should pose no problem. It sounds much like the tribal dances I learned in my village as a child."

Valentin chuckled. "I'm not sure our glorious tsar would delight in that comparison. I really wouldn't mention it to him if you should happen to fall into conversation with His Majesty."

"I thought you told me that protocol forbids casual chats with the tsar."

"It does, but there are exceptions to every rule and it will help our cause if the tsar favors you."

"Is that possible?"

"Quite possible. Alexander always has an eye for the ladies."

Nicholas didn't turn around but his voice cracked through the room. "You might remember you're preparing her for acceptance in the imperial ballroom not the imperial bedchamber, Valentin. I have no intention of acting the cuckold."

Valentin glanced back over his shoulder. "You know Alexander never goes beyond a casual flirtation. He's been remarkably faithful to Catherine."

"I have no desire for Silver to prove the exception."

Silver turned at the door to gaze gravely at him. "I wouldn't take your money and then dishonor your name. It is not my way."

"How comforting," Nicholas said ironically. "For God's sake, get her out of here, Valentin."

Silver still hesitated, her troubled gaze fastened on Nicholas's tension-taut back. Then she turned and followed Valentin's gentle urging to swiftly leave the room.

The parlor was silent except for the crackle and hiss of the logs in the grate.

"I suppose you know why my wife has this sudden desire to go to court?" Nicholas asked Mikhail without turning around.

"Yes," Mikhail answered.

"And you don't intend to tell me?"

"No." Mikhail paused. "But it is not the same desire that drives your mother."

"Then what in hell—" Nicholas broke off and was silent for another moment. "This isn't going to be easy for me. I'm not a patient man."

"I know."

Nicholas reached out, his hands closing on the edge of the marble mantel. "She's so damn wary of me. It's even worse than it was before she lost the baby."

"She does not trust easily."

"I know, but . . ." Nicholas's words trailed off. "I guess I'd hoped for something more."

"She is no longer asleep. You said that was what you wanted."

"Yes." Nicholas glanced at him over his shoulder and smiled faintly. "She's awake and I thank God for it. God and you, my friend. Whatever is ahead, it can't be worse than standing by watching her as she was before."

"I cannot know what is ahead."

Nicholas's glance sharpened. "You still have apprehensions?"

"Yes, but it is done now."

"What's done, for the sake of—" Nicholas broke off and muttered a curse seething with frustration. "All right, all right, I'll ask no questions." His grasp on the mantel tightened. "For now. But I don't know how long I'll be able to keep to this docile role you and Silver seem to want me to play."

"Docile?" Mikhail's lips quirked as he gazed at Nicholas. There never had been any sign of meekness in the Nicholas he had known through the years. As a boy he had been wild and, growing to manhood, he had become even wilder, more reckless. His willingness to temper his recklessness for Silver's sake said much. "I would not be so foolish as to expect you to be docile."

"Unfortunately, my wife doesn't appear to be so perceptive regarding my character." Nicholas whirled away from the fireplace and strode across the room. "I've got to get away from here." At the door he asked over his shoulder, "Are you coming with me?"

"Where are you going?"

"Didn't you hear her? I'm neither needed nor wanted at the moment. Perhaps we'll go to Apothecary Island and drink good Cossack vodka and listen to the Gypsies." He motioned to the footman standing in the hallway. "Our cloaks, and tell them to ready a boat." His dark eyes were blazing then as he turned back to Mikhail. "And perhaps I'll find a woman there who requires neither docility nor patience. I'm sick to death of both."

"Perhaps," Mikhail said mildly. "I do not suppose it matters to you that it is foolish to go out tonight? It is snowing hard and getting colder by the minute. The river may freeze over."

"Good." Nicholas shrugged into the fox-lined cloak the footman was holding for him. "I could use a little ice to cool me." He whirled toward the door. "Are you coming?

"Yes." Mikhail took his cloak from the waiting servant. "When have I not followed you?"

Nicholas didn't answer. He had already turned and was striding out the front door of the palace into the stinging, snow-laden wind.

*   *   *

In a fellowship of free men
Never shall a quarrel rise.
Volga, Volga, Mother Volga,
Take the beauty as your prize!

The words of the song were bellowed in a tone half mournful, half belligerent, and the baritone voice rendering them was unquestionably that of Nicholas's.

"Hush now." It was Mikhail's low voice. "You will wake the house."

Silver sprang from her bed, grabbed her robe, and ran across the room. She threw open the door she had left ajar when she had retired for the night a good six hours earlier.

Nicholas was standing, no, swaying, in the hall outside the door. Mikhail's arm around his shoulders was half supporting him. Star-shaped crystals of snow dusted Nicholas's golden hair, and he was obviously very, very drunk. "Ah, my sweet bride, how kind of you to stay up to welcome me home from the storm."

"I didn't stay up for you. Why should I do a foolish thing like that? If you're idiot enough to go out in the ice and snow and risk frostbite and—"

"You were worried about me." A delighted smile appeared on Nicholas's lips.

"I was *not* worried," Silver denied, her eyes blazing. "I just thought it lacked courtesy not to tell Valentin or me where you were going."

Nicholas bowed and Mikhail caught him as he lost his balance and would have fallen. "My apologies. I went to Tania's on Apothecary Island, where the Gypsies play and the vodka flows. . . . I would have invited you to come along, but you were busy." He waved his hand vaguely. "Did you learn the polonaise?"

"Yes."

"I'm sure you do it very well. You have a grace beyond—"

"Go to bed. You're drunk as a skunk."

Nicholas looked pained. "You have a cruelly eloquent way with words. But you've raised an interesting question. Do you suppose skunks do become inebriated, Mikhail?"

"I have never seen one. Come along, Nicholas. It is late and you are tired."

"I'm not tired." Nicholas began to sing again.

"Shhh." Silver stepped into the hall. "That caterwauling will wake Etaine."

"I'm not caterwauling, I'm singing." Nicholas said with dignity. "It's a fine Cossack song about Stenka Razin, a very intelligent man who threw his bride into the Volga to avoid displeasing his men. They thought she had robbed him of his senses."

"He obviously had no more sense than you do to lose." She flinched as he began to bellow again. "Hush. You sound like a coyote with a bellyache. Etaine will wake and—"

"She can't hear me. Etaine sleeps with her door closed," Nicholas said. "Only my firebird can't stand to be confined and leaves her door ajar every night. Do you know how many times I've passed your open door and thought about . . ." He trailed off and shook his head to try to clear it. "What was I saying?"

"That you were tired and wanted to go to bed," Mikhail told him. "Let me take you to your room."

"I don't need help." Nicholas drew himself up majestically and shrugged out of Mikhail's grasp. "A Savron can drink anyone under the table. Vodka is nothing to . . ." He swayed and Silver instinctively stepped forward to steady him.

He smelled of fresh air, tobacco, and something else, something cloyingly sweet.

She suddenly planted one palm on his chest and pushed him away with such force that he staggered and would have fallen if Mikhail hadn't caught him. "You stink of perfume."

"Do I? I don't remember. It must have been sweet Gypsy Tania." He sniffed before nodding solemnly. "I smell it too. Very heavy. Heavy breasts . . . heavy thighs . . . heavy perfume."

"Bed," Mikhail said quickly. He lifted Nicholas in his arms and carried him down the hall as if he were a misbehaving child. "Open his door, Silver."

"For God's sake, let me go," Nicholas protested. "I'm no infant to be scooped up and put to—" He suddenly began to laugh. "Mikhail, you big fool, I'll find a way to . . ." He trailed off and began to sing again.

Mikhail stopped before Nicholas's room and looked back over his shoulder at Silver, who had not moved from where she stood. "The door?"

Silver reluctantly marched down the hall and threw open the door. "You should toss him out in the snow to sober up." She wrinkled her nose distastefully. "It might wash some of that foul stench off him."

"The perfume is not so unpleasant." Mikhail crossed the room, placed Nicholas on the bed, and began to unbutton his coat.

"He stinks." Silver stood in the doorway, glaring at both of them. "I will not go near him."

"Then go back to bed. I have no need of you."

"I will." Silver remained in the doorway, watching Mikhail take off Nicholas's coat and toss it on the bench at the foot of the bed. "I certainly wouldn't help a man who acts like a pig who's swilled too much at the trough."

Nicholas broke off singing. "Now I'm a swilling pig . . . Have you ever heard a more tender wifely discourse, Mikhail?"

"Never." Mikhail stripped off Nicholas's shirt and dropped it on the floor by the bed.

"She's a firebird, you know," Nicholas whispered

confidingly to Mikhail. "She can soar to heaven or rend a man with her claws. Which do you think . . ." Nicholas closed his eyes. "She's a firebird."

"Fairy tales." Silver crossed the room to stand over Nicholas. "I may not have a clever tongue to tell pretty stories, but I don't drink until I have no sense or fornicate with whores who smell like—" Silver broke off and drew a shaky breath. She couldn't remember ever being this angry in her entire life. It made no sense to feel this wild aching sense of betrayal. Nicholas did not belong to her. She was staying with him only as long as it took to find out who had caused her child's death, and nothing else should occupy her attention during this time. Why should she worry about who Nicholas bedded?

Nicholas opened his eyes; they held a curiously wistful expression in their ebony depths. "Fornicate. What a deliciously wicked word." He gazed into her eyes. "I wanted to fornicate tonight."

Pain lashed through Silver. She couldn't stand to know. She blocked the thought almost before it began and turned and almost ran toward the door.

"But I couldn't . . ." His words were almost inaudible, only a faint breath of sound, but they resounded in her ears like a great bell. She stopped and whirled to face the bed.

Nicholas's eyes were closed again, and at first she thought he was asleep. He turned on his side, his lean, powerful body as supple and graceful in relaxation as it was when he was fully alert. "It's a curse. After the firebird touched me, I couldn't . . ." He was asleep.

Mikhail pulled the heavy velvet coverlet over Nicholas and stood looking down at him with a tender smile on his lips. "He's going to have a head as big as a *Hitman*'s samovar in the morning."

"He deserves it." Silver's voice was oddly lacking

in conviction because the relief bubbling through her was making her a little lightheaded. He hadn't bedded that faceless Gypsy woman with the heavy breasts and thighs. "He shouldn't have guzzled so much liquor."

"Sometimes there are reasons why a man drinks too much."

Silver's hands slowly closed into fists at her sides. Guilt? Oh, Lord, let it not be guilt. Let Nicholas not be the one who was responsible for the potion that had taken her baby's life. "Yes, sometimes there are."

Mikhail was still looking down at Nicholas. "I know you have a great hurt inside you, but you must not let it blind you, Silver."

"What do you mean?"

"Let yourself heal. Do not keep the wounds open."

"I'll let them heal." She turned away. "When I've finished with what I have to do. Good night, Mikhail."

6

"**C**ount Marinov requests that you come to Her Highness's chamber at once," Rogoff announced from the doorway, looking straight ahead. "If Your Highness pleases."

"I doubt if he gives a damn whether it pleases me or not." Nicholas, looking in the mirror, finished adjusting his black tie. Once given free rein, Valentin had turned into a veritable whirlwind of activity this last week, he thought sourly. From morning to evening Silver had been subjected to dancing lessons, to fittings for a wardrobe that would stun and dazzle, and to a thorough drill in court etiquette. She had been surprisingly patient and accommodating through it all. He wished he could say the same for himself. Nicholas had scarcely been able to restrain the explosive tension that seemed to be his constant companion of late. He turned away from the mirror. "Tell Count Marinov I'll join him shortly."

Rogoff nodded, bowed, and departed Nicholas's chamber with his typically royal bearing.

It couldn't last long, Nicholas thought as he gathered his white gloves from the table, where his valet had laid them in readiness. Perhaps it was natural that Silver would want to savor the splendor of life at court after her life of humiliation and oppression; he was sure, though, after an initial taste she would find it bitter to the palate. She loved freedom too much to tolerate the mincing hypocrisy of the courtiers.

She was not like his mother.

Sweet Jesus, he *hoped* she was not like his mother. He didn't think he could bear it if he discovered in Silver the same ambitions that had driven Natalya all these years.

A crooked smile twisted his lips as he turned and strode quickly toward the door. He was not in the least like his father. He would never stand by and watch Silver become a demimondaine as Natalya had. If Silver took one step in that direction, he would act swiftly and violently.

Valentin turned away from the gilded oval floor-length mirror and frowned as Nicholas entered Silver's bedchamber. "You took long enough," he said as he stepped back away from Silver and motioned to the plump maid fussing with Silver's hair to leave the room. "I can't do this alone, you know. Tonight is very important and we must be there in time for the polonaise."

"I'm here now." Nicholas's gaze was on Silver, who was looking at herself in the mirror, her back to him. He had seen her tense at the sound of his voice as if she were an animal sensing danger. A sudden jab of pain and frustration knifed through him. Why, in God's name? He had told himself her wariness and distrust would fade in time, but this had not been the case. If anything, she was more on guard with him now than ever before.

His gaze traveled over her. Valentin had chosen

well, he thought. She was gowned in a shade of gray
satin so pale it appeared to gleam like moonlight in
the soft glow of the candles. Against her dusky skin
and dark hair the color was sheer sensual provoca-
tion and echoed the flashing crystal lightness of her
eyes. He felt a sudden tightening in his groin as
desire added dimension to his manhood. He tore his
gaze from her and turned to Valentin. "Why did you
send for me? You appear to have everything under
control. She looks fine."

"I don't look fine," Silver said flatly, gazing at the
low square neckline of the gown that revealed a shock-
ing amount of silken flesh. Hidden stays pushed her
breasts into bold prominence, framing and subtly
offering their voluptuous beauty to the onlooker; below, the tight bodice of the gown accented her slim
waist. The long gray satin gloves that reached past
her elbows gleamed in the candlelight, forming a
sensual contrast that made the flesh that remained
uncovered appear even more alluringly bare. "Why
do I have to wear this paint on my face? If you want
me to look like a whore, the gown alone should be
enough."

"No such thing. Every woman at court wears rouge,"
Valentin protested quickly. "And the gown is very
stylish." He frowned. "Though I shouldn't have given
in to you about the bustle. Madame Lemenov said no
woman at the ball will be without a bustle."

She shrugged. "You said I should be different and I
hate bustles. They make me feel like a camel with a
misplaced hump."

Valentin chuckled. "We certainly don't want to
give that impression." His glance flicked lightly over
her breasts. "And all your humps appear to me to be
in exactly the right places." He turned to Nicholas.
"What do you think, Nicholas? Is that little train as
good as a bustle?"

Nicholas didn't answer for a moment, his gaze riveted on the décolletage. Slowly he lifted his eyes to meet Silver's in the mirror.

Silver felt her breath leave her lungs. Beautiful. Everything about Nicholas was beautiful. In the stark black and white of his evening clothes he was all golden sensuality. Equally sensual, his dark eyes were gleaming, blazing, beguiling as they effortlessly kept her captive.

"Nicholas?" Valentin asked again as he adjusted the train of Silver's gown.

Nicholas forced himself to look away. "Her gown is fine," he said thickly.

"That's not what I asked," Valentin said. "The bustle?"

"For God's sake, what difference does it make?" Nicholas asked impatiently. "Who the hell is going to look at her backside when her breasts are almost tumbling out of the bodice?"

"It makes a good deal of difference," Valentin protested. "We have to strike just the right note. She has to appear original but not unfashionable."

"No bustle," Silver said firmly. "This corset is bad enough. There was no room for the sheath of my knife, and I had to strap it to my thigh. You said if I'd wear the corset, you'd stop arguing about the bustle. I won't look like a camel—"

"You're taking your knife?" Valentin asked, startled. He shook his head. "Silver, you can't take your knife to an imperial ball."

"My knife goes with me or I don't go."

"Forget it, Valentin," Nicholas said curtly. "Let her take the knife. And if you see the lack of a bustle as such a tragedy, we'll just have to give everyone something else to look at to distract them."

"For example?"

"The Savron rubies."

Valentin's lips pursed in a low whistle. "Natalya will not be pleased."

"How unfortunate. I'll be right back." Nicholas turned and left the bedchamber.

"The Savron rubies?" Silver asked.

"They're a part of the Savron family jewels. A great portion of the Savron fortune is derived from jewels mined in the Urals, and the family's personal collection is passed from father to son. When Nicholas came of age and inherited, he took the rubies away from his mother and refused to return them." Valentin shook his head. "They're quite fabulous, and Natalya will want to cut your throat when she sees you wearing them." He brightened. "However, they'll definitely draw more attention to you than the pearls I had in mind."

"Much more attention." Nicholas's eyes were glittering recklessly as he entered the room carrying two large leather boxes. He thrust the smaller of the boxes at Valentin. "Hold this." He opened the other box and drew out a necklace that looked as if it might stain his fingers, if not burn them. He stepped behind her and slipped the jewelry around her neck. His gaze met hers in the mirror, and this time there was no sensuality there, only cynicism. "Rubies suit you well. They look far better on you than they did on my mother." He fastened the catch. "What, no comment? Have I overwhelmed you at last?"

The wide collar of large square-cut rubies intersticed with diamonds was magnificent enough to overwhelm an empress. Silver slowly reached up to touch the necklace with the tips of her fingers. She was surprised how cold they were. The diamonds and rubies blazed with such fierce fire against the duskiness of her throat that they looked as though they might be alive. "It's very . . . nice."

Suddenly Nicholas's cynicism was gone and a smile

lit his face. "Only you would describe a necklace worth a tsar's palace as 'nice.' " He turned and held out his hand. "The tiara, Valentin." The bejeweled coronet was placed carefully on her fashionably coiffed hair before he shut the box and tossed it carelessly on the bed. "You don't need the bracelets or earrings. We don't want you looking like a Gypsy in her bangles."

She stiffened. "Gypsy? Ah, yes, you should be very familiar with Gypsy bangles."

He looked genuinely surprised. "What?"

"Let's go." Silver whirled away from the mirror. "I'm tired of all this fussing. I look passable enough."

"Passable?" Nicholas repeated slowly.

She looked glorious. She was moonlight and flame, a beauty so sensual she would have every man in the Winter Palace panting like a starving wolf, he thought savagely. After tonight she would no longer belong to him alone, but to those sycophants who gathered like leeches around the tsar. For a wild moment he wanted to forbid her to go, to keep her for himself, to tell her that she was his and that he would not permit her to— He stemmed the rush of thoughts and drew a steadying breath. It was only for a little while. He could be patient until she grew weary of the glitter of the court. He picked up the black sable cloak lying on the back of the chair and stepped forward to drape it over her shoulders. "Yes, you look quite passable. Now let's get this farce over with."

"You bring Silver. I'll go ahead to the Nicholas Hall." Valentin tossed his cloak to one of the liveried servants and seconds later began to quickly climb the Grand Staircase. "I want to ask a few questions about who's to be here tonight."

A moment later he had disappeared among the crowd of guests on the landing.

"The Nicholas Hall?" Silver asked as a footman took her cloak.

"The Nicholas Hall is where most of the balls are held here in the Winter Palace." Nicholas's lips twisted. "And, no, they didn't have the good taste to name it after me but after Tsar Nicholas the First." He took her arm and propelled her up the first of the white Carrara marble steps. "There are one hundred and seventeen staircases in the palace, and we're now mounting the Jordan Staircase. It's said to be the most beautiful in the world. Tell me, are you impressed, Silver?"

There was a mocking edge to his tone that prevented her from admitting she was not only impressed but a little intimidated by the massive staircase and the enormous marble columns with their gold-trimmed pediments. On every other step of the staircase stood troopers of the Chevaliers Gardes, their silver breastplates and helmets crested with shining double eagles. Beside them stood other guards in scarlet tunics. "Stairs are stairs," Silver said at last. "They get you from one level to another. Those scarlet uniforms look a little like the clothes Mikhail wears. Are those men Cossacks?"

"They belong to the Cossack Life Guards." Nicholas's lips tightened. "Alexander likes the idea of having a few tame Cossacks around because he has so much trouble with the rest of us."

The guards weren't the only men wearing uniforms, she noticed. A goodly number of the male guests were also garbed in uniforms. Mongol and Circassian officers sported their exotic raiment with a careless elegance that contrasted with the more traditional scarlet and blue tunics and tight elkskin britches of the Hussar officers. "Valentin told me you were once an officer in the army. Why aren't you wearing a uniform?"

"I joined the army because I was bored after I left the Kuban. When I resigned my commission I ceased to regard myself as one of His Imperial Majesty's toy soldiers. I'm a Cossack."

"What's the difference?"

He gave her a sardonic glance. "The difference between your Apache warriors and the U.S. Cavalry. A world of difference, Silver."

"I see." They were now moving down a long hall, passing by variously dressed servants—a footman in snow-white gaiters and black frock coat; an equerry in a rich cape bordered with imperial eagles and a hat with a long scarlet ostrich plume; a lackey dressed in a Polish surcoat with the red scarf on his head clasped with silver. "Are we almost there? I don't see why anyone would want to live in this place, when it takes so long to get anywhere."

"It's just ahead." Nicholas nodded at a door a few yards away toward which all the guests were streaming. "I'll be interested to see your reaction."

She stood in the doorway gazing at the ballroom and was scarcely conscious of the majordomo bellowing out their names. The Nicholas Hall must have been at least two hundred feet long and sixty feet wide, and its gleaming floor reflected the light of thousands of candles in torchères and sconces and in chandeliers hanging like blazing stars from the high ceiling. The delicious fragrance of wood drifted from huge porcelain stoves to blend with the incense several lackeys were swinging in silver censers to perfume the room. Orchids, gardenias, and hyacinths overflowed from silver and porcelain baskets in every corner and cranny of the room.

She became aware that Nicholas's gaze was narrowed on her face. "Well, does it come up to your expectations?"

"I had no expectations." She tried to shrug carelessly. "It's all very grand, isn't it? But then, the saloon on the *Mississippi Rose* was grand too."

"How delightful to see you, Nicholas."

They turned as one toward Natalya. Silver felt the muscles of her shoulders instinctively tense.

"And I'm so pleased that you've finally decided Silver is ready to meet civilized people." Natalya's eyes bored into the ruby necklace encircling Silver's throat. "I see you've decided to deck your little bride with the Savron jewels. Quite appropriate. I hear all savages are fond of red."

"We are," Silver said calmly. "It's the color of blood. We're very fond of that too. You'd be wise to remember, Your Highness."

Natalya snapped her fan closed. "I remember everything I wish to remember. For instance, I recall you told me you were with child." Her gaze wandered to Silver's slim waist. "What a pity you lost the infant. Or was it a pity? Sometimes a child isn't welcome so early in a marriage." She looked up at Nicholas and her voice lowered to silken softness. "And sometimes a child isn't welcome at all."

"And sometimes a child is welcome no matter when it comes." Nicholas's hand closed protectively on Silver's elbow. "If you'll excuse us, Valentin is waiting for us across the room."

"Certainly. I can be very understanding." Natalya unfurled her fan again and began to move it languidly back and forth. "Though I do have trouble understanding why you never visit your enchanting wife's bed if a child is so welcome." Her eyes narrowed with catlike pleasure on Silver's face, drinking in every nuance of the shock and pain she saw there. "Perhaps you'd care to explain, my dear?"

"She doesn't have to explain." Nicholas's tone was fierce, and he hurriedly propelled Silver forward. "It would be best if you stay away from Silver this evening."

"We'll see," Natalya murmured.

They were halfway across the ballroom when Silver spoke haltingly. "How does she know we don't sleep together? Did you tell her?"

"I don't discuss my bedroom activities with anyone." Nicholas said. "In fact, I rarely discuss anything more personal than the weather with my mother."

"Then how did she know?" Silver asked fiercely.

"One of the servants on the island is probably in her pay." He smiled bitterly. "My mother likes to know what's going on. She believes in the adage that knowledge is power."

"Which one? Which servant?"

"I have no idea. Why are you so upset? You'll find purchasing information and gossip is a common practice among these gracious people you wish to emulate." He glanced sidewise at her. "If you find it distasteful, you can always change your mind. We don't have to stay."

"No." She had let Natalya's splinters pierce her and that must not happen again. Their fire was singeing her confidence and ugly suspicion was keeping her from thinking. The servants on Crystal Island could be bought. Was it only information that was purchased or was it something else as well? Perhaps a potion dropped into a cup of sassafras tea? The hot color of anger bloomed in her cheeks. "No, I wish to stay. I can come to terms with these friends of yours."

"That's what I'm afraid of," he said with a lopsided smile. "And I have no friends here."

"You lie," she said coldly. "I'm not blind. I have seen the women looking lustfully at you. You have lain with some of them."

He nodded. "With many of them. Does that bother you, Silver?"

No more than a hot brand laid upon her flesh, she

thought. "Of course not." She raised her chin. "I only noticed. It is nothing to me." She quickened her steps. She had to get to Valentin to put their plan in motion. She must not think of Nicholas in bed with these court ladies or his Gypsies. She stopped before Valentin and smiled with relief. "We are here. When do we start?"

"We've started already," Valentin said. "Every man in the room is looking at you with admiration and every woman with speculation or envy. It's not a bad beginning. Now, if only you can spark the tsar's interest."

The orchestra began to play, and a rustle of expectation whispered through the room. "The tsar is about to make his entrance." Valentin turned his gaze to the doors at the far end of the room. "Do you remember the steps of the polonaise? Nicholas, you must try to position yourself so that when the dance ends you'll be near the tsar and can make the introduction. It's not according to protocol, but perhaps a minor infraction will be overlooked—" He broke off as with great ceremony the door was thrown wide and the tsar and his entourage entered the ballroom.

"Why is he wearing that funny hat?" Silver asked.

"The tsar?" Valentin was startled. "What hat?"

"I think she's referring to the tsar's personal guard." A faint smile tugged at Nicholas's lips as his gaze followed Silver's to the huge Nubian leading the column. "I doubt if Alexander would be flattered. That's Ahmed, a gift from a minor sheikh of Morocco to the tsar. He's wearing his official uniform and the head-piece is called a turban. He was a most awkward gift, since Alexander had just signed a document freeing the serfs. Naturally, he had to immediately free Ahmed but Ahmed refuses to acknowledge it. His Imperial Majesty is directly behind him, walking with Peskov."

"How peculiar." Silver turned her gaze from the giant Nubian dressed in scarlet pantaloons and vest to the man directly behind him. After the colorful grandeur of the palace guard, the smaller Alexander II was a distinct disappointment in his dark blue beribboned uniform and curling mustache. "He looks . . . puny."

"You mean in comparison with the Nubian?" Nicholas's eyes were twinkling. "His Majesty is more of a scholar than a sportsman."

"Where is the tsarina?"

"She's not attending tonight, I understand," Valentin said. "A minor indisposition."

"Good," Silver said with satisfaction. "Then we won't have to worry about her getting in my way."

Valentin gazed at her in sudden apprehension. "In your way?"

Silver nodded briskly. "I've decided that your plan is far too tame if you want me to gain the tsar's interest."

Valentin's apprehension turned to alarm. "Silver, what are you—"

"Don't worry. I'll take care of it." She began to move across the room.

"Don't worry?" Valentin echoed as he whirled around to glare at Nicholas. "Stop laughing. She's turning my careful plans into dust. What the hell is she going to do?"

"I have no idea." Nicholas still smiled. "Why don't we follow her and find out?"

"Oh, God, she's heading straight for the tsar," Valentin muttered. "She'll be lucky if that damn Nubian doesn't chop her head off with his scimitar."

The smile abruptly disappeared from Nicholas's lips. "The hell he will." His steps quickened, his gaze on Ahmed's face. "Let's get over there."

Silver moved quickly through the bowing, curtsying throng. She heard shocked whispers and exclamations as she passed but ignored them as her gaze fastened on the tsar. Alexander had not caught sight of her yet, and his head was bent as he listened to the words Peskov was murmuring in his ear. However, the Nubian's dark eyes were fixed on her with a fierceness that caused her to hesitate for a brief instant. Then she drew a deep breath and crossed the last several yards separating her from the tsar and the cluster of courtiers surrounding him. When she was within two yards of His Majesty, the Nubian drew his scimitar.

The tsar heard the hiss of the metal on the leather scabbard and broke off his conversation to turn and stare at the woman approaching him.

"Tell him to put away his sword," Silver said, meeting the tsar's gaze. "I'm not going to hurt anyone. I merely wanted to introduce myself."

Alexander's eyes widened. "Introduce yourself? My dear young woman, it is not—"

"The custom," Silver finished for him with a gesture of impatience. "I know, but that is such foolishness. I don't understand such a custom. We're far more direct in America."

There were murmurs of outrage from the men and women within hearing distance, but a sudden flicker of interest appeared on Alexander's face. "Are you indeed? Then why are you here among us foolishly indirect people?"

The Nubian took a threatening step forward, and Silver whirled on him, her eyes blazing. "One step nearer and I'll cut your heart out with my little knife."

A shocked silence fell on the ballroom. Then Alexander chuckled. "Sheathe your sword, Ahmed. I wouldn't want to see you injured by the lady."

Peskov, beside him, protested. "Your majesty, this is a terrible lack of respect. She must be punished."

"Perhaps." A curious smile touched Alexander's lips. "But I find the lady very refreshing." He motioned for Silver to come closer. "Who are you, child?"

"I'm not a child." Silver kept a wary eye on the Nubian as she took two steps forward and swept the tsar a deep curtsy. "I'm Silver Del—Savron, and I'm very happy to meet you. Will you dance the polonaise with me?"

Alexander blinked. "You wish to dance with me?"

"Very much," Silver said briskly. "Valentin says it's necessary that you find me interesting." She stood upright. "Do you find me interesting?"

"Exceedingly." Alexander's eyes narrowed on her face. "You're Nicholas Savron's bride? I've heard about you."

"That I'm a half-breed Apache and illegitimate? It's all true." She lifted her chin proudly. "I still want to dance with you. I promise I won't step on your feet. Valentin says I'm very good at dancing now. Will you be my partner?"

The tsar gazed thoughtfully at her for a moment and then made up his mind. "It will be my great pleasure." He held up his hand and the musicians began to play the music for the polonaise. He stepped forward and took Silver's hand in his own. "If you promise to restrain yourself from cutting *my* heart out. Do you truly carry a weapon?"

Silver smiled with relief. "Of course. I don't have a Nubian with a great sword to protect me, you see. I must look out for myself."

The couples were forming behind them even as the tsar led Silver onto the ballroom floor.

"My God, she did it," Valentin said as his gaze followed Silver and Alexander's gracefully measured steps. "By all that's holy, look at his face. I haven't seen him so intrigued in the last ten years. I wonder what she's saying to him."

"Whatever she feels like saying." Nicholas sipped from a glass of champagne. "And probably none of the correct, polite things you told her to discuss with him."

"Whatever she's doing, it's working," Valentin said. "Oh, how it's working."

Nicholas set the glass down on the long banquet table. "Perhaps too well. The dance is almost over. Let's go."

"Where are we going?" Valentin followed him across the room.

"To reclaim my wife," Nicholas said grimly. "And to make sure His Imperial Majesty knows the intrigue ends in the ballroom."

"But it's going so well," Valentin protested. "Silver told you she'd permit no familiarities. Why not let her—" He broke off as he caught Nicholas's chilling glance. "Oh, all right. I suppose we've won enough of a victory for one night."

"Victory may be in how one perceives it." The music stopped. Nicholas moved three steps forward and was beside Silver and Alexander. He bowed. "Your Majesty."

The smile on Alexander's face faded as he gazed at Nicholas. "You wish something, Nicholas?"

"Only to retrieve my wife, sir. Silver isn't accustomed to dancing. It tires her."

Alexander's gaze went to Silver. "I would never have known it. She appears to have amazing vitality."

"It's deceptive, I assure you." Nicholas reached out and deliberately took Silver's hand from Alexander's clasp. "As many aspects of life are deceptive. Haven't you found that true, Your Majesty?"

Weariness suddenly robbed Alexander's face of amusement. "Sweet Mary, yes. I can never be sure what is a truth and what is a lie."

"Then you should be careful not to surround yourself with liars," Silver said.

Valentin inhaled sharply and took a half step
forward.

Alexander's face clouded. "Are you suggesting that
I may be foolish?"

"A man who surrounds himself with people he
can't trust is surely not wise." Silver met his eyes
directly. "Why not get rid of them?"

A slow smile lit his face. "It sounds very easy.
Replace deception with truth, dishonor with honor.
Perhaps I should start with you. Would you lie to me,
Silver Savron?"

Silver shook her head. "I hate lies."

"So do I." Alexander turned to Nicholas. "You
have a very charming wife. I find her exceptional."

"It doesn't surprise me." Nicholas's hand tightened around Silver's with blatant possessiveness. "A
blind man can see that Silver has qualities that aren't
common."

The tsar's lips tightened. "You haven't changed,
Nicholas. You're still as disrespectful as ever." Then
as he looked again at Silver, his expression softened.
"But I'll forgive you this time. It's not often that an
ornament such as your bride is brought to my court."

"As long as you realize that it's the court she's to
ornament," Nicholas said bluntly.

Valentin muttered something beneath his breath.

Alexander's lips tightened. "You go too far. You're—"

"Truthful," Silver interrupted quickly. "Honest."

"Arrogant," Alexander added. Then he smiled
grudgingly.

"But yes," the tsar said, "with all your husband's
faults, he's never tried to deceive me in regard to his
views. However, I find honesty far more palatable
when spoken by a beautiful woman." He inclined his

head in a bow. "I look forward to seeing you at all our entertainments, my dear Princess Savron."

"You will give me what I want?" Silver asked.

"The royal favor? Why should I not when it is what I wish also?" His eyes twinkled. "I believe this season is going to prove very interesting." He turned and strode away and was immediately surrounded once more by the men and women of his immediate set.

Valentin expelled his breath in a rush. "*Merde.* I'm glad that's over. I expected him to throw one or both of you into the deepest dungeon at any moment." He drew out an immaculate white handkerchief and dabbed at the perspiration beading his brow. "I don't think I want to be involved in this any longer. It's too hard on my nerves."

"Nonsense," Silver said. "I think it went very well. Though you really should have told me the tsarina's name was Maria."

"Why?" Valentin asked warily. "I guess I thought you knew."

"How could I know if no one told me?" Silver asked reasonably. "The tsar was very surprised when I told him you had said he was surprisingly faithful to his wife."

Nicholas's gaze narrowed on her face. "I'd be curious to know how that comment came to be brought up in the conversation."

"I asked him to show the entire court he favored me and he asked if I meant—"

"What difference does it make how it came up?" Valentin interrupted. "She spoke to Alexander about his *mistress*, for God's sake."

"Well, I didn't know this Catherine was his mistress. I thought she was the tsarina until His Majesty straightened everything out for me. You should have made that clear, Valentin."

Nicholas's lips were suddenly twitching. "Yes, Valentin, how very remiss of you."

"Oh, Lord." Valentin groaned. "*I'm* the one the tsar is going to throw into the dungeon."

"Don't be silly," Silver said impatiently. "He wasn't at all upset once I explained that I understood men were seldom faithful to their wives and that he was no worse than anyone else."

"The tsar of Russia is no worse than anyone else," Valentin repeated dazedly.

"Well, is he?" Silver frowned. "He didn't seem so bad to me. He said I reminded him a little of his Catherine when he used to visit her at school many years ago."

"How . . . nice," Valentin said weakly.

"I don't know why you're behaving so oddly. We accomplished exactly what we set out to do."

"But not the way I planned to do it," Valentin said, dabbing again at his forehead with his handkerchief. "The safe, gradual way."

"I couldn't do it your way." Silver's face became troubled. "Don't you see? If I'd schemed and tried to manipulate the tsar, I would have been just like all those other people he was talking about. But I'm not like them. I need a favor from him, but I won't give him lies to get it."

"Yes, I do see." The hardness had completely vanished from Nicholas's face as he gazed at her. "I suppose I should have expected it."

Silver turned and met his gaze. "You understand?"

"I understand."

"Well, I'm not so idealistic," Valentin said. "And I think it was the height of foolishness to risk—" He broke off. It was obvious neither Silver nor Nicholas was listening to him. They were looking only at each other, caught up in an intimacy, an exchange, that held a multitude of heated emotions and complexities. "Nicholas, it's time for you to withdraw from the ballroom."

"The hell it is," Nicholas said softly, his gaze still holding Silver's. "It's time I danced with my wife."

Valentin frowned. "It would be a mistake. You've already displayed an unfashionable amount of possessiveness with the tsar. You must let the gentleman of the court know they won't have to risk facing you with a sword or pistol if they ask Silver to dance. An idea like that can be most unsettling and damage everything we've worked for."

"And what difference does it make?" Nicholas's voice was urgent, coaxing, and it was clear he was speaking only to Silver. "This isn't what you want." He lifted her hand and pressed his lips to her palm. He could see the rapid throb of the pulse in her wrist and was jolted by a surge of lust. "We could leave now. There's nothing here for you."

Color glowed in her cheeks and her crystal eyes shimmered. "Nicholas, I don't know—"

"I do. Come with me."

She took a step toward him as if drawn by invisible strings.

Valentin sighed. "So much for making you the rage of the court." He started to turn away. "I'll tell a footman to order the carriage brought around."

"No." Silver's voice was a level above a whisper. She closed her eyes for a tenth of a second, and when she opened them the softness was gone though wistfulness remained. "No, I'm staying. You're wrong, there is something for me here, and nothing is going to stop me from getting it." She pulled her hand from Nicholas's grasp and stepped back. "If Valentin thinks it's the wrong thing to do, I won't dance with you. And I won't leave here. Perhaps you'd better do as Valentin says and withdraw."

Nicholas was silent, his tension and anger nearly

palpable. "Very well." He whirled on his heel and strode away through the throng.

Silver gazed after him and a tremor ran through her. The light from the candles in the chandeliers turned Nicholas's hair to golden fire. She knew how angry he was. Zeus ready to hurl his thunderbolt, she thought. Yet just a moment before he had been a sunlit Apollo, warm, loving, drawing her within his radiance with a power she had found almost impossible to resist. She *must* continue to resist. There were things she had to learn before she could trust him.

"You could change your mind," Valentin said softly as his gaze followed hers. "Nicholas isn't pleased. The situation could become difficult."

"No, you're wrong. I can't change my mind." Silver tore her gaze away from Nicholas and forced a smile. "Now, what's our next step?"

"You have to do something." Natalya's eyes were blazing as she paced back and forth across her boudoir. "Do you hear me? I won't *stand* for it."

Monteith gazed at her composedly. "There is no problem."

"No problem?" She whirled to face him. "She's making my life intolerable. That idiot Alexander absolutely fawns over her, and naturally everyone follows his lead." She drew a deep breath. "And follows *her* lead. The bitch shows she has no liking for me."

Monteith smiled wanly. "And you're being rejected by your friends? How sad."

"It's not amusing," Natalya said fiercely. "Do you think I care about them. They're nothing to me. But I won't let that savage rob me of what I've gained over the years."

"And that's why you had Peskov summon me to you?" Monteith leaned back in the chair.

"You have to do something."

"It will not go on much longer."

"It's already been three weeks."

"You have no patience. Soon Silver Savron will have something else to think about besides robbing you of your social victories."

"When?"

Monteith only smiled in answer.

"I must know." Natalya's hands closed into fists at her sides. "I *demand* to know."

The smile faded from Monteith's lips. "Demand? You don't demand from me, Natalya."

"You must help me. You can do it. They listen to you."

"Yes, I could do it." He paused. "But I do not choose to do so. Can you guess why?"

"It doesn't matter why. You must—"

"Be quiet." The words were soft, yet laden with such force that she involuntarily took a step back. "You will listen to me."

Natalya felt a wild surge of rebellion. She would *not* obey him. She obeyed no one. Yet she found herself silent, listening.

"I will not give you what you want because you had the temerity to order me to come running at your call as if I were the most humble lackey." Each word was dropped into the silence with great precision. "Why did you not come to me to plead? You know what I am, what I can give you."

"You've given me nothing so far," Natalya said sullenly. "Nothing but words."

"How easily you forget." Monteith's gaze narrowed on her face. "You doubt me?"

Natalya had an instant of misgiving. "I didn't say that."

"But you do have doubts, I think," he said slowly. "Perhaps it's good that I came here this morning. I thought you were beginning to waver and that won't be permitted, Natalya."

She glared at him. "Do what I ask and I will never waver again."

"You said that once before." He smiled coldly. "You forget your promises as soon as you make them."

"That was different."

"No, you'll always be rebellious and disobedient unless taught a lesson." He gracefully rose to his feet. "Yes, it was good that I came today. Undress, Natalya."

Her eyes widened. "Why?"

"The usual reason you undress for a man in your boudoir. To rut, to copulate."

"You want to bed me?" Somehow she had never thought of Monteith in that way. He had always seemed too cold and ascetic to indulge in carnal romps. Now she looked at him with new speculation. A man who lusted was vulnerable and could be controlled and it would be very valuable to have the means to control Monteith. She smiled. "You find me desirable?"

His gaze raked her coolly. "You're very beautiful and will probably remain so for a few more years."

Chilling fear ripped through her. She *must* control Monteith. She took a step closer. "That's not kind. I want you to be kind to me."

"Neither of us is kind," he said. "Your beauty has only a marginal appeal for me. It's your hunger that I find attractive."

She frowned. "My hunger?"

"For power. I admire the way you've ruthlessly pursued what you've wanted over the years. It shows unusual strength of purpose." He shrugged out of his pearl-gray coat and laid it on the back of the chair. "But you've grown too smug. You've used your body to purchase power and you think you've found a weapon that's indomitable."

"It is indomitable." She reached up and released her golden hair from its pins and it tumbled down her back in a shining stream. She smiled seductively. "Let me show you."

"I intend to let you try." He took off his vest and laid it neatly on top of his coat. "Because you must learn I'm stronger than you are, even in this."

He was really quite handsome, Natalya thought as she gazed at him objectively. This shouldn't be at all unpleasant, and when it was over she'd have what she wanted. She began to unbutton her blue velvet robe. "But first your weapon will be mine," she said softly. "And I think you'll enjoy defeat even more than you would a victory."

The harsh sound of Natalya's sobs were very satisfying, Monteith thought. He would like to lie there and enjoy his triumph a little longer, but that would lack discipline and might encourage her to think he had softened toward her. He sat up and swung his legs to the floor.

"Where are you going?" Natalya raised herself on one elbow to gaze at him.

"Your weeping does not please me," he lied. "It is over. I am leaving." He began to dress. "You're quite accomplished. I might find that useful in the future." He glanced sidewise and smiled as he caught the shudder that ran through her naked body. "Oh, not for myself. I'd find no pleasure in it now that you've been properly schooled. But other men are easier to please. Tell me, Natalya, would you obey me if I told you I wished you to seduce someone?"

She didn't answer.

He buttoned his vest and turned to face her. "Would you?"

She lowered her gaze to the coverlet. "Yes." Her voice was muffled.

"Anyone? Without question? No matter how distasteful you found him?"

"Yes."

Monteith felt a surge of delight so heady he could feel himself swell in stature. "You will do anything I tell you?"

"Yes."

"You will come to me on your knees if you ever wish something from me?" he asked softly. "And you will never demand anything from me ever again?"

"I will never demand anything from you," she repeated numbly.

He deftly tied his cravat before slipping on his coat. "Very good." He smiled. "And if you continue to please me, I'll give you what you want more than anything in the world."

"Thank you." She swiftly reached for the sheet and covered herself. The action had a touch of desperation in it and pleasure welled within him again.

"However, you must be patient. You won't mind letting your sweet daughter-in-law reign for a little longer, will you?"

"No, I won't mind."

He picked up his hat and gloves from the table. "I'm glad we've come to this fine understanding. Good afternoon, Natalya. Peskov will transmit any instructions I have for you." He moved toward the door with fluid grace. "Which I'm sure you'll be happy to obey."

"Monteith."

He turned to look at her inquiringly.

She was gazing at him with stark terror on her face. "What did ..." She stopped and waited until she had the courage to continue. "What did you do to me?"

He smiled. "Why, Natalya, you know what I did to you. The sport of a thousand delights."

"No." She swallowed. "It was more than that. You . . ."

"Yes?"

"You made me . . ." She shuddered and fell silent.

"You seem to have trouble expressing yourself. Would you like me to come back to bed and attempt to clarify things for you?"

"No!" She drew back against the headboard in panic.

He met her gaze. "It's not necessary, is it?" he asked softly. "Because you know what I did to you." He paused. "And you know what I am. *Au revoir*, my dear."

She watched the door close behind him before huddling down beneath the sheets and curling into a tight ball. She did know and she would never forget.

Because Monteith had made sure she could not forget.

7

"If you don't take your hand off my breast I'll put my knife through your palm, Denis," Silver said clearly. "I understand you fancy yourself a fine swordsman. You'll find it's very difficult to wield a weapon with cut tendons."

Count Denis Stepvan laughed uncertainly. "You don't mean that." Then as he met her gaze he immediately jerked his hand from her bosom. "I meant no offense. I thought when you said you wanted to leave the ballroom and see my greenhouse . . ."

"I wanted to see your cherry trees, not your private parts," she said dryly. "I found the idea of flowers and fruit growing here surrounded by all this ice and snow very interesting." She glanced at the large glass-enclosed garden. "I still find it interesting. The scents are wonderful. What is that flower growing beside the door?"

"A hyacinth," he answered, his desperate gaze fixed on her face. "Silver, you must feel something for me.

118

You let me ride with you, dance with you, take you sledding . . ."

"You don't offend me like some of the others, and it's the custom for a woman to be escorted by someone other than her husband." She moved down the path between the rows of cherry trees. "This is a very sensible idea your father had to build this structure. Cherries in the winter. Could you send some to Crystal Island? I like cherries."

"Tomorrow," he promised, following her. "You are cruel. Why do you not admit you want me as much as I want you?"

She looked at him in surprise. "Because I don't want you and I'd be far more cruel to say that I did. You don't really care for me either. Last summer you were trailing at Natalya Savron's heels and a few months before I heard you had a grand passion for Marina Kovalsky."

Stepvan's young face flushed. "It's not the thing to throw a man's past indiscretions up to him. Besides, this is different."

"Until next month," Silver said with a faint smile. "Or next season. Why do you think I chose you? I will last in your affections about as long as the cherries on these boughs."

"It's not true. Just because your husband's passion didn't last doesn't mean that mine wouldn't."

The unexpectedness of the words caught Silver off guard and pain iced through her. She averted her face and quickly shuttered her expression. "I don't wish to speak of Nicholas."

"He doesn't love you." Stepvan took a step closer and grasped her bare shoulders in his hands. "He couldn't love you and ignore you the way he does."

"He doesn't ignore me. He escorts me to every ball."

"And then leaves you and dances with other women or plays cards or—"

"It means nothing."

"I would never leave you," Stepvan said with soft urgency. "I would have to be near you to hear you laugh or watch you move. We could be so happy. Come back to the house with me. We can go in the study entrance and slip upstairs to my bedchamber. I know I can please you, Silver. Let me try—"

"Why not here?" Nicholas's words cut through Stepvan's plea like a slashing saber.

Silver's gaze flew past Stepvan to Nicholas, who was standing in the path behind them, her sable cloak draped over his arm. She saw dark emotions on Nicholas's face. Rage. Death. She instinctively stepped back from Stepvan.

Nicholas took a step forward with the sleek stalking grace of a puma. "Why bother to go to the house?" he asked softly. "I thought the greenhouse might be cold, so I brought Silver her cloak, but it's actually quite warm here. I'm sure Silver would enjoy the earthiness of making love beneath your flowering cherry trees."

"You're mistaken," Silver said quietly. "We didn't come here to fornicate."

"No?" Nicholas's tone was silky. "That wasn't the impression I received when I walked in the door. I believe I was about to have horns firmly planted on my head. That doesn't please me, Silver."

Nicholas at that moment was fire beneath ice, a stiletto sheathed in satin. Silver moistened her lips with her tongue. "He's only a boy."

Stepvan bristled indignantly. "I'm two years older than you, Silver." He stepped forward to confront Nicholas. "You wish to meet?"

"No," Silver said sharply, and hurriedly stepped between them. "This is foolishness. Nothing happened, Nicholas." She smiled bitterly. "Your honor is quite safe."

America's most popular, most compelling romance novels...

Here, at last...love stories that really involve you! Fresh, finely crafted novels with story lines so believable you'll feel you're actually living them! Characters you can relate to...exciting places to visit...unexpected plot twists...all in all, exciting romances that satisfy your mind and delight your heart.

Get one full-length Loveswept FREE every month!
Now you can be sure you'll never, ever miss a single
Loveswept title by enrolling in our special reader's home
delivery service. A service that will bring you all six new
Loveswept romances each month for the price of five—and
deliver them to you before they appear in the bookstores!

Examine 6 Loveswept Novels for

15 days FREE!

(SEE OTHER SIDE FOR DETAILS)

"Tonight, perhaps."

"Oh, for heaven's sake," she said in exasperation. "Do you wish my word? I told you I would not dishonor your name and I have not."

His gaze searched her face, and a little of the tension ebbed from his taut muscles. "How wise of you." He jerked his head toward the door. "Leave us, Stepvan."

Stepvan cast an anxious glance toward Silver. "I'll stay. Silver needs—"

"Silver's needs are only my concern," Nicholas said. "Though I'd really prefer you to stay. It would give me a reason to kill you." His glance shifted to Stepvan's face and the count's eyes widened at what he saw there. "I'm in a mood for killing someone at the moment."

"Go, Denis," Silver said quickly. "This isn't your business. I don't want you here."

The relief on the young count's face was obvious. "Well, if you're sure." He moved quickly toward the door, carefully skirting Nicholas. "But if you need me . . ." The door closed hurriedly behind him before the sentence was completed.

Nicholas's lips twisted. "You must remember to pick a lover with more backbone next time."

"I told you that he's only a boy." Silver frowned. "And he's not my lover. It's only a game to him. They all play the same game at court."

"No one knows that better than I. But some play it in more depth than others."

"Well, I have not."

"I wasn't sure." He took a step closer. "Just how involved have you become in the game, Silver? You've gotten what you set out to get. You're *La Belle Sauvage*, the tsar's favorite. I wonder what price you've been paying for all this when I haven't been at your side."

"Not my body. I'm no whore, Nicholas."

"No, but you do like a man's hands on you." His dark eyes were fixed intently on her face. "And you love it when he comes into you and—" He broke off and drew a deep breath. "I know how much you love that, Silver."

But not with any man, she thought. Only with Nicholas. Her knees felt suddenly weak as she remembered the wild fullness, the rhythm . . . She swallowed. "I think I'll go back to the ballroom."

"Not yet." He took a step closer. "I'm beginning to like it here. The smell of earth and flowers reminds me of something. Oh, yes, that night on the bank of the Mississippi. Do you remember that night, Silver?"

She didn't want to remember, but the pictures came flooding back to her. Soft moss beneath her naked back, the smell of the river, Nicholas's face in the firelight as he plunged and twisted, lifting her with every stroke. Her breasts swelled suddenly against the satin of her bodice, the nipples hard and pointed as they pressed against her silk camisole. "I remember."

His gaze flicked over the upper slopes of her breasts bared by her gown. "You're not exactly dressed modestly now, but you wore even less then." His lips curved in a smile that was infinitely sensual. "And later you wore nothing at all. It's been a long time since I saw you like that. I *want* to see you like that."

She felt the muscles in her stomach clench and an ache begin to throb between her thighs. Her hands formed slowly into fists at her sides. "No."

He lifted a brow. "Why not? You've often told me there's no shame in nudity, and it would give me pleasure. Haven't you heard that it's a wife's duty to give her husband pleasure?" He turned and spread the sable cloak on the earth beneath the cherry tree nearest the path. "The fur will be softer than the moss on the riverbank." He took off his black dinner coat and threw it beside the cloak. "And we won't have to worry about dispensing with your virginity this time. It should be much more pleasurable for you all around."

"I don't want—" She stopped as she met his knowing eyes. "I won't do this."

"I think you will." He smiled crookedly. "You want me. You're as hungry for me as I am for you. It will be good for you, I promise."

"No, you're angry."

"Yes, I am." Something wild and hot flickered in his eyes. "I've been angry for many weeks, and it's been growing worse every day, every night. I'm angry and raw and frustrated, but I won't hurt you. It might even make it better for you. You can't deny you like it wild."

No, she couldn't deny it, Silver realized helplessly. She wanted to be touched by him in any way he chose to touch her. Wild or gentle. Soft or hard.

He read the conflict in her face and acted quickly to overcome it. He took her hand and pulled her toward the bed of fur he'd fashioned for them. "Come," he whispered. "You want it. I'll stop if you don't like it, I promise." He pulled her down to her knees on the cloak. "I keep my promises, Silver."

"I know." His hands were on the hooks at the back of her gown, swiftly loosening them. He was so close she could feel the heat of his body, and his warmth was melting her, turning her bones to liquid. She was trembling, she realized dazedly.

She felt a sudden coolness as the material parted and then heard his exclamation of disgust. "My Lord, a corset."

She laughed breathlessly. "Valentin and I made a bargain, remember? A corset for no bustle."

"Blast Valentin. You're the only sensible woman of my acquaintance, and he has to try to spoil you."

Nicholas drew back. "My hands are shaking so badly it will take forever to unlace the damn thing." He drew the gown down from her shoulders to her waist before touching the boned satin corset that cinched her waist and ended just below her breasts, lifting them and throwing them into voluptuous prominence against the silk of the low-cut camisole. "But maybe we can find a way . . ." He slipped the camisole from her shoulders and then slowly pushed it down. Her full breasts jounced saucily, framed and lifted by the corset. She could feel herself swell beneath his gaze, her nipples becoming so sensitive that she experienced a tingling sensation with every breath she drew.

His eyes darkened as he looked at her. "Yes, I'm sure we can find a way," he said thickly. He unbuttoned his shirt and took it off. His hands grasped her corseted waist and tightened slowly. The warmth of his hands through the satin binding her came as an odd sensual shock, and she inhaled sharply. His gaze moved from her breasts to her face. "I didn't hurt you?"

"No." Her answer was scarcely audible. She felt as if her breath were as constricted as the flesh beneath his hands. "I just feel . . . bound."

"So do I." His gaze fell to the hard column pressing against the tight material of his trousers. "But it's not unpleasant . . . is it?"

She shook her head.

"And your breasts are free." He took her swollen breasts in his palms and shook them gently. She gasped as desire tensed every muscle in her body.

"You like that?" He shook her again, watching her lips part and the color steal into her face. He twisted her nipples teasingly. "And that?"

His head bent slowly and his lips closed on one taut nipple. He sucked delicately and then more strongly. His words were muffled against her breast. "And this?"

"Yes." She closed her eyes, her breasts rising and falling with every breath. "I feel so . . . full."

"You are full, beautifully full." The planes of his cheeks tautened with hunger as his mouth pulled at her. "You're even more beautiful than you were before. Fuller. More ripe."

Because of the baby. The thought came like a sudden frost, freezing her. Her body had changed because of her little girl and her little girl was gone.

She stiffened and his gaze moved to her face with sudden alertness. "What's wrong? What did I say?"

"My baby." She pushed him away with all her strength. "My baby."

He understood instantly. "You can't stop living because you lost the child, Silver. You've got to put the experience behind you."

Mikhail had said something like that, she remembered. But she couldn't put it behind when she didn't know who had killed her baby. She had learned nothing yet. She didn't even know if Nicholas had . . . The thought was too painful to bear, and she blocked it quickly. "I can't do this, Nicholas."

"The hell you can't. You can't stop—" He broke off and was silent a minute, struggling against pain and frustration. "Listen, Silver, why are you punishing yourself like this? Why are you punishing me?"

She was quickly putting her clothes in order and didn't look at him. "I'm not trying to punish you. I just can't let you . . ." She stood up in a flurry of silken skirts. "Not with you."

He slowly rose to his feet. "Why not with me?"

She turned and almost ran toward the door.

"Silver!"

She turned and looked back at him, her eyes glistening with tears. "I can't trust you. Don't you understand? I can't *trust* you."

He looked as if she had struck him. Then his lips

twisted in a mirthless smile. "So much for time and patience." His eyes were as hard as ebony jet as he gazed at her across the greenhouse. "All right. I'll let you run away this time. But I warn you, Silver, if not with me, then with no one else. I won't have any other man so much as put a hand on you as Stepvan did. You'll be the most circumspect of wives. No more rides alone with any man, and if you're in another man's company more than two minutes, you'd better be more closely chaperoned than the tsar's oldest daughter."

A flare of anger banished her tears. "And if I'm not?"

"You won't like it," he said softly. "There are more brutal ways than I've chosen to use to tame my firebird."

"Threats?" Her eyes blazed at him. "I haven't noticed you being circumspect with your Gypsies and those fawning countesses and . . ." She trailed off with a sputter. "And I'm *not* your damn firebird. I'm Silver Dove Delaney."

"You're Silver Savron," he said coldly. "And you'll damn well remember it."

"The hell I will!" The door slammed behind her with a violence that threatened to shatter the glass panes of the greenhouse.

Nicholas drew a deep breath and snatched up his shirt and thrust his arms into the sleeves with scarcely leashed violence. *Damn her.* And damn the lust that was twisting his guts and the pain her words had sent needling through him that was even worse than the hunger for her body. Why couldn't she trust him? Was she afraid he would give her another child that would die and she would be hurled back into that deep well of despair?

The thought brought an aching wave of sympathy that served to cool the fury and jealousy exploding inside him.

Patience, he told himself. He'd try to give her more time to find her way through the maze of distrust and suspicion she felt for him.

He pulled on his coat with a jerky motion. But, by God, she'd better find it soon or he'd damn well find it for her.

"You should not be here," Mikhail chided as he set the cup of hot tea down in front of her on the crude wooden table before taking his place opposite her. The chair squeaked protestingly under his bulk. "If you wanted to go sledding, you should have tried one of the slides on the estate of a nobleman. This one is for the common folk."

"And who's more common than a half-breed?" Silver asked flippantly. "I like this one better. These people aren't afraid to show how much they're enjoying themselves. Besides, I'm not sledding today. I've brought Etaine." She gazed at the platform at the top of the forty-foot wooden slide across the street from the tea shop and waved to Etaine, who was settling herself on a sled preparing to make the wild icy descent. Etaine smiled and waved back before gripping the handles at the front of the sled. "Do you think the lords and ladies of the court would welcome the daughter of the owner of a circus? They accept me only because I'm an oddity who amuses them. I won't have Etaine hurt by them."

"I did not realize it was she you were protecting." Mikhail studied Silver's face thoughtfully. "I can remember a time when you would have rushed in and done battle to make them accept her."

"Etaine would be the first to be hurt in the melee, and acceptance from those people isn't worth any child's pain." She took a sip of tea and changed the subject. "Do you see those two women sitting across the room? One of them is dressed in pink and the other in blue. Is it some kind of uniform? I have seen women dressed like that before on the streets."

Mikhail's gaze followed her own to the two laughing young women sipping tea across the room. The women's sheepskin coats were open to reveal the traditional bright blue and bright pink embroidered *sarafan*s and on their braided hair rested diadem-shaped *kokoshnik*s of matching blue or pink velvet. He hesitated. "Yes, it is a uniform."

"What kind? Are they housemaids to a great house? Our housemaids don't dress like that."

"No, they are not housemaids."

"Then what—" She broke off in astonishment as she saw Mikhail's face. "You're *afraid* to tell me. Why would you be afraid?" Then understanding came to her. "They're nursemaids?" she whispered.

He nodded. "Wet nurses. It is the traditional uniform. The woman wearing pink is nursing a girl, the one in blue is nursing a boy. The amber beads about their necks are good luck amulets to ward off illness."

Silver had been expecting his confirmation, but it still brought sadness in its wake. "Don't look so worried. It's not as if someone else wouldn't have told me eventually." She lowered her lids. "It's all right, Mikhail. The pain is still there, but it's like the throb of an old wound; it's not raw and bleeding any longer. I try to think of my baby with love not sorrow. She deserves love."

"That is good. You have learned a great deal in the past months."

"Not enough." Her gaze swung from Etaine's sled, flying down the ice-covered ramp, to Mikhail's face. "I still feel bitterness toward her murderer and I've learned nothing about what I came to court to find out. Either no one knows anything about the doctor and his activities or they won't talk to me." Her hand tightened on the wooden cup. "But you know something. Help me."

"I cannot," he said gently. "I told you all I could, Silver."

"But it's not enough," she said in frustration. "Why? Who are you protecting, Mikhail?"

Mikhail turned his head to look at Etaine, who stood at the bottom of the slope, laughing. "I did not say I was protecting anyone."

Panic flowed through Silver. Who would Mikhail protect if not Nicholas? "Tell me, Mikhail."

"Etaine is getting in line again. We may be here for a while," Mikhail said. He glanced at Silver's cup. "Let me get you more tea."

He would say nothing more, she realized, and her frustration was mixed with relief. If he would not say the words, she could not be sure Nicholas was guilty. "No, I've half a cup left."

"You are sure? It is cold sitting here with nothing to warm you. Nicholas would not want you—"

"Stop it," she said firmly. "I don't need you to coddle me." She smiled bitterly. "Nicholas has probably told you to stay close and make sure I'm not given an opportunity to stain the family honor."

The big Cossack shifted uneasily and his chair squeaked again. "Silver, I do not want—"

She held up her hand. "I know. It's not your choice." She smiled with sudden recklessness. "And if I wanted to see Count Stepvan or any other man alone, I would do so even if Nicholas set the entire palace guard to watch me. It just doesn't happen to suit me at the moment."

"I hope you will not do that." Mikhail's expression was troubled. "Nicholas's temper is—" He hesitated before finishing. "Uncertain right now."

"I wouldn't know about that," she said with a brittle laugh. "He hasn't seen fit to exchange more than a few words with me for the last two weeks. Not that it matters to me, but the tsar is wondering why he finds Apothecary Island so much more attractive than the Winter Palace."

"He feels more at home there."

"With his Gypsy with the heavy thighs?" She drained the rest of her tea in one swallow. "Not that I care. It's nothing to me whose bed he sleeps in." She set the cup down on the table with a resounding thud. "Gypsies or countesses or—" She broke off as she saw Mikhail suddenly stiffen. "What's wrong?"

"Monteith." Mikhail jumped to his feet and started for the door. "He is standing beside Etaine in that line."

"Dear Lord." Silver's gaze flew to the queue leading to the steps of the slide. Monteith was dressed in a gray cloak trimmed with a lighter gray fox collar, his fair hair shining in the sunlight. He was smiling with infinite satisfaction at his daughter. As Silver watched he reached out one well-shaped hand and touched Etaine's cheek. "No!" Silver was on her feet running after Mikhail, bolting across the ice-encrusted street, narrowly avoiding the hooves of the horse of a *drozhki* driver. "Etaine!"

Both Etaine and her father looked up at her call, Etaine with relief, her father with no expression whatsoever.

Mikhail skidded to a stop and scooped Etaine up in his arms. "I think we will go now. It is too cold for you."

"It seems you have a protector, my dear," Monteith murmured. "Does Savron think this bull can keep me from you, Etaine?"

Silver drew up beside them and spoke before Etaine had a chance to respond. "What are you doing here, Monteith?"

"Isn't it permitted for a man to take a stroll through the streets of the town?" His gaze never left Etaine's face. "And stop to speak to the child of his loins. Have you missed me, Etaine?"

"No." Etaine looked fearlessly at her father. "And I won't come back to you. Not ever."

"Ah, such determination. Such spirit. You're coming along quite nicely." He smiled with genuine pleasure. "I hadn't hoped for such progress. I think you may be ready to return to me."

"Then you think wrongly." Mikhail's arms tightened around Etaine. "She goes nowhere with you."

Monteith ignored him, gazing at Etaine with something like pride in his expression. "Yes, you may be ready," he repeated softly. "You're to be congratulated, Silver."

"I don't know what you're talking about," Silver said impatiently. "But you'll continue to stay away from Etaine or I'll—"

"Etaine knows what I mean. Don't you, my dear?" Etaine met his gaze steadily. "Yes."

Monteith's smile deepened. "And you're not afraid?" Etaine drew a trembling breath. "No."

"Of course you're not. You're of my blood."

Something beyond the words spoken between father and daughter frightened Silver. "Monteith, I want you to leave and never—" She broke off as Monteith turned to look at her. His light eyes held emptiness ... a void that was no void because it contained something incomprehensible.

"It doesn't matter to me what you want, Silver. You've given me what I need. I thought you would. That's why I let Etaine go to you."

"If you try to take Etaine, I'll fight you," Silver said fiercely.

"But I've known that from the very beginning, from the first moment I saw you at the circus in St. Louis. It was only a question of time before the struggle between us began. Fight. I shall enjoy it." He paused. "But I will win, Silver. No matter what you do, I will win." He turned back to Etaine. "Until we meet again."

He moved quickly then, striding through the crowd around the slide as if the people were butter and he the hot knife.

Silver felt drained and her knees were trembling. Monteith's aura of power lingered though the man had disappeared from sight.

"He's going to kill me now." Etaine's voice was curiously without emotion.

"No," Mikhail said. "We will not let him hurt you."

"You may not be able to stop him." Etaine moistened her lips with her tongue. "He's changing. He's stronger than he was before."

She was right, Silver realized with sudden panic. Monteith was different. It was as if a light within that he had carefully kept shaded had been allowed to burst forth at last. It filled her with sick terror. "We'll stop him, but I don't think we'll risk you leaving Crystal Island until we do." She tried to smile. "Perhaps we'll ask Nicholas to have an ice slide built for you there."

"That will be nice." It was clear Etaine was abstracted, her gaze still on the crowd into which her father had vanished. "I'd like to enjoy myself before—" She broke off and turned and walked with Mikhail toward the waiting troika.

Silver felt another chill pierce through her. Before what? Before Etaine was killed by her father? But they wouldn't let that happen. They would watch her and guard her so that *couldn't* happen.

She hurried after Etaine and Mikhail. She must talk to Nicholas and Valentin.

"We'll double the guards," Nicholas said briskly. "And set a watch on the dock. She's safe here on Crystal Island and Mikhail will never leave Etaine's side when she is off the island." He turned to Valentin.

"It's been months since we set the investigators to work on Monteith. Why haven't we heard something?"

Valentin shrugged. "They sent word they were finding little trail to follow. Since Monteith seemed to be making no move, I didn't hurry them, but there should be some word soon."

"What good will it do to find out what Monteith has done in the past?" Silver asked hotly. "It's what he does now that's important. We have to keep Etaine away from him."

"We will," Nicholas said quietly. "She's safe here on the island. I promise you, Silver, we won't let Monteith get her."

Silver felt a little of her panic leave her. If Nicholas gave his word, he would do everything under the sun to keep it. She released her breath shakily. "He frightened me so."

He looked at her in surprise. "It's a rare occasion when you admit to being frightened."

"He was . . ." She gestured helplessly. It was no use; there were no words to convey what she had sensed in Monteith. "We have to be so careful of her, Nicholas."

"We." His lips twisted. "I suppose I should feel flattered you trust me in this instance, at least."

She looked uncertainly at him.

He shook his head wearily. "Don't worry, whatever is between us doesn't concern Etaine. I want to keep her safe as much as you do."

Her shoulders straightened and the moment of vulnerability was gone. She turned and walked swiftly out of the study.

Nicholas's hand swept over the desk with sudden violence, hurling account books, letters, and inkwell to the floor.

Valentin eyed him warily. "I take it this display isn't because of Etaine."

"She closes me out," Nicholas said harshly. "Why the *hell* does Silver close me out?"

"Perhaps if you spent more time with her."

Nicholas laughed shortly. "So I can watch her dance and flirt with other men? I came close to killing that pup Stepvan a fortnight ago."

"Silver doesn't flirt," Valentin said. "She's just . . . Silver."

Nicholas knew what he was trying to say. There was no artifice in Silver's magnetism. She was supremely natural in her vitality, passion, and beauty. Nicholas stood up and headed for the door of the study. "Whatever she does, it makes every man at court nuzzle around her as if she were a mare in heat. Well, I'm tired of watching it. You can escort Silver to the Bal Masqué at the palace tonight."

"You're going to Tania's again?"

Nicholas's eyes were blazing recklessly as he glanced over his shoulder. "Oh, yes, I'm definitely going to Tania's."

"I'm not going to stay long," Silver told Valentin as she entered the Winter Palace. The hall was crowded as usual with men and women wrapped in rich furs, and she suddenly felt like a forest animal caught in a glittering, brilliant trap. Bal Masqué they called this event, but no one had yet donned masks, she noticed wearily. They probably wanted to make sure no one made a mistake about who was wearing what splendid costume before they entered the ballroom. "I want to get back to Etaine."

"Mikhail is with Etaine," Valentin said gently. "And you know he wouldn't let an army take her away from him."

"Yes." She shifted restlessly. "Still, I don't want to be here. I'm tired of all of this. It's beginning to smother me."

"It would be polite to stay until after the polonaise. Then we can slip away."

Her lips curled. "Why should we worry about politeness? Nicholas didn't bother to come at all."

And that was the heart of the matter, Valentin thought. After he had been forced to tell Silver that Nicholas had once more gone to Apothecary Island, he had noticed the instant change in her demeanor. She had been silent all the way from the island, but he had been able to feel the waves of tension and unrest she emitted. Blast Nicholas! He should have realized Silver was upset, on edge after that confrontation with Monteith. "After the polonaise," he coaxed.

She nodded wearily. "Very well. I suppose it doesn't matter."

Valentin shrugged out of his cloak and handed it to a waiting footman. "I see Dzosky on the first landing. He's Nicholas's attorney, and I'd like to speak to him about hurrying the report on Monteith before we leave tonight."

"Well, then go on and speak to him." She unfastened her ermine cloak and slipped it off. "Get it over with."

Valentin turned and moved swiftly across the crowded foyer and then up the Jordan Staircase.

"You look quite charming, my dear."

Silver turned to see Katya Razkolsky smiling at her and consciously braced herself.

"But I can't place who you're supposed to be," the countess continued silkily. Her gaze traveled down the sweeping skirt of Silver's white velvet gown. The hem of the gown together with the underlying red ruffled petticoat had been lifted and was caught beneath the crimson velvet sash at Silver's waist, revealing an occasional glimpse of crimson knee-length velvet boots embroidered with pearls in an exquisite floral design. "You're always so original. My own costume appears mundane in comparison." She glanced down at her pink shepherdess gown. "But then, I've always believed it's safer not to be too bizarre."

Silver gritted her teeth at the biting sarcasm in the other woman's tone. Katya had never let an opportunity slip by to insert her claws since that first night at the Summer Palace when Nicholas had introduced them. But tonight Silver was in no mood to put up with the woman's snide remarks. "I'm Diana, the huntress," she said curtly. "I must go now. Valentin is waiting for me on the landing."

"Valentin?" Countess Razkolsky toyed with one of the auburn curls left artfully loosened to emphasize the turn of her cheek. "Not Nicholas? I'm afraid our Nicholas may be neglecting you. What a pity. Nicholas is such a magnificent lover, isn't he? I remember how especially beautiful he was one weekend at my husband's hunting lodge." She moistened her lower lip with her tongue. "His body so smooth and sleek in the firelight and his stamina ... Ah, so like a young stallion. He couldn't get enough of me. Of course, I had to share him with many other women. Nicholas was so much in demand." The countess smiled with delicate cruelty. "And still is. I'm afraid you must wait your turn, Silver."

A red haze of blinding rage descended before Silver's eyes, and she felt as if she had suddenly gone deaf. She could see the other woman's lips move, forming words that dripped more poison, but she couldn't hear them.

Nicholas had lain before a fireplace in some woodlands hideaway with this woman, plunging into her, stroking her, turning her this way and that to make her feel every inch—

She mustn't think about it. She had known Nicholas had had many lovers in the past, but she hadn't realized how painfully, how bitterly she had resented those other women until Katya had started detailing her experience with Nicholas. The pain was overpowering, but the anger was a conflagration burning everything in its path. Her grip tightened on the red velvet crop in her hand. She wanted to lash the woman's face and go on striking, striking, and striking. . . .

Silver grappled with her rage. She must control it. She must do nothing to damage the Savron name. But Nicholas had probably had a hundred, no, a *thousand* mistresses he had touched and to whom he had murmured sweet words of love. . . .

She was jolted by fresh pain, and with it came fresh tendrils of rage. Why should she care if they thought Nicholas was a cuckold? Even now he was probably bedding his Gypsy wench in some room in the inn on Apothecary Island. Why should she be the only one to maintain respectability?

Katya's acidic monologue was continuing, and Silver found she could no longer stand it. "Be *still!*" Silver's voice was trembling with fury. "Do you think I care if Nicholas was your lover? Do you think—" She broke off and whirled around, snatching her white ermine cloak back from the footman. She stalked across the white marble foyer and then up the stairs of the Jordan Staircase.

"Silver?" Valentin turned from the man to whom he was speaking as he caught sight of her expression. "Why do you have your cloak?"

"I'm not staying." She passed him, her gaze raking the guests crowding the staircase. Then she caught sight of Denis Stepvan in the upper hall and started up the second flight of stairs.

Valentin was immediately at her side. "Then I'll escort you home."

"I'm not going home, but I shall have an escort. I won't need you."

Valentin's gaze followed hers and he muttered a curse under his breath. "Don't do this, Silver. Nicholas is just barely holding on to his control. Don't do something that will enrage him."

"Angry?" She turned to look at him, her eyes glittering in the light of the thousand candles illuminating the hall. "Warn Nicholas. *I'm* the one who's angry."

"Let me go with you. You don't need to involve Stepvan."

"No."

"Silver—" Valentin abruptly lowered his voice to make it difficult for the guests around them to hear his words. "You're not going to be foolish enough to go to Stepvan's lodgings here in the city?"

"No." Her smile was a mirthless baring of teeth. "I'm going to Apothecary Island."

8

"**Y**ou won't like this place," Stepvan warned Silver uneasily as he helped her from the troika. "It's not a place for a lady. If you want to go to see the Gypsies, why not let me take you to the Samarkand Inn? At least it's fashionable. Tania's place is visited by peasants, Cossacks, women of no virtue."

"And you think the ladies at court are different? I've found few women there who lay claim to virtue. They seem to take pride in how many men they can take between their legs each week."

He laughed. "Lord, what an unruly tongue you have." His voice lowered. "You don't want to stay among these peasants. Let me take you to a place where we can be alone."

"No." Her gaze was on the long low wooden inn a few yards distant. The sound of hoarse male laughter, a woman's throaty voice lifted in song, and the music of a violin drifted toward them in a dark, sensual stream. "This is where I want to be. Come along."

Stepvan shrugged and followed her up the two steps. "You won't like it," he repeated.

He was wrong. She did like it. From the moment she opened the door and stepped into the large, crowded room, something about Tania's struck a chord that vibrated within her. She liked the smell of the wood smoke, the dimness of firelight, the sound of a woman's melancholy voice rising to the soot-blackened timbers crisscrossing the low ceiling. The only lighting was provided by the massive logs burning in the huge stone fireplace that occupied the entire wall at the far end of the room. Shadow flames danced on the other three walls, while firelight played on the faces of the men and women sitting at the scarred, crudely crafted tables.

The women in the room were dark, dusky-skinned with bold eyes and wild hair loose about their shoulders. They wore similar clothing—gaily colored skirts and embroidered blouses revealing a generous amount of cleavage. On the contrary, the dress of the men was diverse. Uniformed soldiers, elegant dandies, and coarsely garbed peasants rubbed elbows in the room.

Suddenly a crash of splintering wood joined the wild cacophony of conversation, song, and violin as a chair was turned over and two bearlike men wrestled playfully to the floor, both laughing uproariously. Yes, Silver thought, she could see why Nicholas liked it here. This place was untamed and honest and free.

"Would you like to leave?" Stepvan asked anxiously. "You might be hurt."

"I won't be hurt." Silver's gaze searched the smoke-filled room. "Do you see Nicholas?"

Stepvan's eyes widened. "Nicholas? You expect Nicholas to be here? Why didn't you tell me?"

"Because had you known, you would not have

brought me. You were willing enough to seize the opportunity to commit adultery with his wife, but I think you're not willing to face Nicholas again."

"I'm not afraid," Stepvan said quickly. Then he grimaced. "I'm lying. Your husband's reputation with sword and pistol is—"

"There he is," she interrupted. Her gaze fastened on Nicholas with fierce satisfaction. He was sitting at a table by the fire, one booted foot resting on the edge of the table, his chair pushed back and balanced precariously on its back legs. He gazed moodily at the singer sitting on a stool on the hearth a few feet away. Silver was surprised she hadn't immediately seen Nicholas. He was a figure of light in the dim, smoky room. The tunic and closely fitted trousers he wore were of beige doeskin bleached so pale they appeared white and clung to the strong muscles of his body. Framed against the fire, his tousled golden hair appeared as radiant as a desert sunrise, but the expression on his handsome face was dark. He looked moody, sensual, utterly cynical.

"He doesn't appear in very good temper," Stepvan said uneasily.

"Good. I hope he'll soon be in even worse temper." A fresh stream of anger bubbled through her as her gaze moved to the woman singing. Was this the Tania of the heavy breasts? She was certainly displaying enough of them in the off-the-shoulder blouse she wore. The scooped neckline barely managed to cover her nipples. Silver impatiently tossed the hood of her ermine cloak back from her head. "Let's get his attention off that fat cow," she said, linking her arm through Stepvan's. With her free hand she picked up an earthenware bottle from the table next to them. She ignored the protests of the soldiers from whom she had confiscated the bottle and balanced it in her right hand.

"What are you going to do?" Stepvan frowned in apprehension. "Silver, you're not—"

The bottle sailed from her hand with forceful accuracy, missing Nicholas's head by a scant two inches. It smashed against the stone of the fireplace behind him with a loud crash and a large splash of red wine.

"What the hell!" Nicholas's foot on the table stiffened and he pushed quickly away from the table. The chair teetered wildly and then fell over backward, landing Nicholas in a heap on the floor.

The room exploded with laughter.

"Dear God," Stepvan whispered in horror.

Nicholas was getting to his feet, cursing vehemently, his gaze searching the room.

Then he saw Silver.

She felt a thrust of sheer savage joy as she noticed how he froze at the sight of Stepvan at her side. She met his gaze defiantly and smiled sweetly.

"He'll murder me," Stepvan said with absolute certainty.

"No." She withdrew her arm from his and took a step back. "But you'd better leave now." She watched Nicholas begin to move slowly and with great deliberation across the room toward her, his eyes never shifting from her face. "You've done what I wanted you to do. I don't need you anymore."

He hesitated. "I'll stay. He's angry. I don't want to leave—"

"Go," she ordered fiercely. "I didn't bring you here to get you killed. This is between Nicholas and me. I don't want you here."

Stepvan took a look at the approaching man and decided on prudence over gallantry. "As you wish." He backed hastily toward the door. "This isn't at all wise, Silver."

She didn't care if it was wise. The blood was pounding through her veins in a wild, heated stream and she felt alive.

A blast of icy air behind her signaled Stepvan's hurried departure, but she didn't look around. She was vaguely aware that the room had suddenly grown quiet, the people at the tables watching Nicholas as she was. Then he was standing in front of her and she inhaled sharply at what she saw in his eyes.

"I've told you before you should choose a lover with more courage, Silver," he said softly. "One who won't desert you when you have need of him."

"I don't need him. I don't need anyone."

"So you tell me." He smiled faintly. "You may change your mind." He turned his head and issued a crisp order in Russian to a tunic-clad servant hovering nearby. As the man scurried away, Nicholas turned back to face Silver. "I congratulate you. I'm sure your Apache relatives couldn't have tossed a tomahawk with greater accuracy. I take it you're throwing down a challenge?"

"If you wish to take it in that way. I was only showing you that you will not dictate to me what I will and will not do." She paused. "Or who I will do it with."

"Indeed?"

Her cheeks were burning. "Why should I be careful of your name when you've copulated with every woman in St. Petersburg at one time or another?"

"Not quite every woman." His tone was mocking. "I'm sure I must have overlooked one or two. However, my amorous activities are not in question here. You will not take lovers, Silver."

"Why not? It's not fair that—"

"But who said life was fair to women?" he cut in cynically. "You should have learned by now that a balance is rarely struck." He glanced around the room. "Now, consider these good men watching our confrontation. They would do nothing to help you no matter what I did to you. They sympathize with my humiliation at your hands even though it amuses them. They would even help me if I chose to punish you."

"Then they would soon find themselves lacking in male parts."

"So fierce." His dark eyes glittered recklessly. "God, I'm glad you're fierce. It would rob me of satisfaction if you'd grown tame." The servant to whom he had spoken previously appeared at his side with a doe-skin coat and held it until Nicholas had shrugged into it. He nodded at the servant and the man faded away among the tables. Nicholas casually slipped his hand into the pocket of the coat and then smiled. "But I think it's time we left this place and went to a more private battleground."

"I don't want to go," she said defiantly. "I think I like it here."

"I can understand how it would suit you, but we shall leave." His smile deepened. "Do you know how they keep falcons from attacking their masters? They bind their limbs." He drew a length of thin strong rawhide from his pocket. "Do you think it would work with a firebird?"

Nicholas must have instructed the servant to place the rawhide in the pocket, Silver realized. "No. You're very fond of bonds, aren't you? You ordered Mikhail to bind me once before. This time, if you try to do it, you'll lose—"

"Are you about to threaten my manhood again?" He shook his head as his fingers swiftly manipulated the rawhide to form a loop. "I wish you'd refrain from doing that. It makes me very uneasy." He glanced up to meet her eyes. "You're wrong. I hate to see you bound, but if it's the only way. . . . I think these bonds may work very well." He took a step nearer, and her muscles tensed as she readied herself for the struggle to come. "But not alone. It's strange that you mentioned the way Mikhail brought you to me. Mikhail loves freedom, too, but he has wonderful instincts and he knows about falcons. Did I tell you they do one other thing to hold a falcon captive?" His eyes were sparkling with excitement. "They hood them, Silver."

Darkness enveloped her as two strong arms encircled her from behind, binding her arms to her sides. A blanket, she realized furiously, that damned servant again.

"No!" She struggled wildly, kicking backward. She heard a yelp as her boot connected with her captor's shin and she felt a swift rush of satisfaction.

"Hold her! I don't want her hurt." Nicholas's voice. Nicholas swiftly grasping her wrists, slipping on the rawhide loops and pulling them taut. Her boot swung forward and this time connected with a solid thunk. Nicholas gasped with pain. "Christ, are you trying to cripple me?"

"Yes." She swung her foot again, but he evidently managed to dodge it, for she heard laughter and shouts of encouragement which she doubted were for her. Nicholas was right, she would receive no help here. Well, she didn't need help.

She lowered her head and charged forward. Nicholas muttered a pained oath as her head struck against his chin. It hurt her head a little, too, but the knowledge that she had hurt him eased her pain enormously.

"Enough. You're going to kill us both."

"Only you." She swung her boot again. This time he failed to avoid it and she heard a low exclamation. It was wildly gratifying. She laughed and swung her booted foot again.

"Oh, no, my little savage."

She was suddenly thrown over his shoulder. The wool blanket pressed against her face smelled of smoke, wine, and garlic, and she fought it. Nicholas's arm was around her knees, preventing her from using her feet. She was helpless and the knowledge caused her to struggle even more desperately.

She heard Nicholas give a terse command and the door was opened for them.

"Let me go." She enunciated every word through her teeth. "I'll punish you for this."

"That sounds familiar. You've been punishing me since the day we met." He was striding down the steps and she heard the clop of hooves on the ice-crusted snow and the silver tinkle of bridle bells. "And I've just realized that's what this is all about." He threw her onto the seat of the troika and climbed in beside her. "Punishment. That's what it's always been about."

"Let me go." She tried to wriggle off the seat.

"Oh, no." His hands jerked her back on the seat and he gave a crisp order to the driver. The troika started with a lurch and a flurry of bells and soon the sleigh was skimming smoothly over the snow. "Not until I have you where you can't get away. It's gone on too long. And you know it. No matter what other reason you gave yourself, that's the real reason you came to Tania's."

"No!"

"Yes." His tone was as rough as his hands holding her captive. "But it's done. One way or the other, all the questions are going to be answered and all the conflicts settled between us." He pulled the blanket off her head and the sudden cold stung her face. His face in the moonlight was as harsh as the stark, snow-bound landscape passing rapidly on each side of them. "Tonight."

"And where the devil do you think you're taking me?"

"To Crystal Island. We're going home. Where else would a man take his wife?"

*   *   *

"Let me down. This is foolishness."

Nicholas strode rapidly through the garden, his grasp holding her immobile. "You're mistaken. This is self-preservation." He paused before the oak door in the high brick wall and fumbled in his pocket. Then Silver heard the click of the key in the lock and the gate swung open. Nicholas closed the gate behind them, locked it, and dropped the key back into his pocket. He began walking down the path toward the small stone cottage in the center of the private garden. The bathhouse, Mikhail had called it on that day so long ago, Silver remembered vaguely. Then a wave of pain rocked through her. That was the day her baby had died. No, not died, that was the day her baby had been murdered.

She began to struggle again, fury raging through her. "I want down!"

"In another few minutes." Nicholas's tone was grim. He swung open the door of the bathhouse and strode into the room. He set her down and turned to light the candle on the table next to the door. The sudden illumination revealed a room in amazing contrast to the grandeur of the palace. There was no furniture other than the small table by the door and a wash-stand on which a simple white china pitcher and bowl rested. The only notes of luxury were the tawny pile of fox and beaver furs spread on the floor before the huge stone fireplace and an exquisitely carved teakwood chest against the wall to the left of the hearth.

Nicholas turned back to her, pulled a knife from the sheath in his left boot, and cut the rope around her shoulders. He pulled the blanket away from her body and tossed it on the floor. "Give me your wrists."

"I'll give you nothing."

He reached out, took her wrists, and cut the raw-hide binding them. "There, you're free."

She whirled and started for the door.

"However, the walls surrounding this garden are sixteen feet high, the garden door is locked, and it's very cold out there. I'd stay here if I were you."

She turned to face him. "Give me the key," she demanded.

He shook his head. "Neither one of us will leave here until everything is said." He walked over to the stone fireplace and knelt to light the kindling beneath the large logs that were laid ready on the grate. He soon had a crackling fire blazing and sat back on his heels, gazing at the leaping flames. "Have you ever been to a bathhouse, Silver?"

"No. The key."

"That's right, they're not popular in America as they are here in Russia." He nodded at the door across the room. "That's the steam room. It's the practice to stay in there for a time and then when you've had enough to come back to this room."

"I'm not interested in this, Nicholas."

"You will be." He didn't look away from the fire. "Do you see those linden switches in the corner? After the steam bath it's the custom to take turns switching each other to stimulate the flow of blood beneath the skin. Then we go out into the garden and roll in the snow. It takes the breath from your body and is very invigorating."

"It sounds idiotic to me."

"You think most things Russian are peculiar or idiotic, don't you? This is no different."

"I want the key."

He rose to his feet and turned to look at her. She was standing very straight, her spine taut with an unbearable tension, her eyes blazing at him with fury. "That's not what you want." He turned and strode to the corner of the room, picked up one of the linden switches, and turned to face her. "*This* is what you want."

For a moment the anger in her eyes was tempered by surprise. "You're going to beat me? I'll fight you. I won't let you—"

"I have no intention of beating you. After what I saw that bastard Bassinger do to you on the *Mary L*, do you think I could ever bear to strike you?" His expression was unutterably weary as he crossed the room, put the switch in her hand, and closed her fingers around it. "This is for you." He smiled crookedly as he gazed into her eyes. "You want to punish me? Do it. The only thing I ask is that you tell me why."

She moistened her lips with her tongue. "I don't want to whip you. Just give me the key."

He shook his head. "The key is in the pocket of my coat." He took off the doeskin coat and folded it carefully. He turned back toward the fireplace and tossed the coat on top of the furs on the floor. He fell to his knees on the coat and began to loosen his belt. "You won't get the key. You're a prisoner, Silver."

"No!"

He pulled the tunic over his head and tossed it aside. His naked flesh gleamed in the firelight, the webbing of scars stark and white on the bronze of his back. "There, I'm helpless before you. You could even pull your little knife and plunge it in my back. Why didn't you try to use your knife before, Silver?"

"Because I didn't choose to use it."

"I think it was because you wanted this to happen. You wanted us to come to this point."

"Lies!"

"Whippings aren't new to me and that switch can do little damage. Igor used a knout on me. Go ahead. Punish me. But then tell me why."

Why was he mocking her like this, she wondered furiously. Didn't he realize how angry she was with him? Her voice was shaking as she said, "You think I won't do it. I will. I won't be kept here against my will."

"Then try to take the key. Use the switch."

She didn't even realize she'd obeyed him until the switch cracked against his back. Shock that was curiously like pain tore through her.

"That was scarcely a tap," he taunted. "You can do better than that."

Rage rose within her again in a red tide. The switch came down harder.

"Again." He looked into the fire as he laced his fingers together before him. "You'll never get the key that way."

She *would* get the key. The switch whistled through the air and came down with all her force on Nicholas's naked back. Pain. Why was she feeling the pain as if the switch were striking her?

"That's better," he said quietly. "Did it feel good to let your anger out? Revenge is sweet, isn't it? But for what crime are you taking revenge? Is it because you're a half-breed? Are you punishing your mother for bearing you? Or old Shamus Delaney for rejecting you? Or is it all the people who have been cruel to you? There have been such a lot of them, haven't there, Silver?"

Her throat was tight and agony was exploding within her. "I only want the . . . key." The switch seemed almost too heavy to lift and her hand grasping it was shaking. "Give me the key."

"Perhaps it's really me you want to punish after all. I held you prisoner. I took your virginity. I caused you to be beaten and abused by—"

"Nicholas . . ." Silver raised the switch and then let it drop nervelessly from her hand to the floor. Tears were running down her cheeks and each breath was a sob. "Please. Give me the key."

"We both know this isn't about the key." He turned

his head to look at her over his shoulder. "Why?" he asked softly. "Tell me why now. I've borne the pain. I deserve to know."

"I . . . can't."

Her glittering eyes held torment, agony, and something else.

"I *deserve* it, Silver."

"I don't want to say it," she whispered.

"Tell me."

"My . . . baby . . ." She stopped, fighting the sobs that were racking her body, struggling for words. Then she burst out, "Did you kill my baby, Nicholas? Did you murder my little girl?"

He gazed at her stunned, uncomprehending. "What?"

"Did you do it?"

He rose to his feet and turned to face her. "I suppose the fault could be mine."

She went still, her eyes widening in horror. "You did do it?"

"The doctor said that perhaps you weren't strong enough to bear a child. If I hadn't been so lustful . . ."

Relief pierced the sick horror she was experiencing like dawn's first rays of sunlight. "No, that wasn't what I meant. The potion. You didn't give me the potion?"

"What potion?"

"Mikhail said there was a potion made of rye grass put in my tea that afternoon. It made me lose my child." Her voice turned fierce. "It killed my little girl."

"My God," he whispered. There was a long silence in the room. "Why didn't you tell me?"

She didn't answer him.

Pain clouded his face. "You thought I killed my own child?" He smiled mirthlessly. "Well, why shouldn't you? There was never trust between us. Why shouldn't you believe I'd commit murder as well as rape and—"

"You never raped me," she said quickly. She couldn't bear the raw hurt she sensed in him. It writhed inside her, adding immeasurably to her own pain.

"How generous. You excuse me of rape but condemn me of murder."

"I didn't condemn you. I didn't know. You gave Etaine the tea to bring to me in the garden. You hired the doctor and he was known to give ladies at court such potions when they asked for them."

"And you think I was aware of that?" Nicholas's tone was savage. "He was *English*. I thought you'd be more comfortable with him. You were so far from home—" He stopped. "What else?"

She was silent, gazing at him.

"There must have been something else. Tell me."

"I thought you wouldn't want my baby," she said haltingly. "A baby with tainted blood."

He closed his eyes. "Christ, you don't know me at all, do you?" He opened his lids and suddenly his dark eyes were blazing at her. "No, I did *not* kill your child! Why didn't you ask me? I would have told you the truth. I don't lie, Silver."

"I know."

"Then why in the name of all the saints didn't you come and ask me?"

"I couldn't." The tears were again falling and her hands were nervously opening and closing at her sides. "Don't you understand? I couldn't ask you."

"No, I don't understand. Why not?"

"Because . . ." She gazed at him in desperation. "Because I didn't want to know. If it was you, I didn't want to find out. I wouldn't have been able to bear it." Her voice rose. "I wouldn't have been able to *stand* it, Nicholas."

He took a step nearer. "One more question. Why wouldn't you have been able to stand it?"

She shook her head and took a hurried step back.

"Why?" he urged softly.

"Because I . . . I love you." The words were torn from her in wild despair as sobs shook her body. "I love you!"

He crossed the remaining space between them in three strides. He enfolded her in his arms, rocking her in an agony of tenderness. "It's all right, Silver. Shh . . . it's all right."

"No." Her voice was muffled against his chest. "It's not all right. I don't want to love you. I don't want to love anyone. It hurts."

"Yes, it does hurt," Nicholas said gently. Poor firebird. Life had taught her so many harsh lessons, and this had been the harshest of all. "But not all the time. It doesn't hurt all the time. I won't let it hurt you, love."

"You will." Her fingernails dug into the flesh of his shoulders. "You'll go away. Everyone goes away."

"I'll never leave you. Not unless you send me away." His lips brushed her temple. "And even then I'll come back again and again until you get tired of sending me away and let me stay." He held her from him to look gravely down into her eyes. "And if you ever fly away from me, I'll follow you, Silver, across rivers and seas, over steppes and mountains. I'll follow you, I promise."

She couldn't look away from him. What she had been waiting for so long was there shining in his eyes. "Because I'm your wife?" she whispered.

He shook his head. "No." He smiled down at her with a joy she had never seen in him before. "Because you're my love."

She drew a deep breath. "No."

"I'm not permitted to love you?" A tiny smile tugged at the corners of his lips. "I'm afraid it's too late. The deed is done."

She shook her head. "You couldn't love me. I'm not at all lovable. Do you think I don't know that?"

"Attribute it to my peculiar Russian tastes. For I most certainly do love you, Silver Savron."

"My name shouldn't even be Savron. I forced you to marry me."

"Did it never occur to you to question why I gave in so easily?"

"Why should it? I was holding a gun on you."

"And Mikhail was standing in the doorway behind you. He would have taken that little pistol away from you if I'd so much as lifted an eyebrow."

Her eyes widened in surprise. "He was? But why—" She broke off and made an impatient gesture. "That no longer matters. The fact remains that I'm still not gentle or sweet or well mannered. I do what I wish, when I wish. Perhaps you love only my body."

He chuckled. "Only you would make a declaration of devotion so infernally difficult." He cupped her cheeks in his palms. "Listen carefully, do you believe I love Mikhail?"

"Yes."

"And Valentin?"

"Yes."

"Then why shouldn't I love you?"

"I told you, I'm not . . ." She was trembling as if with a severe chill, her entire body shaking. "You can't—" She broke off and shook her head. "Don't lie to me, Nicholas, I can't bear it."

"I'm not lying. I told you I don't lie." He stopped speaking as he realized her trembling was increasing by the second. It was quite comfortable in the room now that the fire was burning high, but it seemed to make no difference to the shudders that were attacking her. He drew her ermine cloak closer. "We'll talk of this later. Come closer to the fire."

"No." Her tone was dazed, her face paler than its usual dusky gold.

His lips quirked with amusement. "You've been saying no to me since the moment we met. I believe it's become a habit that must be corrected." He took her hand, pulled her toward the hearth and pushed her gently to her knees on the furs. "Stay here. I'll be back soon."

"Where are you going?" She wrapped her arms around herself to try to still the shivering.

He smiled. "I'm going to start the fire in the steam room. I think I'd be wise to make sure you're able to pay careful attention to my arguments before I try to convince you of my affection. It seems to have had the same effect as a bullet striking a vital organ. It's evidently as much of a shock to you as it was to me." He turned toward the door he had indicated as leading to the steam area and glanced back over his shoulder, his eyes twinkling. "Think about what I've said. Surely it's not surprising that I should love you. You've always told me you could do anything, be anything." His voice lowered to velvet softness. "So why can you not be my love?"

9

T he door opened fifteen minutes later and a great
puff of steam billowed into the room. "If we're not
quick, we'll have two steam rooms." Nicholas crossed
the room to the teakwood chest against the wall,
opened the lid, and pulled out several towels. Then
he was kneeling before her on the furs to unfasten
the ermine cloak and slip it from her shoulders. He
swore softly. "You're still shivering, dammit."

"No, it's much better now." It was true. She did
feel less chilled though still dazed and bewildered.

"You'll feel even better in a few moments." He
pulled off her crimson velvet boots and tossed them
aside. "And much warmer." He unfastened her gown
and corset. "Can you slip out of the rest of your
clothing while I undress."

"Of course." She stood up and the gown fell to her
feet in a pool of white velvet.

"You look like a Gypsy wench in that red petticoat." Nicholas was quickly stripping, his gaze fixed
on her.

She frowned as fresh annoyance pierced through the bewilderment surrounding her. "You should know. It's clear you have a fondness for Gypsy wenches."

"But I have an even greater fondness for Apache wenches." His eyes were suddenly twinkling. "I've found they have a wildness that never fails to appeal to me." He glanced down at his rigid manhood with a rueful grimace. "Never."

He was completely naked now and she found herself curiously embarrassed. Strange, she had never felt awkward with him before. She looked away, her fingers clumsy as she removed the last of her undergarments.

"No answer? *Merde*, I believe you've turned shy on me. You truly aren't yourself, are you, love?" He picked up the large towel he'd dropped on the furs and held it out. "Come here." She took a step forward and was immediately enveloped in the towel. "There. Now I can see only fleeting glimpses of your delectable person. Does that make you feel more comfortable?"

She nodded, still not looking at him.

He draped another smaller towel over her hair and wound it deftly about her head. "A turban just like the one Ahmed, the tsar's guard, wears." He picked her up and carried her toward the steam room. "Aren't you ever going to speak to me again?"

"Of course. I just have nothing to say." She forced herself to look directly into his eyes. She had never felt so vulnerable in her entire life, completely defenseless and without armor. She saw nothing but gentleness in Nicholas's face, but it didn't help. She quickly closed her eyes again.

"Sweet heaven," he said in exasperation. "Whatever I expected, it wasn't this." He opened the door. "Well, the steam is so thick in here you can scarcely see me if you should decide to open your eyes." He kicked the heavy birch door closed behind him and placed her on a wooden bench before dropping down beside her and gathering her in his arms. "Are you warm at least?"

"Yes." She opened her eyes and saw nothing but a thick wall of steam. Even Nicholas's features above her were indistinct. The feeling of anonymity, of being lost and yet safe in this warm, steamy fog soothed her in some mysterious fashion. She began to relax. "In my village the young warriors would go to the medicine man's tepee to cleanse themselves and dream their great dream. I think that tepee must have been like this."

Nicholas's hand gently stroked the hair at her temple. "To dream their great dream?"

"The dream that was to guide them all the rest of their lives. I always wanted to go to that tepee."

"Because you wanted to dream?"

"No, because they would let no women go there. Only the young warriors."

He laughed. "I should have known."

She nestled her chin against his chest. "I never believed in dreams. I thought it all foolishness. Life is what we carve out for ourselves. Do you believe in dreams?"

"Some dreams, but not the ones that come to us in sleep."

The damp heat was seeping into her bones, and her muscles were beginning to go limp and utterly relaxed. The hot air was heavy, and it was hard to breathe, but that only served to increase the feeling of delicious languor. "What dreams do you believe in?"

"Oh, the ones about firebirds and Apache maidens and—"

"Don't joke."

"I never joke about firebirds." He sat up. "And

now I think I'd better get you out of here. Too much steam at one time isn't good for you."

"I don't want to go," she said lazily. "I like it."

"I thought you would." His tone was amused as he tightened the large towel around her and closed her hand on the folds at the front. "It's a very sensual experience for a very sensual lady. Don't worry, we can always come back later. We have to talk now." He felt her tense beneath his grasp and continued. "It's not going to hurt, Silver. So help me, if you begin to tremble again, I'll spank you."

"We could talk tomorrow."

"Tonight." He opened the door and pushed her gently into the other room. "I'll be right back. I'm going outside."

"To roll in the snow?" She frowned. "That's stupid, you'll catch cold and—"

"I'm used to it, but I won't insist you go with me this time. You'll find the water in the pitcher on the washstand enough of a shock." He was striding toward the front door. "But I can do with some cooling off in more ways than one." His dark eyes were sparkling mischievously as he glanced over his shoulder. "I thought the steam bath would help, but your effect on me is more potent than I imagined." The front door closed behind him.

She stood gazing at the door with a worried frown for a moment before crossing the room to the washstand. She peeled off the towels enveloping her, poured water from the pitcher into the bowl, and dropped the washcloth into it.

Seconds later she gasped as the cool water touched her heated flesh. She persevered and found Nicholas was right, the cold was curiously exhilarating after that first shock. When she had finished bathing she slipped on her ermine cloak and settled down on the furs before the fireplace to wait.

She didn't wait long. Only a few minutes later the door was thrown open and Nicholas burst into the room. He slammed the door shut and stood shaking off snow like a bear waking from a winter's sleep. "I think I've turned into an icicle," he said, striding toward the fireplace.

He didn't look like an icicle. He looked boldly masculine and more vitally alive than ever before. His dark eyes were sparkling, the color in his cheeks high, and Silver felt a surge of pleasure just looking at him. She tried to hide it beneath a casual shrug. "It serves you well." She lowered her eyes as she handed him a towel. "What an idiotic thing to do. No wonder Russians are so peculiar; they probably freeze their brains as well as other parts of their anatomy with this foolishness."

Nicholas ran the towel over the dark hair roughing his chest and then over his lean belly. "My 'parts' seem to be in good working order. Though we most definitely should test them." He took an impulsive step forward, then stopped and shook his head regretfully. "Later." He dropped the towel and knelt beside her. "And you have no idea how difficult it is for me to postpone that particular test. It seems I've waited a thousand years for you to say the words you said tonight."

Her gaze shifted hurriedly to the fire. "Oh?"

"Talk to me. Tell me why you're so frightened. Look at me, Silver."

She reluctantly did so. "I'm not frightened," she denied. "Well, perhaps a little. But not of you."

"Then of what?"

She moistened her lips with her tongue. "It's . . ." She closed her eyes. "This is very strange to me. I've never loved anyone but Rising Star and I knew she would never hurt me."

"And you think I will?"

Her lids opened to reveal eyes glittering like crystal in the firelight. "I don't know. Perhaps you won't mean to but . . ."

"But what?"

"What if you tire of me and go away?"

"I won't tire of you. Not ever. And I'll never go away, I've already told you so."

"Everyone goes away." Her lips were trembling as she tried to smile. "Not that I blame them. I'm not at all lovable."

"Christ, I told you . . ." He trailed off and began to swear under his breath. He cupped her face in his hands. "It all comes back to that, doesn't it? Just because the Delaneys found no worth in you doesn't mean that I don't." His gaze held hers. "I find many things to love in you, Silver. Your strength and your sense of honor, your loyalty and your warmth."

She gazed at him in bemusement. "Truly?" She laughed shakily. "But you said I had no humor."

He grinned down at her. "But we're working on that. By this time next year—"

"Next year?" She experienced a surge of panic mixed with almost unbearable joy. Perhaps she really could allow herself to think of a future with Nicholas. "I don't know. . . ."

"Well, I do," Nicholas said firmly. "Next year we'll—"

"Do we have to talk about that now?" she interrupted. Her hands clenched nervously at her sides. "I'm confused. I never thought . . . This always happened to other people, not to me."

He frowned and then his face softened with understanding. "No, we don't have to talk about it at the moment. I suppose I should give you time to adjust. This is newer to you than it is to me."

"It is?" She gazed at him curiously. "When did you realize you cared for me?"

"Probably from the first moment I set eyes on you and you glared at me in Mrs. Alford's parlor."

She shook her head. "That was lust."

"That, my dear Silver, was destiny." Then as she started to protest he held up his hand. "But perhaps I didn't realize it was destiny until I saw Bassinger trying to whip you to death on the deck of the *Mary L.*" His face became shadowed. "Oh, yes, I realized it then. It nearly tore me to pieces to see that whip come down again and ag—"

"Whip!" Her eyes widened in horror. "I *whipped* you! Dear God, did I hurt you?" Her hands went out, clutching his shoulders in an agony of remorse. "And you say I'm lovable? Would any other woman have been that cruel? Let me see your back. Perhaps you need a salve or—"

"Hush." He was laughing and shaking his head. "I need nothing. That switch was meant to sting, not cut."

"Turn around. Let me see."

"It's nothing."

"Then let me see for myself."

"As you wish, Your Highness." He obediently turned around. "You see, it's nothing."

It was true the fresh pink marks were barely visible, but they still inspired a wrenching pang of regret. She reached out one trembling finger and touched a faint weal on his shoulder. "I didn't mean to bring you pain. It was so wicked of me. I have no gentleness."

"Neither of us has had a great amount of gentleness in our lives. Perhaps we can develop that quality together."

She felt the tears rise to her eyes and blinked to keep them at bay as she gazed at the web of older white scars on his back. It was certainly no gentle hand that had wielded that whip. "Perhaps." She drew even closer and laid her lips on the jagged scar marring his right shoulder blade. She felt his muscles tense beneath the warmth of her lips and turned her cheek to rest it in the hollow of his back. "I promise I will never hurt you again." Her words were muffled but the sudden note of fierceness was clearly audible as she continued. "And I'll cut the balls off anyone else who tries to do it."

His laughter held a thread of huskiness running through it as he turned to face her. "Now, that was a tender declaration. I find it most . . . moving." His fingertips traced the plane of her left cheek. "And I return the vow. Cossack to Apache." His fingers moved with passionate gentleness to the corner of her lips. "Man to woman." His voice lowered to a level above a whisper. "Lover to beloved."

She couldn't look away from him. His eyes held joy and beauty and . . . Even now her mind sidled away from acknowledging that other emotion she saw mirrored there, but she had no such doubts about her own feelings. "Lover to beloved," she echoed softly.

"Forever."

Her brow wrinkled in a troubled frown. "You don't have to promise me forever. I know love seldom lasts for men and that you will probably leave me someday."

"Silver . . ." He gazed at her in helpless exasperation. "How can I convince you that—" He stopped. He could see by her expression that he could never convince her with words. After the life of rejection and lack of affection she had lived, only patience over the years would convince her his was a love that would not fade away. "Very well, have it your way. Am I permitted to say I love you for the present?"

"Oh, yes." Her face blazed with radiance. "That makes me feel wonderful."

"Good." The darkness of his eyes seemed to deepen,

the pupils enlarging to dominate his face. "That's the way I want to make you feel." His hand reached out to toy with the closing of the ermine cloak. "Shall we see if I can make you feel even more wonderful?"

The warmth of his fingers through the softness of the fur caused heat to spiral through her. Her breathing was suddenly shallow, and when she spoke, her voice was uneven. "That would please me very much."

"Not nearly as much as it will please me." He slipped the cloak from her shoulders and it joined the other furs on the floor, his gaze on the hills and valleys of her naked body. When he spoke again his voice had thickened. "As you will please me, love." His fingers threaded through her glossy hair. "There's one more peculiar custom connected with the Savron bathing ritual. Shall I show you what it is?"

She nodded dreamily, trying to fathom the secrets in his dark eyes.

"Lie down on the furs." His hands dropped from her hair. "I'll be right back."

She gazed at him in bemusement as he stood up and crossed to the hearth. He opened the teakwood box from which he had taken the towels and drew from it an exquisitely cut ruby crystal decanter. He set the decanter on the hearth close to the fire and knelt beside it, gazing into the flames. "In the Kuban there was a Turkish trader who came to my grandfather's village once a year bringing many treasures from Constantinople and Athens. The Turks make delightful oils and ointments and my grandfather was particularly fond of this one. So fond that he sent several hundred jars to my father as part of my mother's dowry. He claimed that it has certain properties. . . ."

She wished he would be done with talking and come to her. "What properties?"

"The old Turk called this oil the Caress of Aphrodite. He said it had magical powers."

"Foolishness."

"Perhaps." He slanted her a smile over her shoulder that held both sensuality and amusement, and a hot shiver rippled through her. "However, I believe I should tell you that Igor Dabol is no fool and was eager for many grandsons of his blood. He was sure the Turkish oil would help, as he'd used it many years himself."

"What's in it?"

"I have no idea. Nothing harmful, or my grandfather would have cut the ears off that Turkish trader." He picked up the decanter and the firelight glittered on the crystal prisms. "It should be warm enough now."

Silver found herself gazing in fascination at the ruby-red decanter. The Caress of Aphrodite.

Nicholas dropped to his knees beside her and unstoppered the bottle. A breathtakingly delicious scent drifted from the lip of the decanter. She couldn't place it. Cinnamon, vanilla, gardenias . . . Perhaps a little of all of them and many other ingredients that were a mystery. They mingled to create a fragrance that was wildly intoxicating to the senses. "Lovely," Silver whispered, breathing deeply. "I've never smelled anything so lovely."

Nicholas smiled as he poured a little of the clear oil into the palm of his hand. "I think you'll find it feels lovely too." He set the decanter down on the floor beside them. He rubbed his palms together. "Roll over, love."

"But I want to look at you. Why is all this necessary? We don't need this trader's ointment."

"And I'm trying not to look at you," he said hoarsely. "This isn't easy for me, Silver."

"Then why—"

"Because it's been a long time and I don't want you to be—" He suddenly smiled with beguiling sweetness. "I want it to be very good for you." He gently turned her over on her stomach. "Now, lie still." His palms began to knead her shoulders, rubbing the fragrant oil into her flesh.

"It feels pleasant but I don't see—" She inhaled sharply. Fire. Ice. How could both sensations exist side by side? Yet they did, and something else that was sensitizing her flesh to an excruciating pitch.

Nicholas's fingers were moving skillfully down her spine and the burning became a sensual torment. "The trader said the Sultan ordered his harem eunuchs to massage his chosen concubine for the night with this ointment. Do you suppose he spoke truly?"

She swallowed. "Yes."

"So do I."

More oil, Nicholas's hands squeezing her buttocks, massaging her thighs, the backs of her knees, the curves of her calves. Her entire body seemed to be flowering with fragrance, her flesh ripening to such exquisite sensitivity that the lightest touch of Nicholas's fingers made the muscles of her stomach clench and ignited a tingling between her thighs. She bit hard on her lower lip to keep from moaning as Nicholas began to rub the oil into the curve of her instep. "Nicholas . . ."

"You like that? I remember how sensitive you are here."

She was sensitive everywhere. Her lips parted to permit more air into her starved lungs. "I'm not sure I like your Aphrodite's Caress. It makes me—"

"Hungry, aching, on fire?" Nicholas whispered. "I know. But that's good. It makes what comes later all the better."

"My heart's beating so fast it's hard to breathe." She turned over on her back. "It's—" She gasped.

Nicholas's hands were on her breasts, encircling the round globes with smooth, gentle strokes. She could feel her breasts swell, ripen.

"Beautiful." Nicholas was gazing down at her, his palms cupping, squeezing, releasing and then squeezing again. His head lowered slowly and his mouth closed on the nipple of her left breast. She gave a low cry as she felt the gentle suction begin. Her hands tangled desperately in his hair and she held him to her. She felt a shudder go through his body as he lifted his head to look down at her. His nostrils were flaring with each ragged breath. "Too beautiful. This is . . . *killing* me."

Silver was panting, her breasts rising and falling beneath his hands. "Then stop. Come into me. I need—"

"Not yet." He reached for the decanter. "It's got to be perfect for you."

"It *is* perfect. Come—" She broke off, her spine arching upward off the furs. "Nicholas!"

He was massaging the oil into her mound of curls, parting her thighs to reach into the heart of her womanhood. Silver's fingers dug into the furs and her mouth opened in a silent scream of primitive passion.

"Just a little more," he muttered. "You're so beautiful here. The scent of you . . . You'll like this." His fingers plunged deep again and again and again.

A low sob broke from Silver's lips as her head thrashed back and forth on the furs.

"You're gleaming in the firelight like a golden statue." Nicholas's voice was uneven as his fingers moved rhythmically. "But you're not a statue. I can feel you tighten around me. Try to hold me."

But she couldn't hold him, he wouldn't permit her to hold him. Her hips lunged upward. "Stay."

"You want me?" His gaze narrowed intently on her face. "The way I want you?"

"More."

"No, not more," he muttered. "But enough, thank God. Come." He was lifting her and standing up. "I can't wait any longer."

She gazed at him in bewilderment. "Where . . ." She saw that he was heading toward the door leading to the steam room. "Now? No, Nicholas, I want—"

"The steam intensifies everything." The door opened and billows of steam surrounded them. "You'll see." He kicked the door shut behind them.

Heat. Steam. The wild, spicy fragrance of Aphrodite's Caress.

Nicholas dropped down on the wooden bench and set her astraddle his thighs. His rampant manhood nuzzled against the heart of her. "Can you feel me burning?" he asked thickly. "Are you burning, Silver?"

"Yes." Inside and out she was tingling, her flesh hungering for his touch, for completion. She moved yearningly against him. Why didn't he fill her, give her what she needed? She couldn't see his face in the misty darkness, but there was no mistaking the evidence that he was as wild for her as she was for him. Every muscle of his body was locked and tense, his manhood a drawn bow ready to be loosed.

His hands slid around her, cupping her bottom. "Now?"

"Now." Her fingernails dug into his shoulders. "It has to be!"

He jerked her forward, piercing, plunging into the depths of her womanhood.

Her head fell back, the tendons of her throat distended as she felt the incredible fullness, the feverish, ridged warmth of him.

"Tight," he gasped. He flexed with wild, hungry pleasure and then began to move slowly, deeply, as if savoring every stroke. "I can barely move. . . ."

She tried to help him, but she was so dazed with

pleasure she found she could only accept and accept and accept again. She was lost in heat, surrounded by delicious scent, devoured by Nicholas's hunger and her own. Her fingers kneaded the slick muscles cording his back in an agony of helpless need. "More."

He moved faster, deeper, wilder. His fingers dug into the cushioned softness of her buttocks, his manhood probing, thrusting boldly within her.

The fragrance rising from her heated flesh was as potent as the incense burned in an ancient temple dedicated to Aphrodite, a temple devoted to the same sensual splendor of the rite that Nicholas was performing on her body.

She was sobbing, each breath hot and heavy. She could hear Nicholas's harsh breathing, feel his chest heave with each gasp for air, sense his desperation as he plunged deeper, harder.

The desperation mounted. He gave a low, guttural cry. "Love, please . . ."

Searing pleasure exploded in the hot misty darkness. Beauty. Joy. Nicholas.

Her arms held him tightly. She didn't want to let him go though she was suddenly so weary she collapsed against him.

"Silver."

She was too tired to answer.

"Silver, we have to leave this room now. The steam . . ." He lifted her off him and rose to his feet. He caught her as she swayed unsteadily and swung her into his arms.

She felt deliciously languid, every muscle buttersoft. She yawned. "I can see why your grandfather thought so highly of his Turkish oil." Her flesh was still pleasantly tingling as they left the steam room, though her sensitivity was now enormously decreased. "I'm very good with herbs. I wonder if I could work out the formula."

"I definitely think you should try. I'm sure we'd both find it gratifying." He looked down at her, his eyes gleaming like a boy's. "Are you ready for your snow bath?"

"No!" Her eyes widened in alarm. "Nicholas, you wouldn't—" She broke off as she saw that he was shaking his head and she relaxed. "Just because I approve of one of your customs is no reason to think I'll indulge in that madness."

"Someday." Nicholas strode toward the washstand. "But in the meantime I'll indulge you and let you bathe at the washstand again." His smile faded and his gaze narrowed intently on her face. "Or perhaps we'll bathe each other."

"Another old Russian custom?"

He turned her in his arms and allowed her to slide slowly down the newly hardened muscles of his body, letting her feel every nuance of his arousal. "I believe the ritual I have in mind has no national boundaries," he whispered. "And the appeal is definitely universal."

"Why were you so angry tonight?" Nicholas's fingers threaded lazily through Silver's hair, letting the strands run through them like ebony rain. "You were blazing with rage when you so rudely threw that wine bottle at me."

"I didn't throw it at you." Silver's lips brushed his shoulder lovingly. "If I had, I would have hit you. I don't miss what I aim at. I merely wanted to stop you from looking at that stupid woman. It displeased me."

"Tania?" Nicholas curled one long tress around his index finger. "I was only listening to her sing. She has a very pleasant voice."

"She sounds like a hyena howling for its mate."

Nicholas chuckled. "You're unkind. Tania has—"

"I don't want to talk about her," Silver interrupted crossly. "I've heard enough about the sluts you've bedded."

Nicholas's fingers paused. "Indeed? What other woman do I stand accused of bedding?"

"Katya Razkolsky. When I met her at the ball tonight, she took great pleasure in describing your tryst at the hunting lodge."

"I see." His fingers resumed their stroking. "And that's what enraged you?"

"Why should I care how many women you've bedded?" Then as she met his gaze she nodded reluctantly. It was still proving difficult to lower her defenses and give him total honesty. "I wanted to scalp her." She added fiercely, "And you too."

"Then I suppose I was lucky to come away with just a switching." He was silent for a moment. "What happened with Katya shouldn't hurt you, Silver. It was a long time ago and I was only a boy."

"She must be almost as old as your mother. Such a woman isn't interested in boys."

"You're wrong."

There was such bitterness in Nicholas's voice that Silver raised her head from his shoulder to look at him. "Am I?"

"Oh, yes, very wrong," he said cynically. "Perhaps you haven't been at court long enough to find out that anything new or fresh is grabbed at with greedy hands and that young boys are prizes to many of the older women there. It's not at all unusual for the pages to be summoned to the bedchambers of the ladies of the court."

"But you weren't a page," Silver said. "You're a prince."

"With an ambitious mother who wanted acceptance and was willing to pay for it. With her own body and also with mine."

"I don't understand."

"It's very simple. My father died when I was ten, and my mother sent me away to my grandfather in the Kuban. I loved it there. It was home to me. I was brought back to St. Petersburg only in the summer to make an appearance at court and show the tsar I was well taken care of and not maltreated by my mother."

"You didn't like your time at court?"

His lips tightened. "I hated it. I was treated like a mongrel dog by the other children and ignored by their fathers and mothers. I was a Cossack, a barbarian to them. Dear God, they didn't realize I never wanted to be anything else. I was nearly smothered in those ballrooms. The air was so heavy with perfume I couldn't breathe, and the rich foods made me feel like a slug."

"Your mother wouldn't let you stay with your grandfather?"

He shook his head. "After my father was killed in a duel with one of her lovers she had to appear above reproach. Any decadence is permitted as long as it's done discreetly, but my mother is seldom discreet. She didn't want me there any more than I wanted to come but she—" He shifted restlessly. "It was a long time ago. You don't want to hear about all this."

"I do want to hear it. I want to hear everything about you."

He shrugged. "There's not much more to tell. The summer I was fourteen my mother decided she could make use of me. She began sending me to visit her friends in their bedchambers. Oh, I won't claim reluctance. I was as curious and lusty as any other lad."

"Katya?"

"She was one of them. For a while I felt proud as a bantam rooster. The young Cossack was being petted, demanded by those highborn ladies as if he actually had some importance. If I gave them pleasure, they let me do anything I wanted with their bodies and—'' He broke off as he felt Silver's fingers dig into his arm. ''I told you that you didn't want to hear it.''

''Did you . . . like them?''

''I didn't think about it. I liked what they made me feel. I thought I was a pasha with an entire harem for my pleasure.'' His expression turned bitter. ''Until I realized I was being used. They cared nothing for me. I was as much of a whore as the camp followers of Igor's band who spread their legs for a few rubles. Only what my mother charged was much higher. For every favor she gave her friends, she demanded one in return. In the end I left St. Petersburg and told her I'd never come back.''

''But you did come back.''

''Not willingly. Something happened. . . .'' He trailed off, his gaze fixed moodily on the fire. The silence in the room was broken only by the crackle and hiss of the blazing logs. His shoulders suddenly shifted as if he were throwing off a burden and he turned to look at her. ''So you see, Katya means nothing. They all meant nothing.''

It wasn't true, she thought with fierce protectiveness. That time in his life had taught him bitter lessons and given him deeper scars than the wounds on his back. He had been made to feel without worth and she knew that feeling too well. ''I'll punish Katya for you if you like. I'll punish them all for you.''

The moodiness in Nicholas's expression disappeared as a smile lit his face. ''Such a fierce little warrior. I appreciate the offer, but it all happened a long time ago. No punishment is required.''

''But I want—''

His fingers on her lips silenced her. ''No,'' he said softly. ''I believe in revenge, but I was not without

blame. I was no innocent even as a child. Cossacks—"
He stopped as he saw the tears glittering in her eyes.
He touched one long sweeping lash and found it
damp. "For me?"

"For you." Her lashes lowered to veil her eyes.
"And for our child. What you said reminded me that
evil happens also to innocents. Our baby had no
guilt. She should not have died." Her tone turned
fierce. "But her murderer will be punished. I also
believe in revenge."

Nicholas looked grim. "Mikhail is sure about the
potion?"

"Yes." She hesitated. "He told me he visited court
and discovered nothing, but I don't believe that's
true. I think he found out something he doesn't want
me to know."

"He'll damn well tell me if he knows anything."

"I hope that's true. I couldn't get a word from
him." She lowered her cheek once more to rest on his
shoulder. "And I could find out nothing these past
months about the doctor or who could have bribed
him to have done this thing."

He suddenly lifted her chin to look down into her
face. "*That's* why you wanted to go to court?"

She gazed at him in bewilderment. "Of course,
why else should I go there? It's a very boring place."

"Boring? The most glittering court in the world is
boring?" He suddenly gave a shout of laughter as his
arms closed tightly around her. "*Merde*, she thinks
it's boring!"

"I don't see what's so amusing. You said you had
no liking for court life either."

"But I thought that you . . ." He trailed off and
began to caress her naked back with exquisite gentleness. "You're right, it's not amusing." His lips touched
her temple. "It's a gift from God."

"I don't know what you're talking about."

"It doesn't matter. Not now."

She didn't speak for several languid moments, and when she did, her voice was barely audible. "I can't give up, you know. Not until I find the person who killed our baby."

"I wouldn't want you to give up. We'll find him together."

"Will we?" She was so accustomed to thinking of herself as alone that it felt strange to realize she now had someone to share the joys and the burdens of life. Even though it might not last, it was still extraordinary. She said haltingly, "Thank you. That's very kind of you."

"Kind?" he asked, startled. "For God's sake, Silver. She was my child too. Why shouldn't I want to find the bastard who did this?"

"No reason." She would not let the tears fall. She felt full, bursting with a joy that knew no bounds. She must not let him see how foolish she was being, how much it meant to her to know that she had him beside her in this precious closeness of mind as well as body. Even he would not understand the impact of the knowledge that had rocked the foundations of everything that had gone before. The knowledge that was so simple yet resounded within her like the joyous caroling of a thousand bells.

She was no longer alone.

10

"I want to know, Mikhail." Nicholas's tone was hard. "The time for secrets is over."

"I cannot tell you," Mikhail said quietly.

"Silver thinks you're keeping something from her." Nicholas shook his head. "And God knows I don't know what to think. Why the devil wouldn't you come to me and tell me about the potion?"

"I thought it best not to do so."

"But *why?*"

Mikhail didn't answer.

"This was my child too. Not only Silver's but mine. Does a friend keep silent in such a situation?"

"I will always be your friend."

"Mikhail, dammit. Talk to me."

"I cannot." Mikhail's expression was troubled. "It is not something I can . . ." He trailed off and shrugged his massive shoulders helplessly. "I cannot. If you think this is a betrayal of our friendship, then I will leave you."

"*Merde*, you're stubborn."

"Shall I leave you?"

Nicholas gazed at him broodingly. "No, dammit." He dropped down in the chair before the fire. "But before this is over I may crack that thick stubborn head of yours."

A relieved smile lit Mikhail's face. "You do not believe that I would betray you?"

"I'm not such a fool. You may lack judgment but not loyalty."

"Sometimes judgment is not easy. You know I've never been clever. I can only do the best I can."

No, Mikhail had never been clever, Nicholas thought, but he possessed both honor and almost faultless instinct. Nicholas was torn between frustration and affection as he stared at his friend. "You will say no more?"

Mikhail started to turn away. "I must go now. I promised Etaine I would walk with her in the garden."

"Mikhail."

Mikhail glanced back over his shoulder.

"If you won't help, at least promise that you won't hinder me. I *will* find out who did this."

"I will not hinder," Mikhail said slowly as he opened the door. "I would feel as you do."

The door closed behind him.

So much for the assurance he had given to Silver last night, Nicholas thought wryly. After all these years he should have realized how obstinate Mikhail could be. Now, how the devil could he go back to Silver with no information to give her?

A perfunctory knock sounded before the door of the study was opened to admit Valentin. "Good morning." Valentin warily studied the scowl on Nicholas's face. "Or is it? It wasn't my fault that Silver followed you to Tania's, you know. I tried to reason with her, but she wouldn't listen. You didn't—"

"Drown her in the Neva?" Nicholas asked dryly. "No, she's quite safe. She's only sleeping late."

"Silver?" Valentin asked, surprised. "Silver never sleeps late."

"Well, she is this morning. She was . . . tired."

Valentin gazed at him speculatively, and then a delighted smile lit his face. "I see," he murmured. "You look a trifle weary yourself today. Tania's must have been very . . . interesting. How is young Stepvan?"

"Alive."

"How surprising. Is he going to remain that way?"

"Probably."

"My, you must be mellowing. I hear the gentler emotions do have that effect on a man."

"I'm not feeling very gentle at the moment. Mikhail—" Nicholas broke off. "Did you come here only to see if you were going to have to act as my second?"

"Tut. Tut," Valentin chided with a mocking smile. "I just don't understand you. You're bad tempered when you don't get what you want and in even fouler temper when you do. You're a very difficult man to please, Nicky." Then, as he saw Nicholas's expression darken, he hastily continued. "But as it happens, I did have a reason for coming here other than my concern for Silver. I spoke to Dzosky last night regarding the inquiries we instigated about Monteith. He received a report from London day before yesterday."

Nicholas's eyes narrowed with sudden alertness. "And?"

Valentin's smile faded. "Ugly. Very ugly. It took a long time to gather the information because no one would talk about Monteith in the village where he grew up. He was the son of the vicar, but he obviously didn't inspire any faith, hope, or charity." He paused. "The investigator's report emphasized how afraid people were to talk about him."

"Why?"

Valentin hesitated. "Do you want me to give you the bare bones? You should have a full written report from Dzosky by tomorrow."

"Why were they afraid?" Nicholas asked impatiently.

"Devil worship."

Nicholas went still. "What?"

"Monteith was involved in devil worship. He was rumored to have conducted black masses in the dungeons below the castle of the Earl of Leith. There were all kinds of stories. . . ." Valentin paused. "Several women disappeared during the last two years Monteith was in Yorkshire. They were all young village girls whose bodies were never found. Rumor had it they were chosen by Monteith as sacrifices at his black masses."

Nicholas experienced an icy chill as he remembered the sight of Etaine on the black marble slab in the lion's cage. The scene was a parody of just such a sacrifice. "Could the local magistrates do nothing to stop it?"

"The Earl of Leith had the magistrates firmly under his thumb." Valentin's gaze met Nicholas's. "And evidently the earl was equally under Monteith's control. It sounds ominously familiar, doesn't it?"

"Peskov."

Valentin nodded. "And God only knows how many other men and women of the nobility. According to certain sources, Monteith dealt heavily in promises."

"Promises?"

"Eternal youth and beauty for the women, and wealth and power for the men. Whatever they want as long as they follow and obey him."

Nicholas muttered a curse beneath his breath. "It's preposterous!"

"Of course." Valentin shifted uneasily. "Still, he

held sway over those people in Yorkshire for almost
three years. How did he do it without fulfilling those
promises, Nicky?"

"He's a very clever man."

"Perhaps—"

"What do you mean perhaps?" Nicholas asked in
astonishment. "You can't think there's anything to
Monteith's claims?"

"He's very . . . strange," Valentin said slowly. "And
there's one more thing in the report that's even
stranger."

Nicholas gazed at him, waiting.

"Monteith married a young village girl named Mary
Trask. A year after Etaine was born his wife disappeared just like the others and was never found."

Nicholas's eyes widened in shock. "He sacrificed
his own wife?"

"Presumably."

And a man who would sacrifice his wife would
have no qualms in sacrificing his daughter, Nicholas
thought in horror. He jumped to his feet and started
toward the door.

"Where are you going?" Valentin asked.

Nicholas opened the door. "To Dzosky's office to
get that report."

"But he'll send it to you tomorrow."

"That's not soon enough. I want to study every
detail immediately." He glanced back over his shoulder. "And I don't want Silver to know any of this. Do
you understand?"

"No, I don't understand." Valentin frowned in puzzlement. "Why not?"

"What do you think Silver would do if she thought
Etaine was in that kind of danger?"

Valentin grimaced in sudden comprehension. "Go
after Monteith and remove the threat."

"Exactly."

The door slammed behind Nicholas.

The cloak floated down upon Silver in a coverlet of flame.

"Get up, woman, it's the middle of the afternoon. Are you going to sleep all day?" Nicholas was standing by the bed and grinning down at her. Silver's heart gave a leap of pure joy that dispersed the last remnants of sleep.

Nicholas was dressed entirely in black suede trimmed with lustrous black fox, and his golden hair and bronze skin glowed against its darkness with a radiance that made her catch her breath. Hers. This beautiful creature belonged to her now. It was beyond belief.

When she didn't answer, his brow rose. "Well?" he asked.

She propped herself up on her elbow. "I might decide to get out of bed." She added with a yawn, "Since there's nothing of interest to do here."

"A challenge?" he murmured, his dark eyes twinkling. "You're uncommonly fond of issuing challenges, love. I think I can assure you an interesting time— not in bed this time—but on a ride in the troika. Come. Put on your cloak. Though I should rightly return it to the shop since you've expressed no appreciation for it."

He was right. She had wanted to look at nothing but Nicholas, had noticed nothing but his loving smile and the sheer sensual beauty of him. Now she reluctantly shifted her gaze away from him to the garment he'd dropped over her when he had first awakened her. She smiled in delight. The hooded cloak was incredibly lovely and outrageously extravagant, composed entirely of feathers dyed a brilliant shade of scarlet that curled like soft tongues of flame.

"It's . . . beautiful." Her finger reached out to caress one silky feather. "Where did you get it?"

"Madame Lemenov's. I saw it through the window of her shop on the Nevsky Prospekt. Actually, I saw it two weeks ago, but I was in no mood to shower you with gifts then." He pulled her to her knees on the bed and the covers fell away, revealing her golden nudity veiled only by the glossy darkness of her hair. The smile faded from his face as his gaze traveled over her and his eyes gleamed with admiration. "However, when I passed the shop this morning my mood had undergone a miraculous change and I decided every firebird deserves a few feathers to keep her warm."

A tingle of heat burned through her. "A few?" Her palm stroked the cloak gently. "There must be thousands of feathers in this cloak. What kind of feathers are they?"

"Firebird feathers, what else?"

"No, what are they truly? No myths."

"You and Mikhail." He shook his head reprovingly. "Neither of you have any faith. When one sees a firebird, one must not question." He picked up the cloak and flung it over her shoulders. "Who's to say that a firebird didn't shed these feathers to summon her lover to follow after her?" He fastened the cloak at her neck. "Then all Madame Lemenov had to do was gather them up and fashion them into a cloak for—"

"I think perhaps they're ostrich feathers."

"Nonsense." He pulled the hood over her dark hair. "You have to believe." His eyes were grave as he gazed down at her. "There are so many beautiful worlds open to us, but we may never find them unless we believe."

He was no longer talking about myths, she realized. But didn't he know how difficult it was for her to have faith that his love would last for more than a short time? He *did* understand, and the sadness generated by his comprehension was reflected in his expression as he looked at her. She wanted desperately to banish his sadness, but she could only gaze at him helplessly. "Perhaps someday . . ." She smiled with an effort. "What were you doing on the Nevsky Prospekt today? I would have thought you would have been as tired as I this morning," she said to distract him.

His gaze slid away from her. "I had business to attend to that wouldn't wait." He pulled two shining tresses from beneath the hood and arranged them against the fiery feathers. "Your dark hair looks quite wonderful against this scarlet."

"What business?"

"Nothing of consequence at the moment." He lifted her in his arms and whirled her in a dizzying circle above his head. "Fly, firebird!"

"Nicholas!" It was madness. She laughed helplessly as she clutched wildly at his shoulders. "Stop."

"Why? Aren't you enjoying it?"

The room was whirling around her, and there were only the flaming feathers of the firebird and the golden radiance of Nicholas. Exhilaration spiraled within her, intertwining with a joy so great she felt as if she would float away at any moment. "Oh, yes." She held out her arms as if they were wings, and the cloak of the firebird shimmered in the sunlight streaming through the windows. The laughter bubbled in her throat as the hood of the cloak fell back and her hair streamed behind her in a wild cascade. "Oh, yes, I'm enjoying it."

"So am I." Then he was gently lowering her, letting her slip down his body. Nicholas. The scent of leather, soap, and musk. The softness of fur and suede.

The hardness of taut, locked muscles and fevered arousal.

"Do you believe?" he whispered.

At that moment she could believe anything. In a love that could last forever, in honor and trust and vows. She reached up to touch his cheek with infinite tenderness. "I believe."

"Good." His smile flashed with sudden mischief. He scooped her up in his arms and strode toward the door that led to the hall. "Then let's see if my fire-bird can melt the icicles."

"Where are we going?" She didn't really care. Her arms slid contentedly around his neck as he started down the hall.

"You should pay attention. I told you before that we were taking a ride in the troika. It's a beautiful morning and the woods should look like a fairyland."

"I think I should call your attention to the fact that I'm wearing nothing beneath this cloak."

"I noticed."

"Not even shoes."

"You won't need them." His eyes twinkled as he gazed down at her. "I believe this is the first time I've seen a glimmer of modesty in you. Are you acquiring a sense of decorum?"

She shook her head. "I just thought I'd mention it. My being naked in front of people seems to bother you."

"You're damn right it does." He started down the marble staircase. "And I shall take great pleasure in tanning that delightful bottom if I catch you displaying it to anyone but me ever again. However, I definitely have no objection when we're by ourselves."

"You're going to drive the troika?"

"No. Sergei is driving. I want to be able to relax and enjoy . . . the scenery. Don't worry. I told him if he didn't keep his eyes on the horses, I'd carve a hole in the ice and toss him in the Neva." He reached the bottom of the steps and started across the gleaming foyer toward the front. "The door, Rogoff."

The servant scurried ahead to throw open the door before resuming his statuelike immobility.

Silver's bare feet were peeping from beneath the hem of the cloak, and as soon as they were outside and moving toward the waiting troika, she shivered in the frigid air.

Nicholas looked down at her with sudden concern. "Just a few more steps and you'll be warm under the furs, but perhaps we should go back."

"The cold is nothing. I don't want to go back." She was brimming over with excitement. "You promised to show me a fairyland."

"I did, didn't I?" His smile held pride as well as tenderness as he placed her on the wide cushioned seat of the sleigh and drew the sable robes around her until only her face showed above them. "I should have known a little ice would have no effect on you. Mikhail says you could have been a Cossack." He climbed into the troika and slipped beneath the furs beside her.

Silver noticed with amusement that Sergei was sitting ramrod straight on the driving seat, his gaze fixed rigidly ahead. He was obviously taking seriously Nicholas's threat of immersion in the icy waters of the Neva.

Nicholas gave an order in Russian and the driver snapped his whip. The troika began to move over the snow, first slowly and then faster, then faster still as the horses gained momentum. Within minutes they had left the grounds of the palace and had entered the woods.

Fairyland, Nicholas had called it, and fairyland it was, Silver thought. The boughs of the white birch trees and evergreens held thousands of icicles whose crystals sparkled with all the hues of the rainbow. The colors were so brilliant they dazzled her eyes, and the beauty was so intense she found her throat tightening with emotion.

Nicholas was watching her face. "I keep my promises, Silver," he said gently.

"Yes." She swallowed to ease the tightness of her throat. "I see that you do. Fairyland."

"It's a fitting place for a firebird." He drew closer and his hands were suddenly moving beneath the fur, unfastening her cloak. "But there are too many icicles." His fingers began to pluck teasingly at the nipples. "Can you melt them, love?"

A hot shiver ran through her and she felt a familiar clenching between her thighs. They had made love so many times last night in the bathhouse before they had returned to the palace that she had thought she'd never be hungry again. She knew now she had been wrong. The hunger was back, as sharp as if it had never been satisfied. "I find the icicles very . . ." His hand moved down to stroke the tight curls surrounding her womanhood and she had to steady her voice. "Pretty."

"Do you?" His words were a soft murmur in her ear as his finger searched and then found. She gave a low cry and arched upward, her thighs instinctively parting.

"Does their shape please you?"

She half sobbed as his fingers moved rhythmically, forcefully, within her.

"Does it?"

She couldn't remember what he had asked. She was melting, burning and . . .

"Does it?" he repeated.

"Yes." It didn't matter what the question, the answer would be affirmative.

"And the texture? They're very hard, aren't they?"

She moistened her lips with her tongue, her head thrown back against the furs. "Yes . . . hard."

"Too hard?"

"No."

His fingers resumed their magical play, while the other hand made adjustments in his clothing. "I'm glad," he said softly as he moved over her. His fingers were gone and his bold manhood was pressing against her. "And you have no objection to the length?" He plunged forward.

She gave a low cry. Fullness. Impossible, glorious fullness.

He was gazing down at her. "Objections?" he prompted.

What was he talking about? How could she object when he was a part of her. "Move."

"Too cold?"

She gazed at him in confusion. Cold? She was burning up. "What?"

"The icicles." His eyes were sparkling with mischief. "That *is* what we were talking about, isn't it?"

"Icicles?" She stared in at him in disbelief.

"Ah, love, what am I going to do with you?" He reached up and deliberately tugged at his left ear.

"Jokes? Now?" she whispered.

His smile faded and his gaze narrowed on her face, and now only hunger and raw arousal remained. "You're right," he said thickly. "This is no time for jokes."

He exploded, lifting her to each forceful thrust, his chest moving in and out with the harshness of his breathing. "I may hurt you. . . . Stop me if—"

The troika glided over the snow, the cold stinging her cheeks and Nicholas burning within her. Icicles splintered in sensual brilliant above her, around her, inside her.

She tried to stifle a cry, her fingers digging into the

sable covering Nicholas's shoulders. He moved faster, harder. His breath clung to the air in frosty puffs. His nostrils flared as he sought to take in more air, as his body sought to take in more of her. Fullness. Power. Flame.

"Fly," he urged hoarsely. He thrust deeper. "Fly, love. Now."

She flew, soared, burst toward the sun in a wild conflagration of brilliance. Nicholas was with her, she realized vaguely. Soaring high, higher, piercing mists and clouds, valleys, and mountains until there was nothing left but sunlit radiance.

And Nicholas.

"That was a most inappropriate time to joke," she said reprovingly. "You distracted me."

"Sorry." Nicholas's tongue stroked delicately at her nipple as his cheek nestled more comfortably on her breast. "But I saw no reason not to inject a note of humor. I was very happy." He planted a kiss beneath the curve of her breast. "*You* make me happy."

"Do I?" A burst of joy shot through her. She had the power to make Nicholas happy. The knowledge filled her with a sense of wonder. "Truly?"

"Truly," he said solemnly. He rubbed his cheek back and forth against her like a playful puppy. "Does that surprise you?"

"Yes." She was silent a moment. "I've never worried about trying to make anyone happy before. It's a responsibility. What if I do something wrong?"

He laughed.

"No." Her gaze flew to his. "It's not funny. I'm not like other women. I don't know how to be gentle or kind. What if I hurt you?"

"Then I'll be hurt."

"You won't become angry and leave me?"

"No."

There was silence in the troika, broken only by the clop of the horses' hooves and the tinkle of the silver bells on the harness.

"I'll try to be gentle," Silver said haltingly. "But if I'm not, you'll know it's not because I don't care for you. It won't be because of that, Nicholas."

There was another silence. Nicholas didn't lift his head from her breast, but his voice was curiously husky when he spoke again. "Yes, I do know that, firebird." His lips brushed against her with gossamer tenderness. "And I find the knowledge unmans me." He cleared his throat and raised his head to look at her with glittering eyes. "And the last thing I want is to be unmanned with an unclothed women in my arms."

"I'm sure you'll recover shortly." She frowned. "And I don't like being called just any unclothed woman. I'm an unclothed Silver Delancy."

"Savron," he corrected her. "When will you become accustomed to the idea that you're my wife?"

"It feels . . . strange."

"You'll get used to it. I'll try to make the state as painless as possible." He lowered his cheek once more to rest it on her breast. "As a matter of fact, I wanted to talk to you about that." His tone was casual, almost careless. "I made inquiries while I was in town today regarding a school for you."

"A school?"

"You told me once you wanted to study to become a doctor," he reminded her. "According to Dzosky, there are no suitable schools that will accept women here in Russia, but there's a fine university in Switzerland from which two Russian women have graduated. I told Dzosky to make the arrangements and hire a language tutor to begin—"

"Switzerland. That's very far away."

"You won't be alone. Etaine and Mikhail will be with you."

She pushed him away and sat up. The furs fell to her waist but she didn't feel the icy bite of the cold. She felt only panic rising within her. "But not you? You're sending me away?"

"For God's sake, do you want to freeze?" He fastened the feather cloak around her and pulled up the robes. "I'm not sending you away. I'm trying to give you what you want."

She shook her head. "You don't want me. You're sending me away."

"Silver . . ." Nicholas was gazing at her with aching sympathy. "I'm not a Delaney. I'll never willingly send you away. How often do I have to tell you that? I'm only trying to give you what you want."

"Words." Her voice was brittle. "You will not, but you are. If you don't want to part with me, why won't you come with me?" She edged away from him. "Not that it matters. I couldn't go anyway. I must stay here and find the murderer of my child. You need not think—"

"Hush." He pulled her back within the curve of his arm. "And stop bristling like a porcupine. You *could* leave if you'd trust me to find the murderer for you. Can't you do that, Silver?"

She didn't look at him.

"No, I see that you can't." His lips twisted in a rueful smile. "I didn't really think you would, but I wanted to try. I don't suppose you'd consider changing your mind."

She shook her head emphatically.

"Then we'll just have to postpone your schooling until I'm able to go with you."

"You're not going to send me away?"

He *should* send her away, blast it. He wanted desperately to send her and Etaine out of the country until he could deal with Monteith. The report he had read this morning had filled him with dread. Yet how could he send Silver away when she would regard it as another rejection? He cradled her head against his shoulder and sighed in resignation. "No, love, I'm not going to send you away. I'll go into town tomorrow and tell Dzosky to cancel the arrangements."

11

Silver came suddenly awake, her gaze searching the darkness. "Nicholas?"

Then she relaxed as she saw his nude silhouette outlined against the window across the room. How stupid to be thrown into a panic just because she had awakened and he wasn't beside her. Three nights before she wouldn't have dreamed she would have become so accustomed to having Nicholas in her bed that it felt wrong to sleep alone. The panic that had jarred her awake abruptly flooded back to her as she noticed the tenseness of the muscles cording Nicholas's shoulders and back. "Are you ill?"

"Go back to sleep." He didn't turn around. "There's nothing wrong."

"Don't be foolish. If there's nothing wrong, then why aren't you sleeping?"

He chuckled and turned to her. She couldn't see his features but a little of the tension had eased from his face. "I'll endeavor to refrain from lack of logic in the future." He was coming toward her. "I only had a bad dream and felt the need of a little space to breathe." He slipped beneath the covers and gathered her close. "You can understand such need. You don't like closed doors yourself."

"You had a bad dream last night too. I woke in the middle of night and you were . . ." She paused, remembering the fear she had experienced when she had awakened and found Nicholas, muscles locked, his mouth open as he struggled for breath. "You weren't good. You reminded me of Etaine when she's having one of her attacks."

"I don't remember dreaming last night." He kissed her lightly on the forehead. "Was that when you woke me so pleasurably?"

"I was frightened. I wanted to be close to you."

"You couldn't have gotten any closer. If that's the result of those hellish dreams, then I must find a way to have more of them."

"Don't joke. I don't like waking up and seeing you like that." She raised herself on one elbow to look down at him. "You told me once you had dreams about something that happened a long time ago. About darkness and not being able to breathe . . ."

"Did I? How depressing of me."

"Is that what these dreams are all about?"

"I don't remem—" He stopped. "Yes."

"Always?"

"Yes." He shifted and drew her closer still. "But they come much less often than they used to. Now go to sleep. I told you there was nothing to worry about."

But she *was* worried, and it was clear Nicholas had no intention of discussing the matter further. She would try another trail to the same destination.

"Nicholas—" She paused. "How did you get those scars on your back?"

"That's a depressing story too. And one that happened too long ago to matter to us now."

Yet Silver felt strongly those "depressing stories" caused his horrible nightmares. He needed to talk. Why wouldn't he share the painful memories with her? She wasn't a bloodless ninny to be protected and cosseted from the storms of life. She was the one who wanted to protect Nicholas.

Until she could discover the cause of Nicholas's disturbance she knew another way to protect him. She had discovered it last night and there was no reason the remedy should not work again tonight. She would make sure he was too weary for any dreams whatsoever.

"Well, if you don't want to talk, then I suppose we must find something else to do to amuse ourselves." Her hands began to move gently, teasingly on his body. "Mustn't we, Nicholas?"

"Etaine said you wished to see me." Mikhail's expression was wary as he crossed the breakfast room to stand before her. "I told Nicholas I couldn't tell him what he wanted to know. Why—"

She held up her hand to silence him. "That's not why I wanted to see you. Have you had breakfast?"

"Many hours ago."

"Well, sit down and keep me company while I have mine. Nicholas has gone into town to see his attorney and I may not have another opportunity to question you without him being present."

The faintest smile touched Mikhail's lips. "I have noticed that he wishes to be always at your side these days. It pleases me."

"It pleases me too." She hurriedly began eating her eggs as she felt warmth seep into her cheeks. "I think he may truly care for me."

"Think?" Mikhail asked gently.

"He says he has love for me." She kept her eyes on her plate. "And I—" She stopped. "I feel the same."

"That is good."

"Yes." She forced herself to look up knowing that she was blushing like one of those idiotic simpletons at Mrs. Alford's Select Academy. "But it's not good that Nicholas treats me as if I had no brain and must be protected from unpleasantness. I wish to share everything but he won't let me." She drew a deep breath. "He has terrible dreams."

"Yes, I know."

"He told me once that they were brought on by memories of something that happened in the past." She frowned. "But he won't tell me what happened. He says he doesn't want to talk about depressing things."

"Perhaps that is best."

"No, it's *not* best," she said fiercely. "I want to help him but he won't let me. I can't do anything until I know what's troubling him. You know, don't you?"

He nodded. "Yes, but it would do no good to tell you. You cannot change what is past."

"Let me be the judge of that. Tell me."

He hesitated, gazing at her uncertainly.

"You've kept secrets enough from me. Tell me this at least."

He shrugged and sat down in the chair across the table from her. "What do you want to know?"

"The dreams, the scars on Nicholas's back, everything."

"They are all bound together." Mikhail looked down at the polished rosewood table. "We are friends, Nicholas and I. We have been friends since we were children. Though he was the grandson of a great leader and I was the child of a common whore it made no difference. Not to Nicholas. And not to me. It is important that you know that."

"Nicholas values you a great deal," Silver said gently.

"He was the only one in the village who did when I was a child. I was big and clumsy and as ugly then as I am now."

"I don't find you ugly."

"Neither did Nicholas." Mikhail's finger began tracing the mother-of-pearl lily inlay in the gleaming wood of the table. "And then when I was seventeen I found a woman of the village who also seemed to think me pleasant. Her name was Marika and I married her. On our wedding night I discovered she was not a virgin and a few days later she told me she was three months with child. She had needed a father for the child and a husband to hide her shame and she had chosen me." His lips twisted. "I was a fine choice: lovesick with a young boy's first passion and stupid enough to think a woman could care for me."

"She was the stupid one," Silver said fiercely. "You'd make a fine husband. You should have thrown her out of your house."

"I did not know what to do. I was . . . angry. I shouted at her. She only laughed at me. Then I told her I would denounce her before the whole village. She stopped laughing. I rode out of the village and stayed away for many hours. I tried to think what to do. I am not clever like Nicholas, and the pain . . . I finally returned to the village and learned that Marika had decided to find another way to hide her shame."

"The potion," Silver whispered.

He nodded jerkily. "There were bruises on her face and her lip was cut. She told me she had gone to her lover and he had grown angry with her demands for his help. He had struck her again and again. Then she had gone to the old woman. . . ." He was silent a moment, gazing blindly down at the table. "She died. I was angry and in pain, but I did not want her dead.

I loved her still." He shook his head as if to clear it. "The old woman who gave her the potion was afraid she'd be blamed and denied she had given Marika anything. Many people had heard me shouting at her. They saw the bruises and thought I had beaten her and caused her death. I was brought before Igor Dabol and found guilty of murder. Nicholas was the only one who believed me and he argued and then pleaded with his grandfather for my life. Igor Dabol would not listen, and I was sentenced to death. They began to dig the hole."

"The hole?"

"It is Cossack tradition. A very deep hole is dug in the ground and then they break the legs of the man who is accused of murder. He is thrown into the hole and the coffin of the victim is lowered on top of him. After that they close the grave."

Smothering darkness, Nicholas had said. Buried alive. Silver shivered in horror at the thought. Her own people had fearsome traditions, but none she could think of at the moment to equal this one.

"They broke my legs and threw me into the hole. I lay there in the dirt and knew I was going to die." Mikhail's hand closed slowly into a fist on the table. "Then Nicholas jumped into the pit beside me. Igor ordered him out but he refused to obey him. He said if murder was being done to me it must also be done to him. I think Nicholas believed that Igor might spare us both rather than kill his grandson. But Igor has a terrible temper and he grew very angry with Nicholas. He ordered the coffin lowered and the grave closed."

Silver inhaled sharply. "He buried you both alive?"

Mikhail nodded. "I don't know how long we were down there. It seemed like a long, long time. We couldn't breathe. . . . Then we heard them shoveling away the dirt and they pulled us both out of the pit."

His lips twisted in a crooked smile. "Igor had decided to be merciful. He gave Nicholas forty lashes with a knout, took away our boots, and set us free on the steppes with a storm approaching. He knew we had little chance to survive."

"But you did survive."

"We found our way to the Sea of Azov and sheltered there. After we had both healed, Nicholas and I set out for St. Petersburg. We were exiled forever from the Kuban and there was nowhere else we really wanted to go when our home was taken from us."

"Igor Dabol must be a hard man to banish his own grandson. I find it strange that he would cast off his legitimate heir."

"Do you? I thought it stranger that Igor showed us mercy at the pit," Mikhail said quietly. "It was only later that I realized why."

Silver gazed at him inquiringly.

"I did not tell Nicholas, but I believe Igor Dabol was Marika's lover. He knew I had no guilt and to kill me and Nicholas would have been a mortal sin."

"Yet he nearly did it anyway." Igor Dabol was evidently as ruthless as his daughter, Natalya, Silver thought with a passionate rush of sympathy for Nicholas. It was a wonder Nicholas had been able to maintain the honor and integrity that he still possessed when he'd been brought up by two warring savages who wanted him only to serve their own ends. "I'd like to throw his grandfather into a hole and cover him with a ton of dirt!"

"It is over, Silver," Mikhail said gently. "There is nothing you can do. It is not Igor who causes Nicholas to dream, it is only the memory. As the memory fades, so will the dreams."

"But I want to help him *now*."

"I know, but you cannot erase that part of the past."

"I'm not so sure." She frowned. "How far away is this Kuban?"

"Too far." Mikhail's eyes began to twinkle. "And it would not ease Nicholas's pain for you to ride across all of Russia to try to punish Igor." His smile faded. "Nicholas had much affection for Igor at one time. He has a loving heart and finds it difficult to turn his back on family ties."

"Even when the old bastard buried him alive?"

"Even then."

Silver was silent a moment. "Then I suppose I can't do the same to his grandfather," she said reluctantly.

A faint smile tugged at the corners of Mikhail's lips. "It would not be wise. I know it is difficult to accept."

"But I want to help him, Mikhail," she said in an urgent whisper.

"Then forget about the past darkness and make the present brighter for him."

The wistful expression vanished from her face. "That's your way, not mine. But I'll try it until I discover another way." She smiled gaily, rose to her feet, and tossed her napkin on the table. "And now let's find Etaine and go for a ride in the troika."

"She was going to the stable when she left me. She is worried about the mare that is about to foal. I think she—"

"Your pardon, Your Highness." Rogoff appeared suddenly in the doorway and for once his face reflected something besides its usual stony formality. "It's Mistress Monteith. She appears to have taken ill. Sergei sent word from the carriage house that—"

"Ill?" Silver felt a swift surge of panic. Etaine had

been doing so well. There had been no attacks and the child had appeared to be blooming with health and contentment. "Why didn't he bring her back here?"

Rogoff hesitated. "He didn't think it best. The child seems very ill. She can't breathe."

"Dear Lord." Silver ran from the breakfast room and dashed down the hall. Mikhail reached the front door before her, threw it open, and was down the steps and halfway across the courtyard leading to the carriage house with Silver following at a dead run.

Sergei had placed Etaine in the large troika on a bed of furs and was gazing down at her, his face a mask of misery and helplessness. Mikhail fired a quick question at him in Russian and the coachman answered with equal brevity. Silver reached the sleigh just as Mikhail stepped into it and gathered Etaine into his arms.

"No!" Etaine pushed him desperately away. Her breath was coming harshly, her eyes wild in her flushed face. "I can't—" She twisted on the furs, her slight chest laboring as she tried to force breath into her lungs. "Silver!"

"I'm here." Fear sleeted through Silver as she stepped closer to the sleigh. She had never seen Etaine in these straits. Even the worst attack Silver had witnessed had never been this severe. "It will be all right, Etaine."

"No." Etaine's mouth was wide open as she tried to breathe. "Not . . . this . . . time. Help—" She turned on her side and curled into a ball, her fingers clutching the fur. "Help!"

"Shall I carry her back to the house," Mikhail asked anxiously.

"I don't know," Silver whispered. "It's not like before. She's—" She stopped. She didn't want to put the thought into words, the thought that Etaine might be dying. "I don't know if the steam will help this time."

"I will go for the doctor," Mikhail said.

Silver shook her head. Etaine was panting, fighting for breath, struggling desperately. How long could her heart endure that struggle? "It would take too long for you to fetch him." But she didn't feel confident to handle Etaine's care herself, she thought in anguish. Why didn't she *know* more?

Well, it was not helping Etaine for her to stand there and bewail her own ignorance. "Tell Sergei to hitch the horses to the sleigh. We're going to take her to the doctor. It will be faster. Where are the offices of that doctor who took care of me after Nicholas dismissed Dr. Rellings?"

"Dr. Balvar? Twenty-three Nevsky Prospekt," Mikhail answered. He spoke quickly to the driver in Russian and Sergei scurried away toward the stables. "I will go with you."

"No." Silver settled herself in the sleigh and covered both herself and Etaine with the fur robes. "I want to travel fast and your weight would slow the troika. You follow us."

Mikhail nodded, his gaze on Etaine's face. "Do not worry, little one," he told her gently. "I will break the doctor's bones if he does not make you better."

Etaine didn't appear to hear. Her eyes were closed and tears trickled down her cheeks.

Sergei and four grooms had returned and were hitching the horses to the sleigh. "Hurry," Silver said sharply. "Can't you be quicker about that?" She turned toward Etaine but was afraid to touch her, afraid to interfere and perhaps shift the balance of the battle Etaine was waging. "How did it happen? She was doing so well. I thought she was recovering."

"Sergei said she seemed well when she first came

to the stables to see the mare. Then suddenly she was like this." Mikhail gestured to Etaine. "When we tried to carry her back to the palace she did not want him touching her, so he brought her here."

"I fetched your cloak, Your Highness." Rogoff was standing by the sleigh, her black sable cloak in his hands. "I understood you're going to have to take the little girl to St. Petersburg and I thought you would need it." His gaze went to Etaine and his expression grew anxious. "May I say I hope Mistress Etaine will be better soon?"

If Silver hadn't been so frightened, she would have been surprised. Rogoff had never displayed emotion or loss of dignity in all the months she had been on Crystal Island, yet now he appeared sincerely concerned. Perhaps she shouldn't be amazed, she thought wearily. All the servants were fond of Etaine. Who wouldn't love her? "Thank you, Rogoff, I'm sure she'll be fine once we get her to the doctor."

"If I may make a request? I did a great deal of ice racing on the Neva in my youth. I might be able to save you a little time. Not that Sergei isn't an accomplished driver . . ."

The horses had been secured to the troika and Silver was impatient to be off. "Drive. We need to save every moment we can." As Rogoff scrambled with alacrity into the driver's seat, Silver turned to Mikhail. "Follow us closely, but stop off at the lawyer's office and see if you can find Nicholas and Valentin and bring them to Dr. Balvar's."

Sweet heaven, she wished Nicholas were at her side now.

Rogoff snapped the whip and the troika began to move out of the carriage house. Silver drew a little closer to Etaine, her worried gaze on the child's face. She murmured half beneath her breath, "Bring Nicholas, Mikhail."

*   *   *

Mikhail caught Nicholas and Valentin just as they were stepping into a sleigh on the street outside Dzosky's offices.

"Nicholas!" Mikhail's voice thundered over the myriad sounds of the bustling street as he drew in the horses of the troika. "Here!"

Nicholas turned, swift concern darkening his face. "Silver?"

"Etaine," Mikhail shouted. "She is very ill. She could not breathe."

Nicholas muttered a low curse. "Have you sent for the doctor?"

"Silver said Etaine was too bad. There was not time, so she took the child to him. She said for you to meet them at his office on Nevsky Prospekt." Mikhail jerked his head toward the passenger seats of the troika. "Come, we must hurry. That is a fifteen-minute drive from here."

By incurring the wrath of sleigh and carriage drivers and pedestrians too, Mikhail arrived at the offices at 23 Nevsky Prospekt in less than ten minutes.

Nicholas and Valentin bolted up the steps and threw the doors of the office open while Mikhail tied the horses at the hitching rail bordering the street. He burst into the office a moment later to see Valentin and Nicholas standing in conversation with the bespectacled physician. "How is she?"

Dr. Balvar turned to Mikhail. "I was just explaining to His Highness that I have no knowledge of what he's talking about. No child was brought to me by Princess Savron."

Nicholas whirled toward Mikhail. "When did she leave the island?"

"A good fifteen minutes before I did," Mikhail said. "And I had to stop to find you. She should have arrived here almost an hour ago."

"Perhaps some mischance on the Neva," the doctor suggested. "I'm sure she'll be here shortly."

They waited for fifteen minutes, but Silver and Etaine did not arrive.

When another fifteen minutes had passed, Mikhail left the office to return and retrace the route Rogoff would have taken from the island.

An hour later Mikhail returned to a frantic Nicholas.

"You didn't find them," Nicholas said.

"It's as if the Neva had swallowed them," Mikhail said. "But there were no accidents on the Neva this morning, and the ice holds firm."

"It's not the Neva that's swallowed them." Nicholas's hands closed into fists at his sides.

Valentin's eyes narrowed. "Monteith?"

"Monteith," Nicholas bit out. "It makes sense. Etaine was too well guarded at the palace, so he had to get her off Crystal Island."

"But, Nicholas, Etaine was truly ill," Mikhail said in bewilderment. "How could he—"

"How the hell do I know?" Nicholas asked savagely. "But there's no other explanation, is there?"

Mikhail slowly shook his head. "No."

"Then you think Monteith has Etaine?" Valentin asked.

"Yes, he has Etaine." Nicholas felt cold terror twist his stomach as he remembered the details of the report on Monteith he'd perused only yesterday. "And Silver!"

"Then what do we do?" Valentin asked. "We don't even know where Monteith's taken them."

"We know," Nicholas said grimly. "Peskov. Monteith has a history of using the manor houses of the nobility for his sacrifices. He'll have Etaine and Silver taken to Peskov's estate."

Valentin's eyes brightened with satisfaction. "Then

we gather a troop of men and charge in and get them back."

"Or get them killed," Mikhail said slowly. "That is not the way."

Valentin frowned. "Then what is the way, dammit."

"The Cossack way. We go, we see, we kill where we can. Then when we are sure of our prize and Etaine and Silver are safe ..." He smiled with cold savagery. "We kill the rest of them."

"An interesting strategy," Valentin murmured. "Bloodthirsty but definitely interesting. Though I don't believe I ever heard it recommended when I served in the army. You approve, Nicholas?"

"I approve." Nicholas's smile held the same savagery as Mikhail's as he turned abruptly away. "God, yes, I approve. Let's go."

"Come now, Silver, surely the blow wasn't that severe. Open your eyes and talk to me. I've been waiting for this opportunity for a long time."

Monteith's voice, Silver realized, struggling to fight her way through waves of pain and darkness, was cooing at her ear. She opened her eyes and then quickly closed them again as a bolt of jagged agony knifed through her temple.

"I admit I'm disappointed in you." Monteith's tone was mocking. "I was hoping you'd kill Rogoff. It would have given me such a magnificent reason for oratory at the ceremony tonight."

Rogoff? What did the servant have to do with—
"Etaine!" Silver's lids flew open and she ignored the pain as her gaze focused on Monteith's face. "Etaine. Is she—"

"Recovering nicely." Monteith smiled. "She'll be in fine condition in a few hours. However, Rogoff isn't so lucky. You managed to do considerable damage with that little dagger of yours before he managed to knock you unconscious with the butt of his whip. He was quite weak from loss of blood by the time he delivered you both here to Peskov's manor house. I'll have to reward him handsomely for his trouble."

"I tried to kill the bastard."

"You certainly made a good attempt. Poor Rogoff had no conception of what he faced in you."

"You bribed him to bring Etaine to you instead of to the doctor's office." Silver pushed herself up to a sitting position on the handsome brocade cushioned couch. She glared at Monteith. "I wish I'd cut his throat."

"I didn't have to bribe him. Rogoff belongs to me," Monteith said as he stood up. "If I choose, I shall reward him, but there's no necessity."

"I want to see Etaine. I don't believe what you say about her condition. She was too ill to—"

"Don't worry," he interrupted with a touch of impatience. "I have every intention of taking you to Etaine shortly. I want you to be together for the next few hours. Strength feeds upon strength, and I want Etaine to be very strong tonight." He strolled over to a long window across the room and looked out, the line of his spine perfectly straight, his carriage impeccable beneath his elegant gray coat. "But I wanted this time alone with you first. I've been anticipating our final confrontation for a long time. And don't be foolish enough to believe that it won't be final. I urge you not even to contemplate escape. I have my followers in every hallway of the house, men who belong to me in a way that gives me total sway over them. They have orders not to harm you or Etaine, but you'll not be permitted to get away."

"Belong!" Silver echoed scornfully. "You think you can own people? No one would give scum such as you any allegiance."

He chuckled. "Ah, how I love that fire of yours, Silver. I've never met a woman who pleases me as you do. What satisfaction it would give me to own you." He turned to face her. "But I always knew it would do no good to try. You would never step across the line."

Silver struggled to banish the dizziness threatening to return her to darkness. "What line?"

"Why, the line that separates us. The line that keeps us from joining." His eyes were glittering in the pale classic beauty of his face. "And what a joining that would be, my dear. You could match me, compliment me. Together we would be superb."

"I want to go to Etaine now."

The enthusiasm of his expression faded. "Don't be impatient. I told you she was recovering. What I have done I can undo."

"What *you* have done?"

"But of course." He looked at her in surprise. "You don't think Rogoff simply seized on a lucky opportunity to bring you to me? It was all planned. Naturally, I could leave nothing to chance, as I had to make arrangements for the ceremony."

Ceremony. He had mentioned something before about a ceremony, Silver remembered dimly. She wished the pounding in her temples would stop so that she could think more clearly. "You couldn't have planned Etaine's illness. She was so terribly—" She broke off as she saw his smile. Sick horror rippled through her. "*You* did it?"

He nodded. "I discovered several years ago that Etaine was affected by the pollen powders of certain weeds. They seemed either to bring on her attacks or increase their severity. When I noticed she appeared to be growing out of her affliction, I used them from time to time to bring on an attack. Rogoff merely had to sprinkle a little of the powder on the hay in the mare's stall. Actually, it was more than a little this time. I wanted to make sure the attack was severe enough to panic you into rushing her to a doctor instead of tending her yourself."

She gazed at him with disbelief. "You deliberately brought on those attacks? How could anyone be so cruel?"

"It was necessary."

"Causing Etaine to suffer was necessary? All those years of needless pain and fear?"

"Not needless. It all had a purpose."

"What purpose?"

"Why, to increase her strength of character and develop her courage. To hone away all her rough edges and make her shine like a rare jewel. To make her worthy."

"Etaine *is* worthy. She was always good and loving and—"

"But that wasn't enough," Monteith said gently. "Though all those qualities increased her value in the ceremony, she had to be quite perfect. You helped me there, Silver. Your example made Etaine independent, your strength made her own strength flower. Why do you think I permitted you to visit her when the circus was camped in St. Louis? I feigned disapproval so that Etaine would have something to fight against, but I never stopped you from seeing her. And I even let you take her away and keep her for a while here in St. Petersburg. In fact, I deliberately kept you here to make sure Etaine would reap the benefit of your presence." His gaze was caressing as it moved over her face. "I always knew you were just as valuable as the cats in her preparation for the ceremony."

"What ceremony?"

"The sacrifice." He smiled as he heard Silver's

quick intake of breath. "The sacrifice that she's been preparing for all these years."

"You're going to put her in the cage with the lions again?"

"Oh, no, the lions won't be used. They'd make matters very difficult when the essence is drawn. It will be the usual ceremonial dagger."

"Why? Why would you do this thing?"

"Because of who I am," Monteith said. "You still don't understand, do you? Etaine's death will be no small matter. It will be the culmination of all that I've accomplished."

"You're mad." Even as she spoke Silver knew the charge was untrue. Monteith's gaze was coldly and completely sane. "How could a child's murder accomplish anything but eternal damnation?"

He laughed with genuine amusement. "But, Silver, don't you realize? That *is* the purpose."

She gazed at him uncomprehendingly.

"Hell is where I wish to rule," he explained softly. "But to do so I must show I'm willing to sacrifice the child of my own blood, if not of my spirit. When I was a boy my father, the good vicar, used to quote something from the Bible to me. 'For God gave his only begotten Son.' I knew even then that I must do the same to please my master. He gave me much power when he realized my devotion, but I knew I would not receive his final acceptance until I had given him the same gift his archenemy had sacrificed." He shook his head regretfully. "It was a pity that bitch, Mary, didn't give me a boy, but I realized soon after Etaine was born that she would do very nicely. She shone with an uncorrupted goodness that was quite splendid."

"Which you want to destroy," Silver whispered.

"To sacrifice," he corrected her. "Why do you think

I made no attempt to corrupt Etaine? To sacrifice evil to evil is a much lesser gift than to sacrifice purity to evil. Tonight with all due ceremony I will take Etaine's life and I'll be given mine."

Silver was suddenly once again conscious of the icy void within Monteith that had frightened her before. Now that chasm appeared wider and deeper, glowing strangely.

She tried not to let him detect tremors from the chill that attacked her every limb. "Even if you manage to kill Etaine and me, Nicholas will see that you're punished for your wickedness. Perhaps if you let Etaine go now—"

"No, Silver." Monteith was shaking his head. "Do you think I'm afraid of your husband? I don't doubt he'll try to rescue you. I've studied the two of you very closely in the past months and I know what flows between you. But I'll win no matter what he does. If he appears after I've made my sacrifice, I'll have more power than he could dream and be able to vanquish him without effort. If he happens to succeed in stopping me before the sacrifice, then I'll merely wait until the next opportunity to seize Etaine again. I have enough powerful followers at court to prevent Savron from doing me irreparable harm."

"And what if Nicholas or I manage to kill you?" Silver asked fiercely.

A curious smile carved his lips. "I'd still find a way of destroying you, Silver. Perhaps not Etaine, but certainly you, my dear."

"You can't hurt me. I wouldn't let you hurt me."

Admiration glinted in his eyes. "You sit there, in pain, barely able to stay upright and still defiant. Is it any wonder that I regret losing you?" He shook his head. "It will be a wonderful sight watching you at the ceremony. Shall I tell you what's in store for you, or would you like it to be a surprise?"

"Tell me."

"First, Etaine will be sacrificed. You'll both be taken down to the big circus tent in the meadow. My followers will be gathered there to watch, but they'll not be permitted to participate in the actual sacrifice. However, I've told them they may partake of the essence."

"Essence."

"Blood," he said simply. "I will cut Etaine's wrists and they may each garner a few drops but not too much. She must be alive when the dagger enters her heart."

"You're a monster!" She stopped. There were no words to describe the evil in Monteith.

"How clever of you to finally understand." His gaze met her own. "You're going to witness the sacrifice, of course. I'm only sorry I'll be too occupied to watch your face at the final stroke." He sighed. "But I'll receive compensation later, when you are sacrificed, Silver. You did know you'd have to die also?"

"It doesn't surprise me."

"Not only are you Savron's wife and therefore a potential danger, but the total experience must be very gratifying to my followers. I refuse to let them use Etaine, but their participation in your sacrifice will give them what they need. Many of them are like stupid children, thinking only of lust and blood. You'll provide them with both." He glanced at her as if gauging her reaction.

Silver carefully kept her expression impassive.

"You'll be strapped to the sacrificial table for many hours before you receive the knife. Any man who desires to do so will be permitted to copulate with you." He paused, waiting for a response.

She gave him none.

"I might even take you myself. It's not often I so

favor one to be sacrificed, but you're very special to me, Silver."

"Don't get too close or I'll sink my teeth into your jugular and tear out your throat."

He burst out laughing. "You probably would at that. I shall be most careful if I do decide to spend time between your thighs." He glanced at the rapidly fading light streaming through the window. "It's growing late and I have arrangements to make. I fear it's time we ended our little meeting and I took you to Etaine. Are you strong enough to walk or shall I carry you?"

"I can walk."

"Or if you can't, you'll crawl," Monteith said. "How proud I would have been to have claimed you as one of mine. Come along then."

Silver swung her feet to the floor and then grasped the arm of the couch to steady herself. Dizziness, pain, nausea. She pushed them all aside and forced herself to stand upright.

"Bravo," Monteith said softly. "Now walk across the room toward me."

She knew if she took a step that she would collapse in a heap on the floor and she wouldn't reveal that weakness to Monteith. She stood swaying, gazing at him in defiance. She would bargain for time to gather strength by asking the one question to which she must have an answer. "You said you had kept me here in Russia. How did you do that?"

Some undefinable emotion flickered in his face. "How do you think?"

She braced herself. "I think you bribed Dr. Rellings to give me a potion that would kill my baby and then paid him to leave St. Petersburg so that no questions would be asked. If I were ill, I wouldn't be able to travel."

"That is true. And, of course, since I'd studied you for a long time, I'd know how you would react to losing your baby, how it would devastate you." His voice was coolly objective. "Yes, it would have been a very clever move on my part."

"You *did* do it," Silver accused, her eyes blazing. "And you paid Dr. Rellings to leave St. Petersburg."

"Oh, Dr. Rellings never left St. Petersburg," Monteith said calmly. "He made a trifling but adequate sacrifice."

Her eyes widened in shock. "You murdered him?"

"Sacrificed. You must recognize the distinction," Monteith chided with a faint smile. "His remains are buried beneath that huge evergreen tree that grows beside the summerhouse." He opened the door and gestured mockingly for her to precede him. "If you like, I'll show you the exact spot when I escort you to the circus tent tonight."

Rage rioted through Silver, blinding her, choking her. Monteith *had* killed her baby. She moved toward him, no longer aware of weakness or pain, conscious of nothing but the anger and hatred dominating her. "I'm not going to let you kill me, Monteith. Not until I've killed you for what you did to my child."

"You hate well," he said approvingly. "I knew you'd feel like that. But you can't attack me now without being attacked yourself." He stepped into the hall and indicated the two burly peasants standing guard at the door before adding softly, "And then what would Etaine do without her friend to help her through her final hours?"

His words pierced the haze of fury surrounding Silver. Etaine. She must find a way of helping Etaine before she was free to deal with Monteith.

He effortlessly read her reaction. "She's right down the hall. We gave her a fine room with every comfort." He turned and walked gracefully down the corridor. "Come along, Silver."

Silver hesitated for the fraction of a moment and then slowly followed him toward the chamber door he had indicated.

As soon as the door closed behind Monteith, Silver hurried to the canopy bed where Etaine was lying. "Are you all right? Is your breathing—"

"It's much better," Etaine assured her. "The attack passed soon after they brought me to this room. It's you I was worried about. I thought Rogoff had killed you when he struck you with that whip."

"It's nothing." Still, Silver was glad to sit down on the edge of the bed. Her knees felt as if they were snowflakes on the verge of melting. Her gaze raked Etaine's face and relief rushed through her. The child was pale and appeared exhausted but otherwise recovered. "I'm sorry, Etaine. I broke my promise to you. I thought I could keep your father away but—"

"There was nothing you could do, Silver," Etaine interrupted gently. "I've known all along that this would probably happen. No matter how many guards you put on me, my father would have found a way."

Silver took Etaine's hand in her own clasp. "He told you what he intends to do to you?"

Etaine nodded. "He told me everything. He said I must be brave and accept my death in a fashion that will bring no shame to him."

Silver muttered a curse beneath her breath. "The bastard could have at least spared you the anticipation."

"Oh, no, Silver, all my life he's prepared me for this." Etaine's voice was calm. "Even though he never put it into words, I think I must have sensed what he had in mind for me."

"And you accept it?" Silver asked incredulously.

"No." Etaine's gaze was clear and serene. "That's what he expects me to do. He thinks he's created the perfect sacrifice, but he doesn't realize that in giving me strength he's defeated his purpose. He's made me strong enough not to let him do this to me without a fight." She paused. "He is no longer my father in my eyes."

Silver's grip tightened. "We'll find a way out of this."

"Yes. And Mikhail and Nicholas can't be far." Etaine sat up in bed. "But I think we mustn't count on them. We must plan our own escape."

"There are guards outside the doors," Silver said. "We need weapons, blast it."

"I think we may already have one," Etaine said slowly. "The sacrifice is to take place in the main circus tent in the cage. My father said—" She paused for a deep breath before continuing. "Monteith said that was why he made me do the sacrificial act with the lions all those years. He wanted to make sure I'd become accustomed to the sacrificial table and more easily accept my fate. If they're using the tent, then Monteith must be sending the circus folk away from the grounds for the night." She smiled. "But they won't go."

"You've got to remember that Sebastien and the rest of the circus people are afraid of Monteith," Silver said gently. "And they may not know we're here."

"Rogoff was bleeding badly and thought only of getting to the manor house, so he drove straight through the meadow where the circus is encamped. Sebastien saw us in the troika."

Silver's heart gave a leap of hope. "You're sure?"

Etaine nodded. "I had no breath to call out to him, but I know he saw me and he must have noticed you were unconscious. He may pretend to go away but he'll come back. He'll help us, Silver."

"I know he'll try to help." Silver smiled with an effort. "And if he doesn't succeed, we'll just have to help ourselves."

Etaine frowned thoughtfully. "Sebastien is my friend. He'll find a way to get close enough to speak to us. And when he does, I think he'll be able to give us our weapon."

12

Tall poles crowned by blazing torches bordered the path leading from the manor house to the circus grounds. Hooded, black-robed figures crowded close to the path, their faces masked, their gazes fixed eagerly on Monteith standing in the courtyard with Etaine and Silver.

He alone was unmasked, his black robes flowing gracefully about his lean body as he raised his hand. "What I have promised you has come to pass. Let the ceremony begin."

Chanting rose on the still evening air from the hundreds of black-robed acolytes gathered there. Rhythmic, powerful chanting in a language totally unfamiliar to Silver.

Monteith turned to Etaine. "Your time has come. Are you ready?"

Etaine's voice was serene. "I am ready." She didn't wait for her father but started down the torchlit path, her white robe and matching cloak in startling

217

contrast to the dark-robed figures lining the path on either side of her.

"You see, Silver, she knows this is her destiny." Monteith's face held fierce pride. "My destiny."

"I'll see that you have *no* destiny," Silver said, her gaze following Etaine. "And Etaine is more than you think she is."

"All the better." The chant was rising as Monteith took Silver's elbow and urged her down the path. "Neither of you has proved a disappointment to me. It's all proceeding quite well."

"Are all these people from Alexander's court?" There must have been well over two hundred robed figures lining the path.

"A good many of them. But there are also merchants, soldiers, servants . . . I have power in every circle."

Silver glanced sidewise at him. The aura of power he was speaking about was now almost tangible. She shivered and jerked her gaze back to Etaine. The child appeared to be hesitating, her gaze on one of the black-robed figures. It was only for an instant, and then she continued down the path. Hope soared dizzily within Silver. Had Etaine caught sight of Sebastien? Or perhaps even of Nicholas?

Silver, too, searched the passing faces, but she recognized no one behind the masks and was sickened by the expressions of eagerness and anticipation for the act to come. Yet even as she glanced away she caught a glimpse of the same massively built acolyte fading in and out of the crowd and keeping pace with Etaine's progress down the path.

Then as Etaine reached the perimeter of the circus grounds, she paused again and Silver saw the child's lips move. Silver was too far away to hear the words Etaine spoke, but the large, hooded figure was suddenly gone, merged into the crowd.

"Are you hoping for rescue?" Monteith asked. Silver turned to see him gazing at her with a mocking smile. "There will be none. Peskov has the woods surrounding the estate filled with an army of guards. Accept your fate as Etaine has."

What if that hooded figure hadn't been Sebastien, Silver thought desperately. What if Nicholas had been stopped by Peskov's guards and there was no help for them? She must think of some way herself to help Etaine. Some of those black-robed vultures must have weapons, or perhaps the torches . . .

"No answer? Are you frightened, Silver?"

"I'd be stupid not to be afraid." She met his gaze. "But I don't fear you."

"You lie," he said softly. "You are afraid. Because you know I'm my master's servant."

She refused to look away from him. "I know you're a charleton and a coward who kills children." Fear twisted in her stomach as she glimpsed something leaping behind the emptiness shining in his light eyes. She looked hurriedly away and her pace quickened. "Etaine is entering the tent."

Monteith's attention was immediately diverted. "Then we mustn't keep her waiting." His fingers on Silver's elbow propelled her forward. "I believe I shall let you help prepare her."

The acolytes were now streaming into the big tent. The chant rose higher, fuller, the mysterious words resounding ominously.

Silver entered the tent, watching as the black-robed figures took their seats on the benches encircling the big ring. Etaine was already in the cage, mounting the black marble slab as she had hundreds of times before.

"Do you see how beautifully trained she is?" Monteith murmured as he half-led, half-pushed Silver across the ring toward the cage.

He actually sounded proud that he had trained Etaine to go so meekly to her death, Silver thought in sick disgust.

Monteith entered the cage and strode toward the marble slab where Etaine was already on her back, her hands crossed over her chest. Monteith smiled down at her in approval. "You're doing very well, my dear. I was afraid I was going to have to tie you down and that would have lessened the beauty of the ceremony."

Etaine returned his smile. "I would like to say good-bye to Silver, Father."

He nodded, and motioned Silver into the cage.

"Alone," Etaine said softly. "Please."

Monteith hesitated and then shrugged. "As you wish." He left the cage. "One minute."

Etaine held out her arms and Silver took the child in a close embrace. "Sebastien?" Silver whispered.

"Yes."

"I saw you say something to him."

"I hope he understood. I had time for only one word—"

"Enough." Monteith was back in the cage. "It's time for the ceremony. Silver can stay in the cage if she likes. I need someone to hold the cup."

"No!" Etaine said quickly. "It would hurt me to see her here and I might turn coward. Send her to sit in the audience with the rest."

"Perhaps that would be best." Monteith gestured and a black-robed figure approached Silver. "Take her out of the cage to a place where she can enjoy the spectacle." He caught Silver's gaze. "Such hatred. I don't think I've ever seen such hatred."

"You killed my child," Silver said. "And you're trying to kill my friend. Why shouldn't I hate you?"

"I'm not complaining. I welcome it." Monteith bowed mockingly. "Take her."

Silver was pushed from the cage and across the ring to the first row of benches. What had Etaine said to Sebastien, she wondered desperately. Only one word. What had Etaine told him to do?

The chanting was rising again. Silver's gaze flew back to the cage. Monteith was holding the dagger above his head, the expression on his face exultant. She couldn't wait for help from Sebastien or Nicholas.

The torch on the pole a few feet away from her.

The black-robed man guarding her was as absorbed as the rest of the acolytes in the sight that was taking place in the cage. She would grab the pole and charge forward toward the cage.

Monteith was taking Etaine's wrist and smiling down at her.

Etaine smiled back at him.

Silver took a furtive step toward the torch. She could wait no longer.

Then she heard it.

A sound she had heard so many times before.

And she knew the single word Etaine had murmured to Sebastien.

Lions.

The three roaring lions bounded down the aisle between the benches, racing toward the ring, the cage where they'd been trained to go.

Chants became screams!

Monteith turned and looked up just as the lioness bounded into the cage. He dropped Etaine's wrist.

"Sultana." It was Etaine's clear voice. "To me!"

"No!" Monteith whirled toward Etaine, the dagger raised.

Sultana's charge struck Monteith squarely in the back, her talons ripping the black robe from his body. Then, as he crumpled beneath her weight to the sawdust, her claws tore at his throat, spraying blood on the sawdust.

Silver grasped the torch pole and jerked it from the ground.

"Silver!" Nicholas, dressed in a black acolyte's robe, thundered into the tent on a gray stallion. He spurred forward and threw the torch he was carrying at the cloth wall of the tent. The cloth caught immediately and the flames hungrily climbed the wall.

Monteith's followers were screaming, weeping, scrambling to get out of the tent like a flock of frightened black birds.

Nicholas reined up before Silver and reached down a hand. "Come up. Let me get you out of here."

"No!" Silver hurled the torch in her hand like a flaming javelin into the fleeing covy of acolytes and then turned and dashed toward the cage. "Etaine!"

The three lions were milling around the fallen Monteith, but that didn't mean Etaine was safe. They could turn on her at any moment and savage her.

"Stay where you are, Silver," Etaine's low voice ordered, stopping Silver in her tracks. "They won't hurt me, but they might hurt you. All this smoke and screaming is frightening them and the blood . . ." She carefully avoided looking at her father as she got off the black marble slab. "I'm going to try to lead them back to their cages."

"We have to get out of here. The fire—"

"The lions helped me, they saved my life. I won't leave them to burn."

Mikhail appeared suddenly at Silver's side. "I will help. Tell me what to do, Etaine."

"Oh, Mikhail. I'm so glad you're here." For a moment Etaine's maturity and strength vanished and she was a child again. She shivered as she glanced at the still figure of Monteith on the ground. "I had to save myself. He was going to kill me."

"I know," Mikhail said. "It was a good thing that you did. Now, tell me how to help you get these animals out of here. Sebastien has moved their cages just outside the tent."

"They're taught to follow me. You must just keep everyone else away from them."

"Silver, dammit, will you listen to me? Get out of here!"

Silver turned to see Nicholas beside her again. His golden hair was tousled, there was a streak of soot on one cheekbone, and he was looking at her with intense exasperation. Yet he had never appeared more beautiful to her. She smiled mistily. "You look most peculiar in those robes. I don't think they suit you at all."

He frowned with concern. "Are you all right? Sebastien told me you were unconscious when Rogoff brought you here."

She nodded. "I am well." She was more than well. She was buoyant with joy. She was *alive*. Etaine was alive. She hadn't known how precious her life with Nicholas had become until it had been threatened. Now that the sword had been lifted, she realized how desperately she had feared that life might be snatched from her. She cleared her throat to ease its tightness. "We must help Etaine get the lions back in their cages."

"Monteith?"

Silver's gaze went to Monteith lying on the sawdust. "I think he must be dead. I saw Sultana's talons rip his throat and all that blood . . ." Etaine was leaving the cage and Silver looked away from the body of the child's father. "The fire is getting worse."

Nicholas nodded. "That's what I've been trying to tell you. Will you please get out of here!" He turned the stallion. "Don't argue. I'll ride herd on your little friend's 'cats.'" He called across the ring, "Valentin, get Silver out of here."

"I don't want to get out of here. I want to help—"

Silver stopped as she realized she was talking to the air. Nicholas, Etaine, and Mikhail were now several yards away with the three lions moving jerkily, warily, in their wake.

Silver shook her head ruefully as she watched them go. Nicholas was cosseting her again, but she could not find it in her heart to resent it. She was too full of love and gratitude to worry about demanding her independence at the moment. She had been too perilously close to losing both Nicholas and life to argue with him right now.

"Sil-ver."

She stiffened. That gravelly whisper was unmistakable. She turned slowly toward the open door of the cage to look at the man lying in a pool of blood in the sawdust. Monteith's eyes were open, gazing at her with a power that was fading as fast as his life force.

"Come . . . to . . . me."

"Why should I? You're dying, Monteith."

"I know." A travesty of a smile touched his lips. "And you shouldn't be afraid of a dying man. Come . . . I want to talk to you." With a jerky motion he threw the dagger clasped in his hand across the cage. "See, I'm defenseless."

"I'm not afraid of you." Silver entered the cage and knelt beside him. The lion's claws had not touched his face and his features had lost none of their classic beauty, she noticed. "And I'll be glad to watch you die, child murderer."

"Ah, that lovely hatred," he murmured. "Your code requires my death, doesn't it, Silver? You could no more not seek vengeance for your child's death than you could stop breathing." He smiled. "Am I right?"

"Yes." Silver gazed at him stonily. "And now I have vengeance. You're dying, Monteith. You've lost."

"I have lost but so have you," he said. "I told you that you couldn't win."

"I have won."

"No." He coughed and then was silent, garnering his strength. "Because I did not kill your child."

She froze. "You lie. You said you—"

"I said I sacrificed the good doctor. It was true. But I did not give you the potion. I intended to order Rogoff to do so, but one of my followers became too impatient to wait for me to act and bribed the doctor to give you the potion."

Her hands clenched slowly into fists at her sides. "Who?"

"Who else? Natalya. I think you've suspected it all along. She wanted no child born to her son from a woman with mixed blood. She thought Nicholas might cast you off if she destroyed the child. Then she got panicky and asked me to rid her of the doctor."

"And you obliged," Silver said numbly.

"Since it suited me." His eyes were glittering with malice as he gazed at her. "So you see, I've won after all. Now that you know Natalya is guilty, you will have to punish her. Anything else would be impossible for you." His breath was beginning to harshen and the words came more slowly. "And you will kill your husband's mother." He paused. "Or perhaps you will goad Nicholas into doing it. Matricide."

"No!" she said sharply. "I would never do that."

"But you could never bear the thought of Natalya going unpunished for your child's murder. You could never watch her living her life of luxury knowing what she had done."

"Nicholas has no love for his mother. He would—"

"But he has love for you, doesn't he? A love that would be poisoned and wither away if you took his mother's life."

"You lie! Nicholas wouldn't hate me. She would deserve—"

Yet in spite of all Natalya had done to him, Nicholas had never said he hated his mother.

And Mikhail had said Nicholas had a loving heart and found it difficult to give up family bonds.

Monteith chuckled. "If you don't avenge the death of your child, the poison will corrode your soul and destroy you. If you do avenge it, your husband will know you killed the woman who gave him birth and will learn to hate you."

"No, it's not true."

"It *is* true." Triumph glittered in Monteith's eyes. "And either way you'll be destroyed and I will win. . . ." His lids fluttered and then closed. "A soul like yours will please my master. I've . . . won." The breath rattled in his throat and then ceased entirely.

"No!" Silver's nails bit into her palms as pain tore through her. "Please. Merciful God. *No!*"

"Silver, what's wrong?" It was Valentin's voice behind her at the door of the cage. "Can I help?"

She closed her eyes tightly as panic raced through her. How could he help? How could anyone help? "There's nothing you can do," she whispered.

"We have to leave here. The north wall of the tent has caught and the smoke—"

"I'm coming." She got jerkily to her feet, her gaze on Monteith's smooth, unlined face. Even in death the faintest of smiles still touched the corners of his lips. A smile of triumph. She turned away and moved blindly toward Valentin. "There's nothing for me here."

And perhaps nothing for her anywhere. Not love. Not Nicholas. Not the life without loneliness that had almost been within her grasp.

Only revenge for the murder of her baby.

And the destruction of her soul that Monteith had said lay ahead for her.

"I knew you would come." Etaine wearily settled back in the troika as Mikhail tucked the robes carefully around her. "It was very clever of you to steal those robes and masquerade as one of them, but how did you get through the guards in the woods?"

"Nicholas and I are Cossacks," he said simply. "No one sees a Cossack unless he wants to be seen." He shrugged. "And Valentin is not so bad, a little clumsy but . . ." He trailed off as he saw the lines of strain deepening around Etaine's lips. He was silent a moment, seeking a way to comfort her. "You were as brave as a Cossack yourself," he said gravely. "I watched you walk down the path from the manor house."

"I wasn't brave. I just had no intention of dying." She met his gaze. "He was an evil, evil man, Mikhail. I suppose I should feel sorry he's dead, but I don't. I feel no guilt either."

"Nor should you."

"He was my father. He gave me life but he also tried to take it. The one balances the other." She blinked away the tears. "You're right, I'm being foolish. I'll be glad to leave this place. Here comes Silver and Valentin. I don't think I'll—" She stopped and started to throw off the fur robe. "There's something wrong with Silver. Look at her face."

Mikhail's gaze followed Etaine's. "Stay here. I will be right back." He tucked the robe around Etaine again and started across the clearing toward Silver. As soon as he was within hearing distance, he called to Valentin. "Nicholas needs you, Valentin. He's at the cages talking to Sebastien and making arrangements for the circus people to be taken to Crystal Island."

"Then why does he need me?" Valentin asked.

Mikhail stared at Silver. "After he finishes with Sebastien he's going to fire Peskov's manor house."

Valentin's face brightened. "Now, that's a different matter." He started across the grounds toward the cages at the perimeter of the woods.

Mikhail studied Silver's face. "There is great pain in you. I would like to help."

Silver shook her head silently.

"Then let me take you to Etaine."

"Soon." Her tormented eyes suddenly focused on his face. "You *knew* Natalya had killed my baby."

He went still. "How did you find out?"

"Monteith."

His gaze traveled to the burning tent. "He was not dead? I did not know that he was involved." He was silent for a moment before he nodded slowly. "I was not sure, but I thought it likely the guilt was hers. I questioned her servant, Marya, and the woman was most secretive. I was certain she knew something, but the next day when I returned to question her again, I found the woman had been sent back to her village in the Urals."

"Why didn't you tell me?"

"I could not. It was my fault that Nicholas had lost everything he cared about—his home in the Kuban, the affection of his grandfather. . . . Was I to cause him to lose his mother as well?"

"She's a wicked woman. She killed my child. She deserves—" Silver broke off and her eyes filled with tears. "I don't want to cause Nicholas pain but . . ." She swallowed. "Monteith said either way I'd be destroyed."

"What are you going to do?" Mikhail asked gently.

She shook her head. "I don't know," she whispered. "Dear Lord, I don't know."

She turned and walked quickly toward the troika.

*   *   *

"I think I had more reason than I thought to wish Monteith dead," Nicholas said tightly, his gaze on Silver's face. "What did that bastard do to you, Silver?"

Silver slipped beneath the velvet coverlet of the bed. "Nothing." She cuddled close to him. "Hold me."

"Nothing!" Nicholas's arms automatically tightened around her. "I know you, Silver. You were like a sleepwalker on the journey back to the palace. It was worse than those months after the baby died."

"My baby . . ." A shudder ran through her. "I love you, Nicholas. Please believe me. Whatever happens, I do love you."

"Silver, did—" Nicholas hesitated. "Did Monteith touch you."

Monteith's words had touched her, violated her, perhaps even damned her, she thought miserably. "He didn't rape me, if that's what you mean."

She felt him relax against her. "Then what the hell is wrong? Monteith is dead. Etaine is safe." His voice thickened. "And you're safe, thank God."

"Am I?" Was there any security or happiness in the world? She had thought there might be a chance of happiness with Nicholas, but now she didn't know.

"And I'll keep you safe. Believe me."

He had said that before. *Believe in me. Believe in our love.* But she had never been able to believe that anyone could love her. And if she acted on what she believed with her whole heart to be a just way, would Nicholas still love her? "I'll try to believe." She nestled closer, clinging desperately to his warm, naked strength. "Hold me tight. Will you do that? I need it so much tonight."

"Silver, tell me what . . ." His lips feathered her

temple. "Very well. No questions tonight. Tomorrow will do as well. Go to sleep, love."

A short time later Nicholas's breathing deepened and Silver knew he was asleep.

But Silver did not sleep for a long time. She gazed into the darkness, frantically seeking a solution. She had still not found one when she finally drifted off to sleep as the first rays of the dawn filtered around the heavy velvet curtains at the long window across the room.

13

❧❧

"**I**'m not going to the damn ball without you," Nicholas said flatly.

"You must go." Silver's lips were trembling as she tried to smile. "You told me yourself that Peskov will be trying to influence the tsar against you with his lies. You and Valentin have to be there to tell him the truth about what happened at Peskov's estate last night."

"Then go with me," Nicholas coaxed. "We'll tell our story to the tsar and then come directly back to the island."

Silver shook her head. "I don't want to see any of those people yet. I would only look at them and wonder which of them were there in that tent last night hiding behind masks." She stood on tiptoe and brushed her lips across Nicholas's cheek. "You and Valentin go. I'll be fine until you return."

"I'm not so sure." Nicholas's gaze searched her face. The skin was pulled tight across her high cheekbones, and the faint shadows beneath her light eyes made them appear enormous in her thin face. But it wasn't the physical evidence of strain that worried him so much as the brittle tension he sensed beneath her carefully maintained composure. Tenderness rushed through him in an aching tide as he reached out and gently caressed her cheek with his fingertips. "This can't go on. I want your promise that when I come back you'll tell me what's troubling you. Let me help you, Silver."

Her lashes lowered to veil her eyes. "You can't help me. I'm the only one who can decide . . ." She trailed off and then suddenly turned her head and pressed her lips passionately against his palm. "Go." She whirled on her heel and swiftly started up the stairs. "I must see if Etaine is sleeping. She was very upset today."

"*Etaine* was upset," Nicholas muttered, gazing after her in frustration.

"The troika is waiting, Nicholas." Valentin appeared at his side in the foyer, and he and Nicholas watched Silver ascending the staircase. "She'll be fine here with Etaine and Mikhail," Valentin said.

"I don't want to leave her," Nicholas said. "She's *hurting*, Valentin."

"It won't make what's bothering her any easier to bear to see you sent off to Siberia," Valentin said dryly. "You know damn well that Peskov will try to twist what happened last night to his own advantage. He'll make the burning of his manor house a senseless act committed by a reckless hothead and himself the innocent victim."

Nicholas knew that was true, but it didn't allay his reluctance to leave Silver. Yet what could he do when she wouldn't let him into her confidence? He turned away and shrugged into his cloak held by the footman. "Very well. I'll go. But as soon as I get the opportunity to speak to the tsar, we're leaving."

"It may not be that easy to get his ear with Peskov around." Valentin frowned thoughtfully. "Perhaps I can arrange a bribe to have you seated next to His Majesty at dinner. It's worth a try anyway."

"Do anything you have to." Nicholas strode toward the front door. "Just get me out of the Winter Palace before midnight."

"Shhh." Mikhail put his finger to his lips as he closed the door to Etaine's room and stepped into the hall. He drew Silver a few paces farther down the corridor. "You don't have to look in on her. She went off to sleep right away."

"Good. I was worried about her today, though I'd expected her to be subdued after such an experience."

"It was a day for pondering. She had to come to accept what had happened and what adjustments must now be made in her life." His gaze touched her face. "It was also a day of thought for you, was it not?"

"Yes." She drew a shaky breath. "I'm so afraid, Mikhail."

"I know you are."

"Nicholas is everything I've ever wanted. When I am with him there is no aloneness, there's only joy."

"That is a great gift."

"But Natalya must be punished."

Mikhail was silent.

"I've tried to think of a way out." She made a helpless gesture. "But I cannot."

"Perhaps that's because you see only what you want to see."

She frowned. "What do you mean?"

"You are still a child in many ways, Silver," Mikhail said gently. "Everything must be either one thing or the other for you. Black or white. When you grow up you realize you can't have everything you want. Sometimes there must be compromises. You must choose what is most important to you."

"But I can't. How can I—" She broke off. "It must be either love or vengeance." Silver turned and moved wearily down the hall toward her chamber. "Good night, Mikhail."

"There is one more choice, Silver," Mikhail said softly. "To put childhood aside and become a woman."

Silver stopped with her hand on the doorknob. "That may be the hardest choice of all. I could lose Nicholas that way too."

A moment later the door had closed behind her.

Silver didn't bother to light the candle but moved directly across the room to the window. She stood gazing unseeingly down at the garden below. Decision. She must not remained wrapped in this mantle of uncertainty or it could destroy her as surely as Monteith had prophesied. It must end. No matter how much it hurt, a decision must be made.

"Mikhail!" Silver ran down the first steps of the staircase. "Mikhail, where are you?"

"Here." Mikhail came out of the study to stand in the foyer. "You have need of me?"

"Yes." Silver stood on the landing gazing down at him, her eyes blazing, the color high in her cheeks. "Order the troika while I dress."

Mikhail's eyes widened. "We are going somewhere?"

"Yes, hurry." Silver turned and began quickly to climb the steps. "We're going to the Winter Palace!"

"Your invitation, please, Princess Savron," the plump liveried footman requested politely as Silver swept into the foyer of the Winter Palace.

"I've misplaced it. You know the tsar sent me one." Silver moved past him and started up the Jordan Staircase. "Are the guests still in the Nicholas Ballroom?"

"No. It's after eleven. They've already retired to the gallery for supper." The footman followed her. "Permit me to take your cloak."

"No!" Silver said sharply. "I'll continue to wear it."

"But I must—"

"I said no." Silver didn't give him a second look as she continued up the Carrara marble stairs. "I won't be here long."

He scurried up the stairs behind her, murmuring remonstrances, but it was only after they reached the doors of the gallery that he became more insistent. "This is most irregular. At least, allow me to announce Your Highness."

Silver gave him an impatient glance. "Then for heaven's sake, hurry up and announce me."

The footman sighed with relief and opened the double doors with a flourish. He bellowed, "Her Highness, the princess Silver Savron."

Conversation at the long damask-covered table instantly ceased as Silver walked into the room.

Silver entered the gallery and paused just inside the doors, gazing at the long table forming an open rectangle capable of seating hundreds of guests. Her glance ran quickly down the table, locating and identifying Natalya Savron sitting beside Peskov at the end of the head table. Nicholas was sitting to the right of the tsar with Valentin at his side. Then, looking intently at Alexander, she strode with great dignity across the room.

"My God," Nicholas murmured. He had never seen Silver looking more beautiful, more splendid. There was no rouge on her face, and her shining dark hair hung down her back as straight and unadorned as it had been the first day he had seen her in Mrs. Alford's parlor. Yet the clean simplicity of her toilette served only to emphasize her great beauty. The cloak of the firebird trailed behind her in a blaze of glorious scarlet and she, too, was shimmering, blazing, aflame with a fire that came as much from within as from the surface. Aflame and yet terribly alone in the vastness of the crowded gallery. Something hurtful twisted within Nicholas and he jumped to his feet. He couldn't *stand* to see her that alone. "It appears my wife has changed her mind about attending the ball tonight. If you'll excuse me, Your Majesty, I'll escort her to a seat at the table."

"That doesn't seem to be necessary." Alexander's gaze narrowed on Silver's face. "She obviously knows exactly where she's going. Sit down, Nicholas."

"I don't believe—" Nicholas broke off.

Silver had stopped directly before the tsar and was gazing at the emperor with bold directness. She did not curtsy but stood proudly, her back straight, her chin lifted. "I must speak to Your Majesty."

Alexander nodded. "Your husband has been telling me a rather interesting story, Silver." He smiled sardonically. "According to Peskov, an almost unbelievable story. Have you come to corroborate it?"

"No. Nicholas speaks the truth, but that's not why I'm here." She paused. "You may have heard that last summer I lost the child I carried."

A flicker of surprise crossed Alexander's face. "I sympathize, but I hardly think that's a matter for discussion here."

"My child was murdered." Silver turned and pointed to Nicholas's mother. "She bribed Dr. Rellings to give me a potion that would kill my baby."

Natalya jumped to her feet. "You lie!"

"No, Monteith told me before he died that it was you. He said that you were one of his followers and he killed the doctor to cover your crime."

Natalya gazed entreatingly at Alexander. "Your Majesty, this is nonsense. Surely you don't believe—"

"This is a serious charge," Alexander interrupted. "Why would Natalya do this?"

"To rid herself of me, to get me to leave Nicholas and St. Petersburg. She wanted no grandchild with tainted blood and cares for nothing but her position at your court."

"And have you proof?" Natalya asked mockingly.

"Not that you killed my child," Silver said. "But Monteith told me the doctor's body is buried beneath the big evergreen tree near the summerhouse at Peskov's estate."

For the first time a shadow of fear touched Natalya's face. "Then Monteith must have been the one who did it."

"It was you," Silver said clearly. "You're a murderess and a devil worshipper and now everyone here knows it."

"You have no proof." Natalya's voice was shaking. "No one will believe you."

"They will." Silver's gaze went from face to face of the guests at the table. "They already do."

"No!" Natalya said shrilly. "It's all lies."

Silver shook her head. "You're as much a killer as Monteith."

"I can't punish her without proof, Silver," Alexander said quietly.

"I know you can't." Silver's gaze shifted back to the tsar. "I was going to do that myself. I was going to kill my baby's murderess." She paused, searching for words. "But she's the mother of my husband, and Monteith told me that to do this would be to destroy the love between Nicholas and me. He said he would win because I'd never be able to live here, seeing her come and go, free and smug without avenging my child. . . ." She closed her eyes. "He was right. I do not have a tame nature and would not be able to bear it." Her lids opened to reveal eyes glittering with

tears. "But I will *not* let Monteith win." She whirled
to face Natalya. "I will not take your life, but I will take
what gives it meaning. I've learned that any wickedness may be permitted here, but not if the wrongdoer
is indiscreet. Now that all the court knows you've
killed your grandchild, there will be ugly whispers
and you will soon be shunned like a leper."

"You savage bitch," Natalya snarled. "I'll find—"

"Silence," Alexander cut in sharply. "I don't like
this story, Natalya. I believe we may dispense with
your presence in the future."

Panic robbed Natalya's face of anger. "No, I didn't
mean . . . You can't . . ." She fell silent, gasping for
breath, wildly looking around the table for some
show of support.

There was none.

Silver braced herself and turned to face Nicholas.
His expression was stern and she tried desperately to
smother a sudden leap of alarm. "I had to do this,
Nicholas. I could not let her go unpunished." She
drew a shaky breath. "But I know myself and I will
not be able to leave her alive and unhurt if I'm in the
same city with her. There will have to be an ocean
between us to keep her safe from me." She met his
eyes. "And there will be. When I leave here I'll go
directly to the docks to arrange transportation back
to America for Etaine and me."

"Silver." Nicholas's voice was hoarse. "Listen to
me—"

"No, you listen to me. There's not much more."
Her crystal-gray eyes were glittering in her tense
face. "Remember the tale you told me of the warrior
and the firebird? The firebird gave the warrior up
and flew away into the sun. Well, I'll not give you up
so willingly. I love you too much to—" Her voice
broke and she waited a moment until she could go
on. "I can't stay here. . . . But if you wish to come

with me . . . I know it would mean giving up your
home and your country." She gazed directly into his
eyes. "I cannot promise you a happy ending to our
story. I promise only that I will love you until the
day I die, Nicholas."

Silver's fingers fumbled at the fastening at her
throat. "If that's enough for you, then follow me,
Nicholas." The feathered cloak floated down to form
a brilliant pool of scarlet on the floor, revealing the
simplicity of the pearl-gray gown she wore beneath
it. Her throat and arms were bare of jewels, and she
looked poignantly vulnerable stripped of the magnif-
icence of the cloak. "Come to me," she whispered.

She turned and walked swiftly from the gallery.

She did not glance back as she descended the Jordan Staircase. She was afraid to look back. The stakes
were too high in the gamble she had made tonight.

She heard no footsteps behind her.

She started down the last flight of stairs.

He wasn't coming.

Her train flowed like pale moonlight on the white
marble steps as her pace unconsciously slowed.

She had asked too much of him.

She reached the entry hall and the plump footman
stepped forward. "Shall I summon your troika, Your
Highness?"

"No, Mikhail is waiting." She was scarcely conscious that she had answered him. She moved toward
the front door.

No man gives up his country for a woman.

"Your cloak," the footman persisted. "It's snowing.
You can't go out without your cloak."

"I have no cloak." The cloak of the firebird was
lying abandoned, untouched, on the gleaming floor
in that gallery upstairs. "Open the door."

The door was opened and Silver was suddenly on

the stone steps outside. Snow was falling, and she should have been cold, but she felt only numbness. She could see Mikhail and the troika across the courtyard and started down the steps.

"Why must I always be forced into the position of putting clothes on you?"

She froze. She was afraid to breathe. She was afraid to turn around.

The feathered cloak was placed gently around her shoulders. "When you know I much prefer to remove them."

"Nicholas." She whirled around to face him. "I was afraid—"

"I know you were." Nicholas smiled down at her lovingly. Starlike flakes of snow were glittering on his fair hair and catching on his black dinner coat. "I've discovered you have a great problem with faith. I would have been here sooner, but I had to have a brief word with Alexander and Valentin before I bolted after you."

She held her breath. "What did you tell them?"

He fastened the cloak at her neck. "That a Cossack must always follow a firebird when she leaves a feather to summon him." His eyes twinkled. "Trust you to be so extravagant as to leave a thousand feathers."

She tried to smile. "I wanted to make sure you knew I wanted you."

"I think you made it abundantly clear. To me and to the entire court."

"It's a difficult thing to leave your home. Are you sure you want to do it?"

"I'm sure I want to be with Silver Savron for the rest of my life." He touched her lower lip with a gentle finger. "I think I could soon become acclimated to your Arizona Territory. Its wildness sounds much like the Kuban."

"But you have so many business interests here."

"Valentin will be delighted to oversee them."

"He will not leave here? I'll miss him," Silver said.

"We'll try to coax him away from St. Petersburg eventually."

"Will the tsar—"

"Hush." Nicholas threw back his head and laughed. "Silver, my love, only you would issue an invitation on such a grand scale and then give me a hundred reasons why I shouldn't accept it." His dark eyes were glowing with love as he smiled down at her. "I'm going with you and you can't talk me out of it. You promised you would love me forever and I have to follow to make sure you don't renege on that promise." He lifted a hand to motion to Mikhail to bring the troika around.

"I want you to be so happy," she whispered. "Promise me you'll be happy."

"I promise you that we'll both be happy." Nicholas kissed her gently on the lips. "And that I'll never leave you, my beloved skeptic. Do you finally believe me?"

"Yes." Her eyes were shining with joy as she took his arm. How could she help but believe him now, she thought joyously. How could she help but believe in a love that would last forever and in a life without loneliness. "Oh, yes, Nicholas. I *do* believe you."

"Well, it's about time." His laughter rang out again on the cold night air as he turned to help her down the snow-covered stairs.

And the cloak of the firebird drifted behind Silver in a cloud of flaming splendor as they ran down the steps toward Mikhail and the waiting troika.

Saturday evening 9:15 p.m.
Shamrock

Dear Cousin Maureen,
  I know it's been a long time since you've heard from me, but I truly couldn't help it. I've been on a wondrous journey and have seen some things that would fair knock your eyes out. Where?
  Australia!
  Did you know that Koalas aren't really bears at all? And that there's a great, grand rock square in the middle of the country where you can see almost to heaven itself? Never did I think I'd see such sights when you and I were growing up in Dublin and our finest dreams were of just having three meals a day.
  But I'm getting ahead of myself. You're going to want to know the how and why of it.
  Do you remember when I sent you that long, long letter telling you about the early Delaneys and how they came to America and founded Killara and Shamrock Horse Farm? You might recall a certain scalawag named William who's buried on Boot Hill, the Lord bless his soul.
  Well, as it turns out, William left a wife and child in Australia and founded an entirely new branch of the family. The current Australian Delaneys consist

242

of Spencer Delaney and his three daughters Manda, Sydney and Addie and an interesting family they are. Well naturally when Burke, York and Rafe found out about the family down under they were curious about them. And so the end of it all was that they decided to travel to Australia to meet them. Burke and Cara, York and Sierra, Rafe and Maggie—the entire family. No, that's not right, is it? Because now there's an Arizona branch and an Australian branch. I'm used to thinking of my Delaneys as the only ones.

And they are *my* Delaneys, Maureen. I'm not just a servant to them.

Mr. Rafe took me aside when all this news came and said naturally me and Bridget would come along. For how could they do without us? They were taking Deuce Moran, me, and Bridget and her husband, Couger, too. I admit I bawled like a baby and Bridget was a bit misty eyed her ownself. It would've broken my heart to stand by and see them go without me, particularly with Miss Maggie being with child. Did I tell you that? The baby is due any day now and Mr. Rafe is hovering over Miss Maggie as if she were carrying eggs instead of a fine healthy baby. Such foolishness when she's so hale and hearty. I saw to that. I was the one who took care of her while we were travelling all around the Barrier reef to visit Sydney and Nicholas and then to the movie location near Perth where Matilda and Roman were staying. But it was Mr. Rafe who had to put his foot down when we visited Miss Addie at the station where the girls grew up. Miss Maggie was wild to ride that horse, Resolute, and her big as a house with child!

Deuce Moran didn't come back with us to Arizona. I couldn't believe it myself when they told me he was staying on at the Isle of Charron. He spent most of his time there at the casino which didn't surprise any of us. I've told you what a gambler the man is, and I've suspected many a time that he's not an entirely honest one. While he was at the casino he met an old friend of Nicholas's, a very pretty lady with the queer name of Mandarin and fell like a ton of sod bricks. I have no idea what will come of it. It seems the lady has just suffered the grievous loss of the man she loved and will have nothing to do with Deuce as anything but a friend. I will let you know how his suit prospers. Who knows? Perhaps the rascal will find someone to reform him at last.

We were all very sad to leave Australia. There wasn't a one of us who hadn't formed strong ties with the folk that live there but I know we'll be returning someday. And they've promised to visit Arizona as well when they get the opportunity. In fact, Miss Manda and her husband, Roman, will be visiting Killara next year when they go to the Academy award ceremony and Miss Addie will probably be moving to Kentucky with her brand new husband any time now.

I feel I'm bombarding you with news but there's truly much more to say than I have time to put down right now. I have gingerbread in the oven and I mustn't let it burn. You know how Mr. Rafe loves my gingerbread. By the way, did I remember to thank you for saying the fudge I sent you was "exceptional?"

Oh, one thing I did forget to tell you. Miss Sierra just found out *she's* with child. Mr. York is out of his mind with joy. I get down on my knees and pray every night the child will be strong and healthy. It should be all right for Mr. York's sickness wasn't inherited. Still, prayers never hurt, do they now? I remember what a nightmare we went through with Mr. York's heart ailment. I've never regretted for a moment that I broke that blasted clock with its infernal ticking away of the time Mr. York had left. Though I know I should have had the courage to confess and spare the boys from being punished for me. I guess I was afraid of being sent back to Ireland and away from the family that's become so dear to me. Through the years I truly believe I've made it up to all of them, Maureen.

You asked me once if I ever regretted coming to America and taking the Delaneys to my heart instead of marrying and having children of my own. I never answered you. Perhaps because I did have a few wistful moments when you wrote to tell me of the doings of your two children and now the birth of that fine grandson you're so proud of. Maybe I could have had a more fulfilling life if I'd stayed in Dublin but somehow I doubt it. The years I've spent at Killara and Shamrock have been full of love and the people I've served have a grand, richness of spirit.

Oh dear, Mr. Rafe is calling me. The baby's coming! More later.

> Hurriedly,
> Kathleen

> Sunday morning,
> 6:30 a.m.

P.S. The baby is a six pound girl and just as healthy as she is beautiful. They're naming her Erin after the boys' mother. Must get to bed. I'll write again soon.

> Love,
> Kathleen

P.P.S. The gingerbread burned but Mr. Rafe was so happy about the baby he didn't seem to care at all. I'll make him another batch today to celebrate.

> Kathleen

THE DELANEY DYNASTY

Men and women whose loves and passions are so glorious it takes many great romance novels by three bestselling authors to tell their tempestuous stories.

THE SHAMROCK TRINITY

THE DELANEYS OF KILLAROO

Now Available!
THE DELANEYS: *The Untamed Years*

The birth of the Delaney Dynasty

Iris Johansen sets the historical stage for the love stories of the colorful founders of the Delaney Dynasty that continue in trilogies from all three authors.

DON'T MISS THE ENTHRALLING

by Iris Johansen

Scottish beauty Elspeth MacGregor travels to Hell's Bluff to hire Dominic Delaney to lead her to the magical lost city of Kantalan, but at first he refuses—the last thing he needs is to join a virginal scholar on a dangerous quest.

But Elspeth's fiery will coupled with her silky hair and milk-white skin prove irresistible, and Dominic acts—first with angry lust, then with a searing yet tender passion that brands her eternal soul and bonds them both to a heated and turbulent future.

Through wonders and tragedy, across the untamed splendors of Arizona and Mexico, Elspeth and Dominic draw closer to their dual destiny: to experience the dark mysteries and magnificent riches of Kantalan . . . and to fulfill the promise of lasting love and the birth of a bold family dynasty.

☐ 26991 / $3.95

"**SPLENDOR** is special—refreshing, riveting, fascinating. I loved it and hated to see it end."
—*Johanna Lindsey*

BANTAM
SHOP-AT-HOME
C·A·T·A·L·O·G

Special Offer
Buy a Bantam Book
for only 50¢.

Now you can have Bantam's catalog filled with hundreds of titles plus take advantage of our unique and exciting bonus book offer. A special offer which gives you the opportunity to purchase a Bantam book for only 50¢. Here's how!

By ordering any five books at the regular price per order, you can also choose any other single book listed (up to a $5.95 value) for just 50¢. Some restrictions do apply, but for further details why not send for Bantam's catalog of titles today!

Just send us your name and address and we will send you a catalog!